Dasha

D. F. Whipple

ISBN: 1-4196-5581-7
ISBN-13: 9781419655814

Library of Congress Control Number: 2008905154

Visit www.booksurge.com to order additional copies.

AUTHOR'S NOTE

This novel does not depict actual characters or events, and any similarities with real people or circumstances are entirely coincidental. A work of magical realism, *Dasha* wraps reality and fantasy together in a lighthearted, yet penetrating, exploration of life's so-called objective reality.

Readers with a background in philosophy may detect a barb at ontological monism in the previous statement, and they would be correct. However, those who are looking for a lively, humorous and satirical tale of lovers in Central Park should keep reading, because this is not a mere novel of ideas.

That said, I want to thank some people who shared my journey of writing this novel. First my mother, who despite a successful career and a harried life always found time to read my drafts, and who strengthened me with faith.

Additionally, I need to thank a professor of literature, Shakespeare scholar and author Robert Thomas Fallon, whose edits and comments were invaluable. I also want to thank J. C., a distinguished professor of literature, whose brilliant insights and an important suggestion added heft and clarity to the text. My friend K. B. made worthwhile contributions and offered suggestions that made it into print. Columnist R. B. suggested several details that lended the book more immediacy and impact. And my publisher BookSurge deserves praise.

Now let's get moving.

Listen, now. Closely. Something's stirring...I think I hear someone now.

D F Whipple
June 2008

But Abraham had faith, and had faith for <u>this</u> life.
- Soren Kierkegaard, *Fear and Trembling*

This book is for Mom.

CHAPTER ONE
Manhattan July 2007

(1)

Brisk air swept across the face of a man in his late twenties who, torpid and wincing, struggled to lug a backpack and duffle bag down the steps of a brownstone on Manhattan's Upper West Side. It was Saturday afternoon. The woman who watched him, prim and attractive, her hair tousled in the breeze, feigned disinterest. Yet she remained on the landing, holding a puppy. The dachshund squirmed in her arms while she stroked it gently, but the dog's efforts were futile: both dog and man needed to separate. The woman owned the apartment, and Carl Moretti was out.

The young man's crimson-hued face and crinkled eyes bespoke anger over the situation, which after the recent layoff and nasty breakup, entailed finding himself about to live on the street with no hope of servicing his considerable debt. He felt no self-pity, though. In fact, his attitude was marked by stridence and defiance, although the reality of his circumstances – the painful string of rejections – weighed on his soul.

He saw no recourse. Despite his looming poverty and homelessness, the young man's eyes maintained a certain liveliness – even to the point of liberation – as if somehow, in the midst of defeat, he would still win.

How, he didn't yet know, but he knew he needed to press on.

"Carl, darling, tell me you won't sleep on the street," Lisa Foley purred with a sarcastic pout. The dog continued its struggle as she stroked her fingers along its back.

"If I do, it'll be on your conscience!" he retorted, huffing. He slung the JanSport backpack over his right shoulder, intending to scramble.

"What's it like to sleep on the streets?"

"I don't know. What's it like to work 'em?" Satisfied, he began walking toward the park.

Her eyes flared.

The pooch squirmed.

As often happens with such affairs, Carl scarcely saw the life meltdown barreling toward him, and when it hit, he initially felt more shock than pain. There had been warning signs along the way, but the culmination of events and her response to his efforts precipitated a drastic change of fortune. Her response over his job loss had been sympathetic, if prickly, but gradually she became cool, then insolent, in tone. Within days, Carl knew they were through; now it was official. Looking toward the swaying greenery of Central Park, he shoved his hands into his wrinkled, chino pockets, bit his lip, and glanced longingly at the dog.

He avoided Lisa's stare.

Determined not to show weakness, which he feared would manifest itself in rage, he maintained an indifferent air while his innards churned. On the one hand, he felt confused and lost. On the other, he had never felt so resolved and determined to move on. Under her menacing presence, he remembered their platitudes of love and devotion; now their promises make him need to spit.

He did, but again he didn't look at her.

2

Jaws tense and eyes bitter, he could scarcely find a more emotional fulcrum for directing his energy at this moment than her. Yet she was not the problem, and he knew it.

Me, he ruminated. Then he brushed off the thought.

Carl's resolution was tempered by a looming sense of doubt, but it was not a question of the future. At the moment, he felt he had none. Instead his doubts lay in the present. How should he feel? Angry? Disappointed? Anxious? Terminal? And beside the question of how to feel, the larger riddle of as what eluded him. As a jilted lover? An unemployed bachelor? A stricken-down victim of urban cruelty, like the losing end of a holdup? An itinerant who could be rolled over like so many sacks of onions?

The question of as who didn't enter the picture.

So prickly was his inner sense of value, and so ready was he to press onward, he dismissed the question as irrelevant. He blocked it from his mind. If anyone asked, he could state his name, his hometown, his vocation, his life's dreams, and everything of a concrete nature was well-resolved. But the question of as who, whether fighter for justice, or son of the Moretti family, or citizen-at-large, or something more nondescript, remained unbearable. Who was he to answer such a question? Did he even have a right to ask? So the question of as what crept into his soul and quivered, but the question of as who remained at bay.

After several moments of aimless darting, his eyes landed tepidly on Lisa's. He forced a smile. "Take care of the wiener dog. I'll miss him."

"The weiner's mine now," she announced, grimacing.

Suddenly, a window opened two floors above her, just to the left, and their neighbor Cynthia, who often dropped by with casseroles and even picked up their paper when they were away, leaned her crimson locks outside and rested her forearms on the window sill. "Go get 'em, Lisa!" she cried in a cross between a cheer and a sting. "What did he do? Cheat on you? Act like a jerk?"

"None of the above," Carl's ex replied, tossing her hair in showy fashion and heaving a sigh. "Nothing wrong at all, I'm afraid. I have no excuse. But nothing right, either."

Her voice sounded cutting to him.

Despite his presence of mind and dignity, Carl blanched, dwindling energy escaping through his beet-red cheeks.

"And the poetry? What about the poetry?" Cynthia asked.

"She read my poems?" the stricken man asked, incredulous.

Lisa folded her hands and pinched her cheeks, as if embarrassed. "Oh, the poems. How could I forget? So sweet, so innocent.

> "Really honey, your words
> were quite pretty,
> But no male can tame
> my romp in the city."

Carl felt a tremor through his body, but caught himself, calmed his stomach, took a tiny breath, and kept his composure, then crafted a response. Once he'd arranged it, he replied with a dismissive air,

> Your words are like
> poison your heart's like ice,
> Soon you'll see when
> your man's not nice;

He'll wine you and dine
you and take you to bed,
Then rip out your soul before
chopping your head.
His words will be harsh,
and his cruelty your kind,
Next time we meet, you'll
have lost all your mind."

"Bravoooo!" Cynthia exclaimed, clapping her hands.

At this point, a street hustler approached Carl on the sidewalk, stopped, and looked him over. "That's it, man. Don't let her toss you around," the stranger approved. Black and clean-shaven, the interloper's clothes were clean, although frumpy, and his eyes shined bright and alert, begetting a certain aura.

Feeling the wound, Lisa swallowed hard, gathered a quick breath, and stretched her back higher. She started to lecture Carl, but taken off guard, she thought better of it. "Never mind. You're not worth it." With that, she turned on her heels, pried open the heavy door, and proceeded back inside.

Carl frowned in Lisa's direction, then turned away, hoping to never see her again. Then together the two strangers headed toward Central Park West. "If I can't live there, I'll make it a camping trip," Carl huffed. "How's that sound? More fun than living with that wench. Besides, I need to have trees again."

"What do you mean?"

"Oh...um...so I won't think about failure. Hard to do that when you have nature around."

"Failure? Man, you don't know the half of it about failure. You breathing?"

Carl grabbed the strap that was slipping off his shoulder. "Yea. So what?"

"Then you're not failing. But I hear you. I've been where I can see you are. Had my own ways of coping. By the way, name's Richard."

Carl nodded.

A taxi ambled by, but Carl paid the sound of engine and rolling tires no heed.

They walked to the end of the street, crossed to the opposite sidewalk, then headed north toward the 72nd Street entrance of Central Park. The silence might have been awkward, but having adjusted to Manhattan, Carl felt no particular discomfort with his itinerant companion. "Yea...need to cope," Carl continued. "Moved here from Cleveland eight months ago. That makes me a transplant, I suppose. I'd been there for a year after graduating...computer science...programming. Carnegie Mellon...out in Pittsburgh. Company out there gave me the hard boot. Said they had business problems. Then I found a job in IT here. Reinsurance company. That's the story, you know? Country kid from upstate New York gets a degree, moves to the big city. It was all so la-di-da at first. The chick and I...we hooked up...we've known each other since high school. Her family's loaded. She sees me in New York now. You know. We did the parties, the restaurants. Had it all planned out. Hardly knew a soul in this cow town myself except for that windbag. Then last week, my boss marches me into his office and says I'm fired. Why, I asked. Why not, he says. That's called a quip. Unless you're taking out your...never mind. What does he care how good I am? He can hire two guys for the price of one he says. It's a global labor market he says. Yada, yada. Screw him. Now I have to go back for an exit interview day after tomorrow. I'm still officially on the payroll for three weeks. They've got something else on their minds, though. Not sure what it is, but I'm sure it's lame."

"Alright. Alright. I'm feeling you. That's a story. I've heard worse, but yea…sorry to hear that…really am. Never like to hear about another man's troubles. I say everyone has what's his and it's his. You can't take that from him just because you want to. That's stealing. I know a lot of guys doing hard time for stealing less than a man's livelihood. I say you have yours and I have mine and that's way it should work. Y'know?"

Carl nodded in a perfunctory way, but turned silent until they reached the park entrance. Thoughts crept into his head, but whereas a week before he would have categorized, analyzed, and filed his ruminations away, at this point he could only shove them aside, let them lie – perhaps, let them die.

"You broke?" Richard asked.

"Almost. I can hang on for a few months, but I'll need to economize. Don't wanna ask my parents for more money 'cause they'll flip. Who wants to deal with that on top of everything else? I could draw unemployment…but have to wait until I'm off their payroll. Besides, I don't like taking handouts. No offense by the way."

"No way…a man who takes care of himself. That's what I am. You know that, right? What, you sleeping in the park tonight?"

"Yep," Carl replied.

"Got any friends in the city?"

"Nope. What I mean is, no one I feel comfortable calling and saying hey, I need to live in your apartment…you understand."

They turned north, trees and grass all around them now.

"Okay, okay. Listen, I know a place," said Richard, brightening the mood. "Don't sleep there myself anymore, but you'll get back on your feet. I know you will. The will is in your eyes." They kept walking. "You know what I used to do as a kid when I was down and out? Like when my father ran off on my Mom in the dead of night? She was crying...so stricken with grief and pain and all that?"

"No. What?"

"Found a friend. She used to come in through my bedroom window."

"Really? What age were you?"

Richard became more animated. "No, no. Listen. Back when I was a kid, I had an imaginary friend. Still do, but she doesn't come around anymore. If I needed her I could summon her up." He snapped his fingers. "Just like that. That's what you need, man."

"Interesting...but I don't know. I think I need something real."

"And what might that be? No, really, she was exciting because man, you don't know what it's like to live with a free mind until you've freed it. But your reaction...I expect it. You do computers and all that. A man who clings to his reason. That's exactly what I'd expect someone like you to say. But you best not use your head as a security blanket. You know what I'm saying? No offense."

"Course not, just that I've never had an imaginary friend. Maybe I should have, but it sounds a little odd. To be honest."

"Yep, I know who you think you are. You keep an even keel. But tell me. What's your name?"

"Carl." The reply was hesitant.

"Carl. Okay. I know you don't know who I am, but I always like to address the person to whom I'm speaking." Richard paused, edging closer. "Tell me. Do you even know what's real? I mean, if that woman back there didn't make you question it, then you are the first guy I've met in a long time who's looked at his woman, sneering and jarring him like that, then said yea, this is reality. This is my life and that's it, now just cope. Look, okay, I see you're not really listening to me. What I'm saying is, my man, many people around here today, in Manhattan…they rush around, get all torn up about this and that, so focused… this isn't reality. They're so real, it's unreal."

Perplexed but interested now, Carl pulled the strap back onto this shoulder and looked at his new acquaintance. "Hm. Maybe I'd benefit from this imaginary friend, as you say. But nothing like that's ever happened to me. People don't just pop out of thin air."

"Until they do. Maybe she will. I don't know. All I'm saying is, if something like that ever happens, you take her in. Appreciate what you've got, not what you don't have back there. Look what she threw away. You going to do that, too? Maybe when you were a kid you weren't ready. Maybe she's lying out there in wait somewhere. Maybe she's watching over you right now. Maybe she's every bit as complicated as you are. Maybe she is The One. You get my drift?"

"If The One falls down from the sky like that, I'll plead for another planet."

They walked onward.

The air hung thick and steamy over the neighborhood. Rising temperatures had trapped odors in the stone, brick, and soil landscape of the Upper West Side, and suddenly, with the full impact his predicament sinking in, Carl accepted the full weight of his problems for the first time. Nevertheless, he remained focused on the matter of finding a new place to sleep, and brushed off his larger concerns as a mere annoyance. How did I get into this mess? Clueless, he called himself, before applying the word to her.

Women called him handsome, although at the moment he looked hugger-mugger and grungy, having neglected shaving for six days and a proper shower for two. Stress had made the common task of hygiene feel onerous and heavy, as if a razor would be more than his heavy heart could bear. The blade might nick him; he hadn't slept much. His eyes retreated deep into their sockets, and bulbous sacks hanging by hemp ropes from his eyelids, he scuffled along the sidewalk, shoe laces untied. Only his shiny, mutt-brown hair and emerald eyes, which despite his sullen mood couldn't help revealing a subtle, inner light, betrayed the charm and magnetism he would otherwise exude.

Carl glanced back in the direction of his ex's apartment, head pounding with angst. Plug-ugly, he reasoned, recalling her menacing expression and hard-boiled eyes. Then his breath constricted and shortened, and he winced, grimacing as if to fight off a stomach ache. He felt depleted, yet not entirely empty. Catholic, he still had God on his side, he reasoned.

His shoulders drooped under the weight of his baggage, half of which cut garnet streaks in his fingers. Passersby paid no attention. A man walked by their right and Richard tried to coax a coin from him, but the man wouldn't oblige.

"God bless you and have a nice day!" the hustler shot back, ambiguously.

"You call yourself an entertainer?" Carl asked, casually.

"Whatever pays the bills and won't land me in jail, that's what I am."

They approached a row of benches. Carl continued lugging his belongings, but his face became strained, even thoughtful. He took in the surroundings: rollerblades, bikers on ten-speeds, women in business suits, cars. They all whisked through the park, leaving trails of memories and fumes in their wakes. The air seemed cooler amongst the greenery, but almost as toxic. Carl's uncombed hair, down to his shoulders and with a hint of blonde – this came from his mother's Irish side – hopped around his face. Lanky but lean and otherwise healthy, his frame evidenced a routine of working out in the gym and general concern about health.

The skies were bright. Live music wallowed from the direction of the pond, and birds chirped effusively, although not at a pitch that could drown car engines and rumbling skates. Leaves rustled in a steady, but muted breeze, and occasionally he caught the scent of roasting hot dogs.

"How much you make hustlin', Richard?"

"Excuse me?" the man responded, "You ought to note:

"I'm a man of integrity,
may I have the acquaintance
Of your best patience and raise
your expectations,
Add gloss to your grey fence
and provide a persuasion
To find the rhyme
in your passion's occasion?"

"Hey, that's good. You make that up on the fly?" Carl asked, digging his pockets for a quarter. Carl held it out for the man.

"Hell, no. It's part of my repertoire. Here, keep your quarter," Richard said, producing a dollar from his own pocket. "Take this. I feel sorry for you." Carl accepted the gift, not wanting to offend his sidekick again, and with that, Carl sat on the last bench.

"I'm done walking," Carl said, determined.

"That's alright. That's alright. Your spot's right over there... in those bushes. It's a safe place to sleep. But now I need to be heading home to Brooklyn."

CHAPTER TWO

They parted on good terms. Richard promised to check up on Carl in the coming days, but the displaced young man wasn't sure where he would be in an hour, let alone days from now. It was a sincere goodbye, nonetheless.

The wind picked up, whipping Carl's oily hair and tickling his face, and rather than let his bags mingle with the ants and other insects on the ground, he decided to prop them against the park bench, throw his arms out wide, and take in the surroundings. *At least I'm on vacation*, he mused. Seated on the hard, wooden planks and soaking in an occasional trickle of sunlight, he contemplated the circumstances. Now twice unemployed in less than two years out of Carnegie Mellon, with stellar grades and marketable skills under his belt, but a net worth only a mother could love and cash flow that would crash in three weeks, he faced the daunting task of finding new work—suitable, well-paying work—before needing to file bankruptcy. Two of his friends had recently gone insolvent, insisting it was an honorable thing when mounting school debts weren't matched by job prospects. Still, the thought made him shudder. *Wasn't I always someone who never quit? Who never let failure be an option?* The pressure made his skin feel tight and his throat restricted.

He drew in a long breath, then exhaled slowly.

Bicyclers rolled by, casual but focused.

Carl had $537 dollars in his checking account and $75 in savings, plus another $6,500 and change in his 401k. After taxes and penalties, he'd be lucky to see half of the retirement money, which he'd need to withdraw without further delay. They would hold the funds until the end of the month according to plan rules. His student loans amounted to $60,000, plus he had $22,000 in credit card debt. He still couldn't believe how quickly the credit card obligations had piled up. He had needed over $8,000 to finish graduate school, needing most of the money for rent and food, having depleted his student loan limits. Then the move to New York, including furniture, incidentals, and the security deposit Lisa coaxed him into paying, cost another $9,000. The rest of the debt came from an ill-fated trip to France. His Manhattan employer, Frontier Reinsurance, enticed him into spending the first three months of his tenure in their Paris office, where, despite his best efforts, he managed to deplete his paychecks faster than he earned them. He took the obligatory trip to Nice, for one thing; his boss insisted it should be part of the experience. *Optimism*, he recalled his manager lecturing. *If you want to fit in around here, you need to spend the money.*

His previous employer, a bank in Cleveland, also canned him without notice. Now a glimmer of hope lay within a downtown Manhattan recruiter, who said she might be able to help. They already had a meeting scheduled for Friday, the day after the exit interview, but the situation seemed slippery.

Payments were coming due next week, Carl remembered, but rather than focus on the pressing matter of money, he pushed his concerns into the back of his mind, closed his eyes, and tried to take in a few rays of sun. He sat like this for half an hour, feeling alone and contemplating little more than his shallow breath and the wind.

He often stewed over his problems. Needing air, he drew in a long, salutary breath, and gazing into cobalt skies through rustling leaves, he sighed, then wished, "Please God, if ever you picked a time to show me my...you know...this imaginary friend...let it be now." He listened for a moment, but no one responded.

Carl fell asleep.

In the midst of his dreams, he imagined himself in the same setting: light, afternoon air, a rustling of leaves and muted sounds. But somewhere else. Somewhere distant, yet close. Somewhere painful, yet comforting. Somewhere unlike New York, and somewhere important. To him. The juxtaposition of these feelings, while seeming to take him in two directions, managed to calm him, and a sense of anticipation and wonder emerged.

A flutter awakened him.

Startled, he popped open his eyes, blinked, and searched both left and right, missing her entirely. He stared for several moments in either direction, trying his best to focus in the suddenly dim light—had a storm cloud rolled in? He rubbed his cheeks, hoping for sentience, and cleared his throat as if to clear his mind, too.

Then he saw her.

She was about his age, with smooth, buttery skin, dazzling eyes, a lithe figure that danced and pirouetted over pointed slippers like a ballerina. She wore a sequined, embroidered, and turquoise dress that curved into delicate pleats: the folds bloomed above her thighs. She eyed him gracefully and with a playful grin, taking in his mood, his expression, and his soul-stricken eyes. Then, with a twist of her waist and raising her toes to a point, she raised a wand in the air and rapped its tippy-top star on his crown.

"There you go!" she snapped, eyes alive and curious. "A scold for your sullenness!" Then turning aside, she exclaimed to herself, "Oh! Look at him! After all these years, he looks… oh! So exhausted! Forlorn! The poor dear. They say these past few years he's been getting worse and worse. What to do? Here I am now. Matters will get better…and I had to be the one to answer his cry. When they told me I knew I must. Fie! Fie! Look at him! They were so kind to let me go. Perhaps, indeed, only I can raise his spirits. But it's best I haven't revealed myself to him until now. When he was younger it would have been far too complex. Now he can take me. Enough prattling on, though! Here goes something!" She turned back to him. "You sit here in the park by yourself and the rain is coming and you don't wear your jacket? Do you want to catch a cold? You're asking for it, you know."

Hearing the flirtation in her voice, his face flushed and his adrenaline picked up. *Who in the world is this gorgeous little vixen? Do I know her?* he wondered. At no time since he had moved to Manhattan had he been addressed with such kindness, heart and sympathy. Suddenly, the urban air, already better in the park, seemed fresher and more nourishing, and seeing her engaging smile, his troubles melted a small amount. He also had an uncanny feeling they had know each other their entire lives, but he couldn't quite place her anywhere specific.

Deep-feeling and hazelnut-dark, her eyes sparkled at him.

"Have we met before? I feel I know you from somewhere" he asked, his voice puzzled yet weary.

"Aha!" she exclaimed, tapping him on the head again. "No peeking into the past! That will be a penalty for you! Now you owe me infinite favors for…hm…infinity," she added, dismissing her thought with a coquettish toss of her hair.

"That's more time than I'll give you," he parried.

"And who says time is yours to give?" she queried in gamely fashion. "That includes me. Do you feel I'm yours to take?"

"I'm taken."

"Taken aback? Or taken by me? You're dreaming. I prefer older men. Men in their hundreds, at least," she responded, cryptically.

"Sure. Plenty of them around. Good luck."

"Oh!" she exclaimed, rapping him on the forehead with her wand. "You test your fate."

His face turned cross. "Can't test what's already decided," he replied, dejected, averting his eyes from hers. "Furthermore, who do you think you are poking me like that? We barely know each other. Although this is a park, I'm not public property."

She pressed her lips together in mock disgust, then, suddenly smiling again and batting her eyes, she twirled in place, reached up to the sky, then leaned down to his eye level. "How do you know your luck's out? Is your life over yet, huh? Are you listening to me? I'm speaking. What kind of man would say such things unless he were standing on the edge of a roof, fifty stories above the sidewalk, planning to jump as soon as he spied a clearing in the crowd? Huh? Huh? Humph. You're looking so grim...so lost. Come back, my little lamb. Here, let this cheer you up," she continued, leaping in place and twiddling her toes. "Do you see? I almost have wings."

"You're a dancer. That much is clear."

"Hah! You think you know this? What is so clear to you except your mood? You think you're so smart you can say what I am. But you have no idea." Sensing her taunts were getting to him, she peered into the sky, and heaved a big sigh. "Once I knew a man. His name was Mark Andropov. A dashing man, and a charming name. Yes? He grew up in Moscow. He was brave, and he served with distinction in a garrison stationed in Siberia. I missed him terribly. When he rode off to war, he vowed that if he died, it would be with honor or he would not return. This was his oath, I'm afraid. In the end, his wounds were no worse than mine," she added, voice trailing off.

Perplexed, Carl studied her. "Who's this Mark Andropov? Are you hinting this is me? What...do you think I'm someone else...or was...or something?" He experienced a strange feeling of déjà vu.

"You think I goad you?" she squealed, elated. "No! I'm not so base and thoughtless! I would not come up to a stranger in casual encounter if I had this lack of respect. It's not my nature. I am stubborn, careless, determined, warm, charming, beautiful, tossy...as fits my protean nature...when I want to change I will...and my mother says I'm deep-feeling, strident but shy, and my heart enjoys laughter. And lightness. And my feet dance like this. Does this not describe me?" she boasted, lingering on her words and posing for him.

"Modest," he joked.

"Yes, modesty would be my best trait if I weren't so pretty." Once again, she drew a deep breath, but this time she gazed over his head, and announced,

"I play and pray and live for the day,
Tomorrow, they say, shall soon pass away."

"What's your name?" he asked, quieter now.

"Dar'ya."

"*Ochin priatna*," he responded, recognizing her name as Russian.[i]

Her eyes bulged. "You speak Russian?"

He nodded. "Studied it in college. You live in New York, I take it?"

"Hm! I live neither here nor there, but guess if you dare," she taunted.

"No idea."

Once again, she brushed her wand against him, this time even more gently. A gust of wind fluttered by, sweeping their hair to the side, and with a suddenly grunt, she spun on her heels, stretched her arms around herself, and came back to her original position, arms now folded across her chest. Her dress rustled in the wind.

Carl looked her up and down, taking in her delicacy and beauty: her radiant hair, chestnut-fire glow, and a bashfulness that masked a deeper sense of depth and self-connection. Or a connection to something else. How did this fair woman arrive so unexpectedly in his life, on a tuft of wind, playing a note from the infinite instrument of God?

She turned away, embarrassed by his inquisitive eyes.

But looking her over, he considered her terribly appealing. Peculiar, yes, but he found her demeanor far too refreshing to consider her unbearable or odd. "You're a mysterious one. And treacherous," he said, hoping to get a rise from her. "Where are you from? You have a Russian accent…did I meet you in Moscow? And why are you suddenly here with me?"

In response to the sudden barrage of questions, she feigned a gasp. "Wha…? Why would you, my little lamb, ask such personal questions?" Crossly, she rapped him again with her wand. "You best ignore such things."

"How can I ignore what's staring me in the face?"

"Aha! Now you ask. This is a sound question for which, perhaps, I may answer you in time. Are you sure you want the answer, though? What is your name?"

"Carl."

"Hm…I like Mark better. But you don't know half the truth. And who are you to make such pronouncements about my nature? I'm not some shrew."

"Shrewd, yes. I never said shrew. Although a teaser…most definitely. I've known many." He painted on a smile.

"And I have not known such men who appear then disappear like the wind? Do I appear so young and naive? The innocent girl with the basket of flowers appearing before the big, bad wolf? We're the same age, don't you think? Tisk, tisk!" she continued, wagging her finger. "We'll have none of that! If you want to know more about me, better to ask than to tell."

He scratched his chin. "You have this old-fashioned way about you. Are you trying to convince me you're from a past life?"

"Bah!" she cried, scolding him with her wand. "In time… in time."

He continued scratching his chin as he ruminated. *Hardly seems a waif. Nor insane. She's far more cunning and sly, and overall, despite her flights of fancy, quite predictable. Evil? No, but untrustworthy…maybe.* He drew in a deep breath, then let it out in a giant, exhausted huff. *On the other hand, she's a live one. Probably wandered down from the Upper 90s or higher…west side. Maybe dances at Julliard…Lincoln Center? Those feet are like rockets: she could tap them in the air and fly away. Her skin is porcelain come to life, and the way her dress wraps over her shoulder is a work of art. Her lips are musty and intense. Worth a kiss, maybe. And those eyes…they might be saying take me, but it's difficult to say. She rejects my advances.*

She tapped her feet on the grass, then rubbed her toes—as if to caress a few blades. With a sniffle and a snort, she dangled her hair to one side, and glancing at his weathered expression from the corner of her eyes, seemed to laugh as she spun around again, then returned to base. "Do you like the way I dance?" she inquired, nonchalantly. "I rather like to twirl."

"Indeed. Indeed...yes...but you could have done it with more elegance," he teased, beginning a puckish grin.

Taken aback, she scolded him with a quick stare, but as if forgetting at once, she twirled again. "Do you like my eyes?" she asked.

"I'll give you a pass."

She smiled, seeing the understatement of his compliment.

For a few minutes, they said nothing. A crisp wind blew across the park, presaging rain. Thunder rumbled in the distance like so many barrels rolling into a pit. The sky darkened, basking the lawns in torpid hues, and off in the distance, water began to drop onto the ground. Only minutes before crowded and lively, the road became desolate, then empty. Smoky fog wafted through the trees.

All the while, she didn't stir. She stood in her place, neck arced, eyes askance, playing with her sleeves with her fingertips, contemplating something and breathing the wet, summer air. Watching her quietly, he judged she was both peaceful and restless, content yet concerned, and from the way her thoughts stirred behind the calmness of her eyes, he felt that the storm approaching must be...her.

She wiped a tear from her cheek, and it began to rain. From his vantage point, she looked vaguely familiar, but he searched in vain to find the source of this suspicion. Had they worked together? Gone to college together? Met once on the beach? Bumped elbows during some late night revelry? He hadn't the foggiest.

"Am I imagining you? Who are you?" he asked suddenly.

Insouciant, she took his question in stride. "Hm...I'm your love faerie. Now don't be silly. Wait, look! Over there! Ask that man," she answered. She proceeded to wave in dainty but determined fashion, her strong thighs holding her up as she craned toward a passing stranger. But the man, whose head was covered with a fedora and whose face pointed toward his brisk-walking feet, didn't look over.

Carl coughed and waved his hand. "Excuse me...excuse me," he said, catching the man's attention. "Am I talking to a beautiful young woman?" Then realizing how foolish he sounded, he immediately turned red.

"Yea, right, Mack! Sure you are. Whatever you say," the man replied, rolling his eyes. The stranger walked away quickly.

Dar'ya straightened up, then raised her chin. "See? He said yes." And with that, she crossed her arms across her breasts, cast a knowing smile in her companion's direction, and alighted on the lawn. She crossed her legs, Indian style. Several pigeons pecked toward her, a response she soaked up with radiance. One came close enough to pet, but she simply made a face, turned her head away, and rested a cheek in her hand, which was propped up by an elbow that dug into her knee.

"You shouldn't feed them. They'll get fat and croak," he said.

"They will turn into frogs?" she teased. "And who are you to notice fat?"

This put him on guard. "Meant nothing by it. Now...do I actually know you from somewhere?" he asked, probingly. "I mean, you're acting as if we've known each other our entire lives."

With this, she drew silent and held her breath. Her moist lips tensed and grew dry, and her once-vibrant gesticulations turned to stillness and reserve. She drew even more into her lungs, as if to heave a sigh, but instead spoke as her breath left her, voice darker and more intense. "I cannot answer this."

"Can't? Or won't?"

Her face creased, revealing delicate lines around her mouth and eyes. "Don't be so strict with me!" she complained with a subtle pout. "If there is some past connection, as you say, between us, then it will bubble up in our hearts. That is how I have set things out."

"Really."

"Uh-huh."

Feeling the strain of their conversation and not knowing how to proceed, Carl leaned further out of his seat and, without looking directly at her, began to imagine women he knew in the past. *Beth McCandless? No, she's living in Seattle. Allison Powers? No, she's a bookworm...no way she's a dancer now.* And on and on he went through his list of women he has once kissed, scrolling through and rejecting each, all the while feeling a vague sense of wonder, even humor, over this situation. *If I kissed her, how could I forget her?* Finally, he looked toward her face, and seeing the light in her eyes, smiled faintly. "Uncle."

"I'm not your uncle."

"It's an expression."

Dar'ya lifted on her toes, a bashful expression appearing over her face, and then, as if to hide her face in shame, she twirled again. Once she returned, her expression was even more radiant than before. "I knew that. You think I don't know such things?" she asked with a twinge of concern.

"I know nothing," he said, repairing her honor.

They fell into silence.

Dar'ya shifted in place, eyeing him thoughtfully. "Are you worrying about work? Men are always stewing over their job, as if there's nothing else!" she exclaimed, exasperated and crinkling her forehead.

Carl sighed. "Maybe I'm not...maybe I am. But I'd rather not talk about it."

"Okay. You don't talk to strangers, either," she replied, feigning hurt feelings.

He eyed her closely, catching a glimpse of the sparkle in her pupils, then realizing she was mocking him as therapy, rather than degradation, he suddenly felt warmth and air in his chest, and with a ray of light creeping into his soul, he managed a broader smile. "You're a vivacious one," he said, examining her, then folding his arms across his chest. He started to laugh. "You don't give up, do you? Shouldn't you try to relax?"

"*Les gouts et les couleurs ne se discutent pas,*" she retorted, blinking in exaggerated fashion.[ii] "*Monsieur,* why would a damsel in distress like me, upon meeting a knight in shining armor, ever stoop to *trying*? Anything? Am I not something you would like to catch? Like a furry little creature? A kitten, perhaps?"

"I hate cats."

Dismayed, her face turned crimson as she rapped him again with her wand. "Hm, there!" she said, wagging an index finger. "That will teach you to speak to a lady with such proud words." Her face softened and she turned aside, pretending his eyes would not follow her. "You see? I can ignore you at will. A man? Hah...would not pay a kopeck for one![iii] They are all the same, yes? They give you flowers," she sighed languidly, "and then they sing you these songs like they're lovers in a pastoral comedy, and then, of course, they line up in a row and ask for your hand, and you must shoo them away because you don't love them. Eh...are you listening to my sermon, young man? You are, good...I don't know, there are so many scenarios: maybe I love one but his fortunes have turned, or his parents do not approve of me. This is impossible, but such complications exist, you know," she added, distractedly, as if reminiscing. "And you? How do you win over a lady?"

"I don't, so you're barking up the wrong tree," he said at once, surprising himself with his candor, yet also realizing in a dark corner of his soul that he would let no woman—no one so lively and beautiful, to say the least—so deep into his life when so much self-repair was needed, unless he knew her. "Sorry...no offense. What I meant was...I...to be honest...I am broke, homeless, and unemployed. I haven't showered in two days, my face is becoming like tangled wire, and on top of that, I was dumped today by my girlfriend and living mate. And I have no prospects."

She yelped at this bluntness, but quickly recovered; an expression of concern grew on her face. "That is all so sad and unfortunate. It's true. Now I have to pity you," she said, making him feel worse.

"I'm a catastrophe. Stay away. My life's gone up in flames."

"Flames of passion, or destruction? I see the latter. Well, then...I was mistaken," she said, suddenly straight-faced, "I did not realize I was in the hospital ward visiting a wounded man of war. Yes? You feel this way? But I have seen such men in my time, and far worse, I think they looked more forsaken than you."

He frowned.

"Cheer up!" she sang, playing with her hair. "Maybe your luck has changed for the better."

He thought for a moment while she watched for his response. The wind softly blew their hair, splashing their faces in silk, and both man and woman breathed quietly, feeling exhausted now.

"Where do you live?" he asked, resigned to her presence. "Really. I mean it."

"Here and about," she replied, suddenly vulnerable and demure. The light in her eyes danced with her feet, while the expression she wore projected a sense of restraint and caution. "I don't live here. That much I can tell you."

Surprised, he shifted back on the bench, slid his hands under his thighs, and blinked. "Then where are you from?"

"That's a different question."

"True. Let me guess. New Jersey."

She shook her head. "Nope."

"Boston."

"Nope."

"California?" he said, taking a long shot.

"No, no, and no to all the above!" she cried with a cryptic humph. "You may properly say I come from where you may be going. If you're lucky and good."

He wet his lips, thinking. "And where might that be?"

"That is your choice."

"Excuse me," he said, "but this conversation is unlike any I've ever had, yet at the same time, I must say you seem entirely sincere...even warm, and...and I...I don't know...what to make of you."

She giggled, then replied,

"We once knew love both high and low;
We lived out east, o'er plains of white and snow."

"You rhymed. Do you know why my ex threw me out?"

She grimaced. "No, but I don't care. It's her loss."

This response, although coming from someone he barely knew, had its appeal, and in his heart he felt, at the very least, a sense of connection with this darling. Truth was, he was even taken aback by her forthrightness and even, dare he think it, her interest in him. It was clear from her body language—the smoky stares, her twitching toes, the frequent spins and even her blushing—along with her soothing words of confidence and concern, that she was coming on to him in some way. But, at the same time, she maintained her distance, perhaps for a good reason, as if something beyond her control prevented her from revealing the purpose behind her appearance. He sensed she had sought him out somehow, yet at the same time, she only wished for a passing glance, or wanted to keep circumstances, if not distant, at least under control. The tension within her became his, as well. While he wanted to dive into this chance to find someone who would accept him in his stricken state, he felt he must maintain his cool, lest he fall in too deep or scare her off.

It rained, then stopped.

"You got wet in the rain," he said.

"I laugh at the rain. I laugh in the rain. It's all the same," she said with a clever grin. "And you? Do you care if you get wet?"

"Not really," he said, shaking his head.

She nodded, as if to her own thoughts. "It's nothing to be wet. I have seen men drag themselves through mud and hail and cannon fire, some with nothing to eat. There is nothing to this wet if you are not shivering and cold," she said, voice trailing off.

"You've seen hard times."

She turned a cheek to the side. "Hard times...good times," she said, lips softening. "You must have had good times, too. Yes?"

His face glowed with her suggestion. "Absolutely."

"*Hresho*. Then you're healthy. I'm sorry to see such a handsome young man in distress. You don't have work?"

"No."

"No, I'm wrong, or no, I have no work?"

"I already told you this. I'm unemployed. At least in three weeks."

"Aha. Then you will find new work?"

"Doubt it."

"What do you do?"

"I'm over-skilled. In technology."

"And this is a problem? Strange place in which you live."

"Strange times, too."

"Yes. Many times are strange...in different ways. If they were strange in the same way, they would be normal."

Hearing the irony in her voice, his mood brightened. Whereas only a few hours ago he felt desolate...abandoned... now he had someone with whom to pass his time. Perhaps a friend, but at least an acquaintance with a sense of what a friend would be. He studied her once again—her face, her silken hair, her shimmering eyes—and imagined what it would be like to kiss her. But as soon as this thought entered his mind, his chest tightened, his heart froze, and the air stopped bellowing in his lungs. "Impossible!" he scolded himself. "No time for wishful thinking." More urgent matters pressed.

"Your mind shifts like the sea," she said, her voice suddenly delicate and tender. "When I look into your face, I see the waves crashing against cliffs...the albatross soaring in the air on outstretched wings, and catching a current, which takes him out of sight. The skies are sunny and grey, like an old man, and the sullen sands lay to rest after a busy day of tossing in the surf. Yes? This is you, yes?" she asked, pensively.

He took in her words, letting them ride the long swells of his breath, and with a feeling of chill, and with the falling light dabbling his forehead, he unfolded his arms and addressed her warmly. "I'm none of these things, but it's a portrait you might paint, watching me from a distance. Right now I think I'm the little conch on the shoreline, wrapped up in his little shell, pondering when the next wave will take me back to sea."

"Yes! Yes! I can see him. And this sea," she asked. "Does it sing? Is it splashing against stone in a voice so loud its words are obscured?"

Since the downpour had drenched the stricken young man and the sun was fading, his teeth began to chatter. "I could pass my time by this sea. But I cannot be in it."

"But you must. You could…of course you should," she said, closing her eyes. "And I would. You must go on vacation there at once. I'll buy you a ticket!" she said teasingly, holding out her fingers as if handing him a slip of paper. "Here, take it."

Carl didn't reach out, but he smiled at her playful nonchalance, wondering when he had last met someone so spontaneous and open. "I will. But be careful of people with whom you give so freely."

"Charming," she replied, ruefully, and feeling she might lose the upper hand. "I'm the sea and the wind and the hallowed stars. I've been and seen all there is to be and to sea I have taken it. Now, I have arrived with the trade winds at your peeping shell, where you can see me. Your heart's content now. For a moment. I think I must be leaving."

"Where are you going?" he asked.

"Where you are, I hope."

"And where's that?"

"Hm!" she exclaimed, blowing her cheeks in mock disgust and gazing past the treetops. "To a cloud. But wait for my return. I'll be back...and don't despair. I'm thinking already about you, and I think, perhaps, I have an idea. We shall see. Oh, you will be so pleased if I am right! And I will find you what you truly need, and perhaps what you want, too. There will be some lovely lady in your life; I think I can feel her presence, and perhaps it will be me?" she added, expressing a sudden thought. "Maybe, maybe not. I've not decided how that shall be resolved...nor how it could be resolved. Matters are complicated, you know. Do you understand? No, of course not. I'm sorry. Anyway, today is a joyous day! The stars are aligned...and you, my furry friend, are going to have Cupid's best at your behest," she said with finality and triumph.

"You're going to fix my life?" he asked.
"I'll find you a wife."
"Surely, you jest."
"Relax. Call this a test."
"Do you have a credential?"
"I'm sentimental."
"Is this consistent?"
"On this, I'm insistent."

She paused, lifted onto her toes, and spun in a circle again, landing in her original place and wearing a mischievous smile. Then she tossed the wand over her shoulder, where it rested lightly. "I once danced at the Mariinsky," she bragged, reaching down and brushing off a leaf that had attached itself to her slipper.

"A ballerina," he noted, impressed.

She responded with a nonchalant shrug. "A former one. Now my legs feel old."

He chuckled at the suggestion of age coming from such a ravishingly beautiful young woman who could not be, he felt, more than his own age of twenty-eight. Noticing the admiration in his eyes, she returned a demure look, her lips at once more full and lush than before. She shifted her weight onto the opposite foot, and with feigned indifference, yet with twinkles in her eyes, she waved the wand across his chest before returning it to her side, and said, "Perhaps I can make your problems disappear. Perhaps I'm magic, yes?" Then she began laughing, as if inspired by her own trickery.

"Your wand. You think this is magic, I take it?"

"You may not take it. It's mine to keep...at least until I return it. Your language is difficult. Yes, you are observant, though. It's a prop; I got it in wardrobe. Right before I left to see you. They gave me my choice and I liked it. Do you like my dress, too? Hmph! I don't need this stick with a star! The powers I can summon need no objects like this. However, I thought it would be fun! Is it not? Do you not appreciate my charms and entertainments?"

Not wanting to play the dupe, he said nothing.

"Hm. A skeptic. There's a need for more romance in you, my dear soldier! You didn't fight your wars to be a sullen, little grump! You can do better!" Eyeing him closely, she paused for a breath.

"Not in this town," he replied.

She pressed an index finger against her lips, then rolled her eyes upward in thought. "It's possible to improve your situation. We'll see. I'll make some inquiries. Find our where to look...see who's available...but...oh!"

At this moment, they heard a light, tinseled chime. It resonated in decrescendo, then lingered in the air.

"Ew...what's that?" she exclaimed with a jolt.

Fumbling with his belt and looking for his mobile phone, Carl replied in hurried fashion, "Must be my cell."

"No, it's my bell." She looked up, drew in a sudden thought, then sighed. "I've got to go. No more pretensions."

"Aww...it was getting fun," he chided.

This pleased her immensely: she drew in a long breath, her eyes glowed softly, and she blew out a phrase in reckless style. "It was fun, handsome, but I must go!" With this, she raised her wand into the air, cast him another glance, then heaved a withering sigh. She tapped her wand on her crown, and—

Bing!

She disappeared.

The wand tumbled, end-over-end, in the air, stopped, then crumbled to the ground. Startled, he stared at the spot where a ravishing young woman had just been replaced by a thin, brass rod that was crowned with a star.

Immediately, and to his shock, she returned, blushing an intense shade of red. "Oops!" she said, flustered and embarrassed. "I forgot my wand!" And she picked it up, and her mood visibly brightened for a moment, then darkened, and with a sudden surge of confidence, she gave him the once-over again, and said, "Stay dry, my little sailor! And ta, ta!" Then—

Bing!

Both wand and faerie disappeared.

CHAPTER THREE

(1)

Carl awoke before 5:00 AM, not needing an alarm clock, which he considered a good thing because he didn't have one. Two days had passed since the dramatic exit from his ex-girlfriend's apartment; he spent the in-between day aimlessly wandering around the Upper West Side. His watch still worked, and the battery might last for another six months, but in the midst of his bush-lined fortress, surrounded by summer foliage and the resplendent architecture that peeked through cracks in the tree line, he also rejected the need to keep time. His foresty existence seemed at once timely—it was warm enough to live here comfortably—and timeless, not least because he'd met this beguiling faerie. *I must be losing my mind*, he thought. *But I saw her as clear as day. Didn't that really happen?*

In the distance, a few taxis honked and tires rolled along the elliptical road of the park, but he barely noticed them.

It took another half hour to wake up, and then he realized he needed to get moving—to do something—because as much as he might need peace, solitude and meditation now, a pressing sense of urgency had overcome him. He must get back into the job market, he realized, and land something before the cold winds of autumn arrived. In his precarious position, he needed to calculate a budget in minute detail. He needed to hit the pavement. Find a job. In short, he needed to live in the real world, no matter how attractive this time off might feel.

With the latter thought, he posed himself a question. Should he clear his mind completely by taking a quick trip, say to the Caribbean, knowing he shouldn't spend the money, but making him, perhaps, more marketable by appearing more content and less desperate? Should he get realistic and move back to upstate New York, where his parents owned a farm...they might accept him into his old bedroom. *No*, he thought, *absolutely impossible. They resented the last time I moved home...between the job in Cleveland and here.* Should he hunker down, get a routine going, and do his utmost to get back on the treadmill when, after all, this was a vibrant economy?

Or so it looked from the outside.

The first order of business was to write out a list of his contacts, which he did on a stray piece of notebook paper that he found tucked in the recesses of his backpack. But in Manhattan, where he was still a newcomer, he soon realized his list contained a sum total of zero. He crumpled up the paper and threw it, disgustedly, on the ground.

Yet the required exit interview at Frontier Reinsurance was this morning, he realized, and between now and 10:00 AM he'd need to clean up at the gym, where he could shower and shave, throw on some decent clothes, and think over his agenda. No doubt, they had theirs.

With this in mind, he searched through his backpack, finding a collared button-down shirt, a wrinkled pair of khakis—the company was business casual, anyway—and a pair of semi-clean socks. He unfolded everything on top of his pack's main storage compartment. He dressed. Then with a huff, he slung the padded strap over his right shoulder and stood up, stretched his arms, and headed for the gym. It would open at 6:00.

It took several minutes to reach. By the time he arrived, the door was open and a small line of early risers was filing inside. Despite the early hour, Carl felt the pulse of the city: the miles of road extending up and down the park, with glowing traffic lights far off into the distance, and taxis, minivans, and cars whisking by while people walked briskly along the sidewalks. It was not crowded yet, but the buzz was unmistakable, even palpable, and even here on Amsterdam Avenue—a relatively quiet stretch of road between Central Park West and Broadway.

He coughed, pressing his anxiety down as best he could, then with resolve he stepped into the club for his morning workout. Inside, the Stairmasters, treadmills, and exercise bikes were dotted with weary strivers who, for better or worse, dragged themselves into the gym three or four times a week— the more foolhardy were here almost every day—at the crack of dawn. Some looked ready to challenge the world, oblivious in headphones and steel-hued faces, while others, drawn and pale, could have used an extra few hours of sleep. Carl scarcely observed them, although on the way to the men's locker room he thought he detected a few glances at his beard.

Carl's first action of the morning was to shave; soon whiskers were clinging to the sink, and he rinsed them away with the back of his hand. He looked at himself in the mirror for the first time in two days: droopy eyelids and dark circles decorated his eyes. Ashamed of his appearance, he saw here a hobo who had dragged himself into a public washroom for his weekly clean-up. He turned on the faucet, cupped his hands underneath it, and splashed the water over his face.

Immediately, he noticed an effect. His expression turned more awake, and gradually a gleam returned to his pupils, a gleam grounded in a rolling sense of connection to this visage, and therefore to himself.

He liked the change he saw.

His workout was uneventful. By the time he exited the gym, dressed in his chosen attire and feeling snappy, even confident, he had burned through two more hours. He turned west, walked to Broadway, then headed south a few blocks to the 72nd Street subway station, where he quickly caught a southbound 3 to 23rd Street, the stop closest to his destination.

Carl stepped into the light, and the squealing, screeching ride on the underground train was replaced by the buzz of Madison Square Park, the hum of food carts and the whizzing of cars. The passenger sign turned green. Tucking his notebook under his left arm, he stepped onto the street and headed briskly for a corner cafe, where he would wait for the appointment.

The office was nearby. Carl rang the buzzer at precisely 9:59 AM, according to his watch, and they buzzed him up without inquiry. Since the building lacked a security post, he walked to the elevator, a relic of the 1940s it appeared, and lumbered up to the fifth floor where he used to work. Now he needed a guest pass. The receptionist was warm and kind, clearly sympathetic, and lacking any desire to make the rounds in his awkward position, he found a seat alongside the wall, feeling silly with the guest pass stuck to his shirt, and grabbed a copy of *People Magazine*—he chose it over a number of business magazines and papers—then proceeded to read.

Fifteen minutes later, Kerry White appeared in a whirl. "Oh, there you are! My apologies…let's go. Jack's expecting you. Come…come. Hurry up. He'll be joining us in a minute.

Here...do you want some coffee? Here. Let's head to my office. Let's hurry, though. I have so many people to see today." She rolled her eyes. Indeed, he thought, he was one of several who had been axed. He followed her down the narrow corridor to her office, where the door was ajar.

A trim, efficient women in her late thirties, White didn't want for energy. Her brown eyes sparkled with doe-eyed, sensual vulnerability; at the same time, her voice was crisp, even tart, in contrast to the silken shine of her hair, her delicate skin, and neat, trimmed appearance. She had a slight Southern accent, but her charm was counterbalanced by a decidedly New York edge. On her desk sat a coffee mug with "Don't Mess with Texas" emblazoned on it. She sat behind the desk, rattling on and eyeing him strangely, as if there were something wrong with him.

"First off, don't worry," she said. "There are all kinds of jobs for people with your skills out there. Things work out for the best. My mother says that." She sipped her beverage. "I was on the phone with a friend who works in HR...a background check company down in Birmingham. They say they can't get enough people...may need to..." Thinking twice, she trailed off, taking a noisy slurp.

Carl began to perspire.

"What was I saying?" she continued. "Oh, yes...jobs, jobs, jobs! So many jobs! Someone like you," she said, her voice suddenly emphatic, "will go straight to the top. I'm sure in no time you'll have an army of programmers working for you."

Finding her words condescending, Carl shrugged and said, "Sure. Unless I get hit by a truck."

She gasped, yet seemed to savor his response. "You'll have health coverage. Don't worry. There'll be no dismemberment on my conscience. No way, José," she stammered awkwardly, attempting to stir a laugh from him, which he partially offered. "This is not a contentious situation. It's a positive. For you and for Frontier Re. I'm glad to see you smiling. That's the whole point!" She fixed her gaze on him for a moment, then turned to the papers on her desk. "We have...let me see right here. Oh yes, I just wanted to make sure...we have you on payroll through the next three weeks, when you officially terminate. Everyone gets this package per company policy. Then at that point, you get an additional two weeks' pay as a discretionary bonus...don't worry, we're calling it a resignation...upon certain stipulations, and I'll get to them shortly. Once Jack arrives. Where is he? Anyway, we have you on the health care package for...for...COBRA. Yes...you're entitled to extend your coverage under the medical plan for eighteen months past the termination of your company coverage by paying a small monthly fee. I think it's $400 now, but at any rate it's a lot cheaper than plastic surgery! I don't mean to be facetious. I'm trying to make this easier for you. I don't know why I said that." Suddenly, she looked at her fingernails as if she wanted to bite them. "Where's Jack? I hate it when he's delayed."

Just then, Jack Baker walked into the room. Stalwart, expensively dressed and in his mid-forties, he conveyed a sense of confidence, albeit a smug version of it.

"Jack...Jack," said White. "We've already discussed the benefits package. Why don't you cover the business side now?"

Nodding his head slowly and smiling to himself, as if absorbed in pleasant thoughts unrelated to his task, yet engaged, nonetheless, Baker leaned against the back wall, his posture languid to the point of a slouch. "Carl. We're sorry it had to turn out this way. Especially so soon. What I mean is, business is what it is. We're professionals. We understand each other."

Carl shifted in his chair, folded his hands in his lap, and managed a wan smile. "Sure. But please, get to the point. Need to spend time on my job search."

Baker raised an eyebrow. With his face turning more sour and his voice darkening, he responded, "You'll need to spend your time wisely in this meeting, or life will get painful for you. Real soon."

"Listen to Jack. Be productive," White added, her voice crass.

A moment of silence ensued.

Baker glanced at his executive underling, noted her complicity then paused, drew a short breath as if to raise the gravitas of his speech, and turned his eyes on Carl, who felt under a microscope—germ-like and squiggling. "Thank you for coming on time today. We're glad to have this chance to have a conversation. You did good work here. That's something you can take with you wherever you go. We're not firing you." He flashed a smile. "And we always regret losing good people such as yourself. But the thing is, and it'll be helpful for you to realize this in your career...there are other good people out there, too. Others willing to do the same job, but for less. That gets me excited."

Carl bit down his anger; he detested this man.

"And the trick to staying in the game is to keep building your skill set," Baker continued. "Which is why we have one more challenge left waiting for you: to train your replacements. It's an opportunity for career growth."

"Oh. You want me to work? You've got to be kidding."

"Do I look like a kidder? I was in your shoes once, and I never would have talked to management that way. Typical now. You know, your generation doesn't appreciate a good job while you have it."

White coughed slightly. "What he's saying, Carl, is we can hire H-1Bs to write code. Based on our skill matching model, we think they can do almost the same work that you can, but for far less money. All within twelve months' time. So why wouldn't we jump at the opportunity? That's a significant bottom line savings for us. One we can't ignore in a competitive marketplace. You understand. Don't look so...I don't want to see you fuming. We've giving you—"

"So you're saying that because I'm less than one year into a new job, where by the way I was building up a database of upgrades for our software...that would've helped us crush our competitors out there...and where I was repairing relationships with your client base...you cut me loose because I haven't already healed the sick and made the blind see. That would be the only way to keep employment at this crap house?"

"Can you *do* that?" she asked in a cutting and sarcastic tone. Baker chuckled, sharing a glance with her.

"No, but I'm always glad to sacrifice myself on the cross of business need."

"Excellent!" Baker interjected, wanting to go with the joke, however phony.

"Really," Carl continued, emboldened. "I did a number of things while I was here on the customer side. In my conversations with Ken Marino...you know how much he spent here last year...I heard all kinds of gripes about our web interface. I stored his comments on a spreadsheet. He says it's buggy, non-intuitive, lacks features he needs. Only I know what your customers want. Mr. Baker, if I can be formal, you're too busy sailing that boat in Maine. And Ms. White, when was the last time you slopped in the trenches?"

White expressed faux shock. With this backlash, she seemed to feel it was only getting fun.

Carl pointed a finger at Baker, looking at White. "Your boss is living in La La Land if he thinks he can run a business like some ancient slave ship. Row, row...do set task as we define it. Don't be creative. No give-and-take. No feedback from the galley slaves. Yea...that's real flexibility for a dynamic world. See how long your scheme lasts."

Her voice cracked. "We can pick up whatever relationships you have. And where's that spreadsheet? It belongs to us."

"Really? How about the file is on my hard drive at home? Hell, I don't remember. And everything else is stored in my brain...which is about to walk out your door."

Offended and ruffled, Baker sneered, "We can terminate you with cause for that. Whatever intellectual property you have in your head belongs to us. You'll need to write it down. But as for your...assessment...of our...business model," he continued, nasty smile plastered across his face, "that's for us to determine."

Not liking the tension in the room, White bit her right thumbnail, then threw down her hand in disgust. "Jack's right. Here's the thing. Your continued employment at this Firm, for the next three weeks, and the severance package I've laid out, is dependent on your cooperation. Your attitude. Because if you decide to march to the beat of your own drummer, well then, we can get the word around to potential employers. It's a small world. You decide."

Baker crossed his arms across his chest, then shrugged as if to say, "what more can I add to that?" His mouth crinkled into a grin as he eyed Carl, whose face was boiling.

Carl huffed, "Yea? Well, I have an appointment with a recruiter tomorrow afternoon. Florence Mirza. She says there may be two companies..." His voice trailed off as White's cheeks narrowed with delight. *Oh, crap. I gave them her name.*

He slumped in his chair, bracing himself for the blow. "There are two companies interested in me."

"Really," White grimaced. "I'm so impressed? Flo and I are old girlfriends...run in the same circles. We're on the same wavelength." She said this with burning, piercing satisfaction.

Carl felt the room getting warmer. "Uh...nothing's certain yet, but I know I'm employable. I'll keep your offer in mind... but you might want to consider upping the ante. My uncle works the casinos in Atlantic City. Know a house bet when I see it. May have to start a new job immediately, too. You don't want to be left out in the cold, do you?"

Baker laughed, superciliously. "We don't. But we can recover. You can't."

This ended the conversation.

Carl left in a daze. Anxious and conflicted, and moreover uncomfortable with their demands, he decided to think things over. Sleep on it. Meet with the headhunter. Decide later. Still feeling the sting from his previous employer, he vowed to fight back.

Even if it meant torpedoing their offer.

(2)

Florence Mirza pressed her back against her tall, leather-bound chair, surveying Carl's face with a skeptical air. Her demeanor and the short clips in which she spoke contrasted sharply with the warm, enthusiastic impression she'd left in their phone conversation. Immediately and deep down, Carl knew she must have spoken to Kerry White already.

Carl sat in the chair closest to her desk, wanting to convey a hint of aggression. Notebook on his lap, he responded to her questions with a confident, even strident, tone of voice. But inside, he risked unraveling. "No, that's not right. I still work there."

"I see. But you came in so suddenly. Why not wait? See what else is out there?"

"I'm looking to make a change. Number one, I want more interaction with customers. More strategy, like a business analyst. To use my master's degree...be more than a coder."

She studied him, squeezing together her lips. "Do you have the experience to justify a move like this?"

Carl leaned forward, emphatic. "Yes. Sure, without a doubt. I can talk with anyone about the client relationships I built up. Technically, it wasn't in my job description, but...you know..." He looked into her face, wanting to see a spark of life.

"Sounds like someone trying to make himself into something he's not," she said, grimacing. "Oh, sure, I can put your skills...what computer languages you know...into my database. And I will. You never know what someone might need. I get sudden calls now and then. But my clients'll never hire me again if I sell a product...that would be you...who doesn't deliver the goods. Try again. What are you looking for?"

Truth was, Carl knew she had boxed him into a corner. On the one hand, he couldn't look for another job exactly like the one he had, because it would raise a red flag. Why would he leave a job to do the same thing, they would ask. It also would demonstrate a lack of ambition. On the other, he felt certain the ladies had talked already, and neither White nor Baker would ever vouch for any claims of expanded job responsibility without Carl's doing precisely what they asked of him. And it all was a humiliation. With skills as hot as his, he questioned whether he needed to let a second company in a row push him around and whether he could continue living like some disk at the end of someone else's yo-yo ring. For a lousy two weeks' bonus. He hadn't made up his mind yet, so he hedged. "Frontier Re has me entering a new project over the next few weeks...if I choose to take it. I'm inclined to, so—"

Mirza frowned. "A project. Mr. Moretti, we need more than a...what...two, three week project...to boost your resume. Show me something I can use."

Her acidity infuriated him. Carl began to shake; she noticed, and he saw she noticed.

"Quickly!" she added, glancing at her watch. "I don't have much time."

Carl harnessed all his reserves of strength, slowed his breath to stave off hyperventilation, and responded with a low, suppressed growl. He knew there was no more time for this game. "Ms. Mirza. With all due respect. Let's cut the bs. Okay? I know you know Kerry White. She told me. And it's abundantly clear from your tone of voice that you've spoken already. So let's talk turkey."

Mirza relaxed, then managed a tone of genuine sympathy. "We did, indeed, speak." She sighed, gathering her thoughts. "And she said, and I'll have to agree, having met you, that you're a difficult cat to manage. Your feistiness, in this setting...I find highly inappropriate. Unproductive."

Carl's pulse quickened. He wanted fresh air. "A popular word this week. But that's preposterous."

"It's fact. Another fact: I cannot recommend you to future employers, on whom my livelihood depends, with...with...this. And they know you checked your personal email from work. Dennis Kucinich! Really...a visa restrictionist. This brands you an outsider in management circles. What next? Ralph Nader? Hm. The two prospects have disappeared."

Protesting, Carl yelped, "But I haven't even rejected their offer! They gave it to me so suddenly…what was I going to do? Oh, hell. What do you care?" he asked, seeing his adversary refuse to budge.

Her visage became cross. "Out! Get out of my office! Now!"

The situation hopeless, and not willing to debase himself further, Carl sighed and stood up to go. "Good luck. You'll need it. And I consider this office…forget it. It's not worth the breath."

Carl marched out of the room.

CHAPTER FOUR

(1)

Feeling a need to recover a sense of power over his own fate, and knowing the company had already smeared him, Carl summarily rejected the offer to train the new recruits. This meant foregoing the meager severance offer and any immediate chances for employment. And since his brief job hunt energies, amidst the suddenness and chaos of his job loss, had led only to Mirza, he had nothing left at the moment. Furthermore, he found it difficult to think clearly under the intense confusion he felt.

Carl spent the following morning in his Central Park hovel. Sulking.

It was Saturday.

But hanging around in the bushes soon became tedious for the normally effervescent young man, and with nothing better to do, and needing to clear his thoughts, he headed out the 72nd Street exit, then south, where he could immerse himself in human activity. As he walked along the Central Park West promenade, then along Broadway once he hit Columbus Circle, the city had its usual bustle, despite the usual migration to the Hamptons, the Jersey Shore, and other, cooler spots; in the midst of the noise, the fumes, and the occasional honking of horns, Carl found the immersion cathartic. He loved the city: its pulse, the flickering trees that stretched toward rooftops above rolling hills of cement, the teeming cafes casually strewn along summer sidewalks, and the pungent yet textured scents of neighborhoods.

He wandered all the way to Chelsea.

Then at 19th Street, he ducked into a gourmet café, hesitated over the $2.95 price of a baguette, and realizing he needed sustenance, took the plunge, wolfing down the bread in a series of gulps. Next he swigged down a fresh bottle of Evian, noted the dent he had made in his dwindling bank account, and with mixed feelings of anxiety and freedom, stepped back outside into the heat. Against a wall, a thermometer read 87 degrees, but with the humidity, it felt steam room hot—too hot to stay outside long—and feeling he needed to keep moving, but not knowing where to go, he crossed into Union Square Park, taking in the quiet, summer tempo of the glade. He strolled past a bustling restaurant, then headed south to the Cineplex. By the time he arrived, he needed another drink of water, which he duly bought from a street vendor.

"Thank you," said the upbeat, gruff voice, which trailed in Carl's mind as he entered the air conditioned box office. Once he reached the ticket line, the young man scanned the film selections, hoping to find something light. But the offerings were the usual summer retreads and action flicks, and noticing his stomach was upset and resisting the prospect of dooming himself to a cramped, narrow seat in a dark theater for 90, 120 minutes or more, he paused, took his longest breath of the day, and glanced around. His sense of anticipation rose; he tried to focus. Where should he go? What should he do? He needed money now. Was there anything he needed to accomplish today, or should he take it easy? He thought about the vibrant city streets he loved so much; they awaited him outside, where the sun was bright and the skies blue and expansive. *Better to be outside*, he thought, stepping back into the oppressive heat.

He walked back to the food cart, bought a hot dog and started to grab a pretzel, but thought better of the latter, judging he needed to conserve the 17 dollars left in his wallet. He left with a bottle of water, too, and two napkins, but he decided to save the napkins for a rainy day.

A taxi nearly hit him as he crossed Broadway. Carl winced, shook his hot dog in the crazy driver's direction, and backtracked to Union Square Park in order to catch a few more minutes of shade. From there, he walked up Park Avenue South as far as 57th Street where, despite his good health, he felt compelled to head west to McDonald's for an iced tea and a place to rest. He chose a table near the picture window that overlooked the street, and in the coolness of the restaurant and despite his choleric mood, he managed to chill, relax, and forget his reason for the walk, which, he knew, was without rhyme or reason.

Even looking at the menu of McDonald's made him worry about money. However, he tried his best to enjoy the drink. *Better fill out that unemployment application now,* he thought, his mind clearer now. He remembered the number was in his backpack and he decided to head straight home from here, fetch it, and make the call first thing on Monday. He managed to laugh when he remembered he lived in the bushes like a common squirrel. *Head home. Yea, right.*

He remained in his seat for another half hour. Then, without thinking much because he felt so numb, he tossed his waste into the trash and left the restaurant.

(2)

Monday rolled in at a summer's pace.

The park was quiet, and the city seemed unanxious to start another work week when the beaches were long and the weekend too short. Under the shade of large maple trees and covered wall-to-wall with verdant carpet, Carl's clump of bushes evoked nostalgia for his teenage camping trips to Philmont, the Rockies, and many state parks around Syracuse. Carl rummaged through his backpack, which was partially obscured by a clump of branches—where he had hidden it. He fetched the number, then turned on his cell phone.

Pressing the phone against his left ear, he stood up.

Off in the distance, a police car sat with lights blinking, apparently questioning someone. Beside it, several boxy and white trucks rumbled down Central Park West. Carl's temporary home felt peaceful and safe, yet the world outside pressed in.

Not wanting to think about this anymore, he called the telephone claims number: 888-209-8124. With the battery indicator on low, he needed to make this quick.

Before long, he had a representative on the line. "Are you working now?" she asked, bored.

"Technically, yes, but I thought I should—"

"How many hours a week?"

"Full-time, but I'm only on payroll for a few more weeks." He went on to explain the situation.

"I'm sorry. You'll need to wait until your official termination date. Then call back this number to open your claim. And to draw unemployment you need to be looking for a job, in the United States, and you need to be working less than four days a week and be earning 405 dollars a week or less."

Carl became frustrated. "That's a lot of buts. How can I pay my COBRA insurance on that amount? Do you have any idea how much debt I have?"

"I'm sorry, sir. You'll have to speak to your creditors about those debts. That's not our department's concern.

Unemployment insurance is here to defray your job hunting expenses, not to help you survive a layoff. Yes, we know you spend the money on groceries...but that's the purpose behind insurance...I don't make the rules."

He gripped his cell phone. "So you're there to get me back on the wagon. When I get tossed into the street like this, it's all on me."

"Like I said, I don't make the rules. And don't forget you'll need to deduct federal, state and local taxes from your check. And you'll need to keep track of all your job prospects, contacts made, and then report your job hunting activity every week."

"My cell phone's running out of juice. How can I make so many calls like that?"

"You can always go to the unemployment office in Queens."

"I can't afford a subway token," he lamented, exasperated.

"You will if you draw unemployment, sir."

Carl threw up his hands in disgust. *They always win. How do I get an edge in this world?* He pressed the phone back to his ear. "You're telling me I'm better off finding a job...and at the same time, you're not actually offering me a job. That's like credit card companies demanding payment on time but pitching your resume."

Her tone went from laconic to annoyed. "We have job postings in our offices. Do you have skills? A high school degree?"

"Yea! Yea!" he shouted. "And a graduate degree in computer science, and four programming languages, and—"

"Then I don't know what you're complaining about."

Carl pulled the phone so close to his lips, he could almost eat it. "Oh yea? You sound so cushy over there. How about my situation? Do you know where I'm sitting now? In my new home on the grass! Sure, opportunities abound for a guy with my skills! That's what everyone says! Cakewalk out there, huh? Lose your job, no problemo," he said, feeling somewhat better vis-à-vis dishing on the telephone rep.

"Sir, I deal with unemployed people all day long. No one's having fun when they're laid off. Frankly, if they laid me off I'd be relieved. But for your own sake you really should try to make this a vacation."

"I am!" Flummoxed, Carl stopped hyperventilating and paused. He took a long breath. *Lady's right*, he thought, gathering himself. *I'm getting way too stressed out. Have to chill. Take in the scenery around here.* He pulled himself together. "Okay. So I call this number when—"

The battery went dead.

Carl cursed, looked at the phone with disappointment, then clasped it shut and placed it back into his backpack. He sat down. Settled on the moistness of the lawn, he closed his eyes. Gradually, fond memories of youth—musty-scented earth, a laugh in the campground, slurping Tang from plastic cups—unfolded from the recesses of his mind. His breath slowed, his pulse lowered, and he gradually fell back into the grass, almost asleep.

Suddenly, he felt something brush against his right knee. Startled, he threw open his eyelids and made a fist, only to hear a sweet, flirtatious voice address him.

"You sleep in my presence?"

Carl looked at her. "Dar'ya...you're back." As his eyes cleared, he saw her languishing against a bush opposite him, arm strewn over the top, tiny skirt dangling over her lean thighs, and one slipper standing at a point to the ground. Her smile was wide and her eyes shined, as if admiring him, and her dimpled cheeks, both crimson and bright, displayed a charming, if not entirely straightforward, invitation. Her figure skater-like dress completed the picture of a woman who, despite her playful manner, presented herself with poise, style, and grace.

"My mind's flipped again," he said to her. At the same time, be felt comforted by her presence, and although he lacked a calendar now, he felt as if he might begin marking time through her steadiness. "Uh...what are you doing here? Last time you...you disappeared into thin air. How'd you do that? You some kind of magician? I thought maybe last time you disappeared it was...I don't know...some kind of a joke. Someone playing a prank. Are you playing a prank? What is this, some Candid Camera show where they play tricks on people?" he stammered.

She laughed warmly. "No, silly. It's me. Your shimmering goddess. Feeling a need to defend your sanity? There's no need. Aren't you glad I returned? Look at me. Am I not dazzling?" she said, having fun. "Am I becoming your guardian angel? That would be smashing! Hm. Perhaps I am. Anyway, it's delightful...why the puzzlement? Can you not appreciate my beauty?" she asked, eyes watering with passion. "Perhaps I can trick you after all...make you obey my magic wand." She twirled her little stick with an insouciant toss of the chin. "Do you...yes, this is so sheik to have you respond this way, my dear Mark. May I call you Marik now? It's more familiar. Oh, this would be so charming. Do I dare call you this? I don't intend to tease. At least not too much." She winked, then suddenly cooled; a glow appeared across her soft-featured face. She peered into the sky. "Hm...we'll see, shan't we not?" She spoke as if people were listening in the air above her.

Carl ran his hands through his thick, scrappy locks. "You are from a different era. Not that it's all bad at all. But it's... forgive my modern English, but it's freaking me out a little."

Dar'ya twirled in place, then returned her gaze to him, this time with longing. "I don't feel this separation. I feel the air again! How it feels against my face. It's almost like heaven. But not quite! Feeling the air again...twirling...all these things we do when we're in...ooh, I shouldn't say that."

Flummoxed, he looked over this ravaging beauty, then darted his eyes away. "I'm not seeing you. This is unreal. Verging on unemployed, living like a hobo, no money...and a beautiful woman sudden appears and has the hots for me? Yep, this isn't happening! I must say, however...at least in my wildest delusion the women are gorgeous. That makes it easier to take, I guess. Um, my dear...by what privilege do you call me by my name Marik? You see, I can play right back. As a perfect stranger, and I say perfect ambiguously...do you get my drift, missus...would I more properly be addressed as Mr. Andropov?"

This raised her ire. "Ha! Mr. Andropov, if that's how I should address you, by what criteria do you assert this relationship as stranger? Are you a man of unimpeachable...and everlasting... memory? Like some clever Sequoia in a distant forest who, upon hearing the whisper of leaves around him, records all these voices he's heard in his cherished rings? So then we may cut him down with our saws and read the lines of his blessed life? No,

> "You're neither forest nor tree,
> nor star-reaching pine,
> But on matters of this, you know
> not who's mine."

Suddenly frigid, she drooped her shoulders toward her chest, and with sorrowful eyes, bit her lips, clicked her tongue, and glanced away, feeling stung yet determined to rise above the wound. "As you wish, Mr. Andropov. Yet now I'm pleased, you must know, because I'm certain your thoughts are genuine."

"And you like real?"

"I'm here. Is that not real enough? Do you believe in me, my dear Mr. Andropov?"

Carl scratched his chin. "Marik. Please, call me Marik."[iv]

Her face muscles softened and her eyes wet. "Yes! Is this not exciting?"

"Why do you say this? What do you mean? Have our paths crossed before?"

She tittered sullenly. "We've no relationship. Yet I am, how do I say this," she continued, pensively, "without revealing my little secret. We've had feelings."

Noticing a sensual tilt to her voice, Carl leaned closer.

"Maybe," she said, tossing the wand over her shoulder, "I should not tell you. What am I thinking...I know, I know, shut up up there...I cannot tell you, my dear. It's simply a duty. Oh, all these duties, would they melt away! But I want you to know, nevertheless...otherwise, why would I travel this time and distance to see you, if not to...excuse me while this woman weighs her thoughts carefully—"

Bemused, intrigued, and somewhat entertained, he listened with wonderment, yet more than an ounce of skepticism.

"Oh, yes!" she exclaimed. "I think it's not proper to tell you of our relationship, which is perhaps in your amnesia... this is not memory loss as you know it scientifically, of course, as you're a brilliant man. You have always been brilliant. Your mother and I, many times, conferred on this. As for my mother, that was a different story, but she had her limitations. Hm."

"Sorry, but I'm not following you," he said, watching her shift her shapely frame against the background of twigs and leaves.

"You never followed me," she snapped. "Never mind." She waved a hand dismissively.

For a minute, she looked away as if in a trance while he began rummaging through his backpack, looking for a pen and piece of paper. She paid little attention, her mind elsewhere, while he continued glancing in her direction, his mouth crinkled in an amused manner. Meanwhile, the noise of the park around them came into focus, as the lunch hour brought hundreds more people to the area.

She wet her lips with her tongue, hoping to look more alluring, and focused her gaze on him, defiance in her voice. "Perhaps you think I'm a lunatic? Yes? Is this your idea?" Bewildered, he shrugged and shook his head. "I see. *Hresho*," she replied.

"You really are Russian. Your pronunciation's beautiful."

Feeling exposed, the color of her face momentarily drained. "*Da*." With this admission, she sank into prim silence, pretending in an unconvincing manner that she would prefer to speak about something else. "This is insignificant when you speak English. America! Ha, I never thought I'd come here. Russian is déclassé, I'm afraid. Better to speak French, *n'est pas*? Or English...I only recently learned to speak English, you know." Gazing away from him, she brushed her eyebrows and batted her eyes, as if looking into a mirror. "And why, my dear Marik, did you bother learning Russian? You are who you are. There's no need."

"It was a requirement for my major," he explained.

Her face immediately soured, cringing like a leather mitt. "And you are motivated by such banal things? I think

(4)

not. I believe you are quite more romantic than you realize. After all,

> "You pen notes and tack them to trees,
> And on love you sing with wondrous ease,
> With bellowing voice rung toward
> heaven so blue;
> From there I've come. Your eyes,
> they are you." [v]

Carl studied her closely, enjoying the rhythms of her voice and the serene manner in which she spoke; her voice emanated from her abdomen and was sincere in tone. "You know who I am, but I don't know you. That makes me feel a little on edge."

With this, she shrieked.

"Sorry. I didn't mean to upset you! It's just that...I don't normally see phantasms in broad daylight."

"I'm not this phantasm. I'm in the flesh. Here. Touch me." He did, and there was no doubt she was a real woman. Taking in his touch, a calmness appeared over her face. "I understand your concerns. But please don't worry yourself. And please don't talk about Russia. Now,

> "Listen, my dear, I'm not some daffy, old hen,
> When such delight I feel to kindle this
> old flame again."

Carl sank back to the ground, trying to understand. *Have we met before?* he wondered. *Did we have a relationship? No... impossible. I only dated Natalia in Moscow, and we broke off on good terms. Is this a secret crush? Or is she someone who changed appearance in some way? But it's all ridiculous! What...am I losing my mind? This could be the end, living in Central Park and talking to people who aren't there! Yet she's here. How could I make all this up in broad daylight? That makes less sense than her appearance itself.*

The questions raced through his mind, but lacking clear memories or information, each thought came to a dead end, and the only sense of her he had left, at least insofar as he could identify, was an odd, engrossing and innate sense of having already bonded with her before. There was something in the way they spoke, so effortlessly poetic and true, as if long ago they had conversed, smiled, and quarreled together in much the same way. This was not to say he trusted her affectations and liveliness, entirely. Despite her spontaneity and heart, she maintained a subtle wall. She wouldn't let him in completely, and he wasn't clear why. Perplexed and intrigued, he decided to address her with, "My lady, you cry tears,

> "Hot and cold. . . n'er one faucet warm;
> But those eyes by your nose,
> They're the eyes of the storm."

She reeled at this sudden burst of verse. She tucked her magic wand under her chin, and with kitten-like grace, fell onto the grass, her thoughts stirring...lingering in faraway places. She snatched the wand and placed it on her lap. "You speak such words to me...as...yes, I do remember well."

A minute passed, then she turned her eyes toward him, muted but burning with desire. She extended her hand in greeting. "My formal name is Dar'ya Ivanovna Konstantinov, and I'm originally from St. Petersburg. You have been there?"[vi]

He nodded. "Yes...in school. White nights, the Hermitage...may I call you Dasha?"

"Yes! Of course we're familiar now. So you've been to the Hermitage. Hm. It's been a long time for me," she said, cryptically. "At least you remember your recent past. I've traveled a great distance to see you, my love, having seen you under duress. You're living like a little rat! Hm! Please, take care. And don't get too chilled; you'll catch a cold."

He promised he wouldn't; after all, it was the middle of summer.

"Yes, it's quite true!" she chirped. "The Cossacks, without land, without home, without country, had it worse than you! I'm a reasonable, compassionate woman...and can sense your misery...and the difficulty of your predicament...and for this, I'm thinking...I can see possibilities for the future...perhaps, I don't know...perhaps I can help you in some way. You're feeling unloved? You're feeling rejected and defeated, and stuck like a little beaver in his trap? Pity, pity. Marik, you should grab your old sword and take on these creatures who hold you down. You truly should."

Carl looked her up and down. *I could never make this up. Must be real. Must be.* "Yea, well...for your information...I'm not stewing in self-pity here. In fact, I'm trying to—"

"Oh, no! No!" she said, eyes brightening. "There's no room for such thoughts. You are an intelligent man. Handsome, strong, kind, considerate. I look at your hands and your eyes and I see this. We ladies notice such things. Your shoulders...they are lean and your body's long, as are your mottled locks of adventurous hair. Eek! Your muscles are big. Do you like adventures?"

He snickered. "Um...I guess so. But not this kind. It depends on the adventure," he replied, wisely.

"Of course, of course! You've had some scathing adventures, Marik Andropov. Hm! All the more reason you'll succumb to my spell!"

"Spell? You think I'm easily smitten?" he parried in gamely fashion.

"Smitten. I don't know that word. But I feel there is no smitten going on here. Once, maybe this was true, but now I'm...oh...if only I could define it myself. What if," she asked, affecting an air of mystique, "I were to tell you everything? What if the place where we met, the time of day, the weather, what you were wearing, the color of your shoes and my dress...what if everything were placed in an orange Hermès box, sealed with a kiss and a note card, and handed to you...would you like to hear this story?"

Not sure where this would take him, he hesitated. "This is overwhelming for me. Maybe we should wait."

Hearing this, she shot him an indignant admonition, then crunched her face like a dried apple. "Hm, we don't want to hear tales of love and woe now? Is this too real for you? Would you prefer I focus our attention on the picayune matters of your predicament and consternation today? Heaven, it's true! Men always worry about business. Perhaps we can find you a job, and then from there we will talk about love? But why wait?"

Carl heaved a sigh. "The subject of love's taboo around here without the former prerequisite. Didn't you get the memo? I see you're from Russia, but here in America one word about love and they'll turn you to stone. It's the Medusa touch of any relationship. You have to dazzle them with your indifference. Show them they're unworthy. Show them you don't care. Or put it this way, as soon as you lay yourself out in any way bare and vulnerable, you would wish you were made of rock for the backlash coming your way."

Confused, she squinted. "Huh? I don't understand this love idea of love turning you to stone. This is silliness." Her voice was low but confident.

"It's all over the western world."

Hot and bothered, she squealed, "Western world? Is this not where love was invented? You expect to find happiness and bliss with this attitude? Am I...yes, I am...I'm talking to a stone instead of a man. I suppose there are no women in this America, either?"

"None," he declared, trying to annoy her enough to end a conversation that made him annoyed.

"Oh! I don't believe you," she said, disgustedly. "What am I? Medusa's chthonic reincarnation?" With this, she stood up and rapped him on the crown with her magic wand. "Perhaps it's not magic you need. Perhaps it's a good whipping."

Seeing the intensity of her fury, which somehow made her face more endearing and real, and noting the vulnerable position in which she had placed herself, he laughed heartily at her expense, knowing she must feel humiliated on some level.

"Boys!" she exclaimed, rolling her eyes. "They can be so mean when they cut you down like so many chaffs of wheat!" With this, her eyes nevertheless shined with admiration; she understood they were sparring, rather than truly fighting, and it intrigued, even excited her.

Carl felt a gradual sense of awareness. Whereas the day before he felt, if not empty, at least shut down, and if not forlorn, at least despondent, now a stirring appeared in his stomach: faint, uncomfortable yet exciting. Concurrently, the world around him—the park and its varieties of trees, its manicured grass, and its glistening waters—seemed brighter...its sounds more immediate. He noticed the effect she had on him, took a mental note and, taking an easy, gradual breath, he watched her animations with intense curiosity.

Feeling his eyes upon her, she glanced back at him, then crinkled her cheeks and dimples with a blush. This moment, she felt, was genuine: gone were the introductory words and pleasantries. They were replaced with realization and a sudden release of pretension.

"I've missed you, Marik Kuzmin Andropov," she announced, faintly. "Ever since your cousin introduced us. But please. Let's drop the formalities. Deal?"

"Okay, but I'm baffled," he admitted, his voice tender. "I dunno. Are you some kind of good witch? I mean—"

She smacked him hard. "I think not! A witch would have turned you into a frog and boiled you for supper!"

His heart leaped. *Oh, no...now I've screwed up.*

"I am not like a witch," she chided. "If I were, I would fly my broom across an orange moon and cackle at you. But instead I am here with you on Earth. It's part of my bargain with the officials," she admitted.

Intrigued, and attracted by their newfound closeness, he leaned backwards, gazing at her face. "And what bargain would that be?" he asked, raising an eyebrow.

"It's so complicated...I had to negotiate my visit. Bureaucrats! Red tape...approvals! Eek! Oh," she sighed, "there were so many approvals needed. These officials, they make such trouble." With this, her face crinkled into a scowl.

"Again, why are you here? I mean now...so suddenly."

Suddenly, she pulled up her wand and rapped him on the forehead. "Don't ask such questions. I saw you were in need. Now accept the gift of my presence and don't be so feisty."

"Sorry."

She looked surprised. "Sorry? There's no reason for sorry. You don't understand why I can't speak to you. I'm under strictures, see...there's so much more to say about this...I... ew...this is stupefying. It's not easy to answer because...I'm afraid...I do not know exactly why I came here myself. To bless you, yes. But whether I was drawn by love or loss, compassion or selfishness, lust or chasteness, I cannot say. My feelings have become much more complicated. I've often asked myself, these past few days,

> "Am I here to dream or dreaming to hear?
> Am I shouting through wind
> or holding a tear?
> Am I dying to kiss or needing to cry?
> Are you heading for heaven or failing to fly?"

Trying to understand her inner conflict, he indulged in a long pause. "I don't know," he said, "but you're resting your feet on my knees. Now I can't get up," he said conclusively, trying to deflect the conversation.

"It was a long time ago that I loved him," she said, moving her toes.

"And who was that? Me?" he asked.

"No one in particular. He passed away," she crooned, softly.

"Did he have a name?"

"Marik."

"That's the name you called me," he said, eyeing her strangely.

She paused, reflecting. "Yes, but it's not you. Now it's someone else."

He studied the creases in her face as she winced over her words. The softness of her skin, bronzed by summer, and the engaging sparkle of her eyes made her at once alluring and untouchable, as if no matter how far he were to dive into attraction and affection, he could never reach her fully. She seemed to hold him at bay, yet exuded deep feeling for him;

the reason—or reasons—for her contradictions eluded him. As he realized he could only go in so far, another realization hit him: his circumstances hardly made him a catch. Therefore, laying himself into the open with a total stranger, however familiar they might feel with each other, would be a risk. And he had more pressing matters at hand. So wanting to stall for time, and for the moment wanting to end the conversation, he tried to wrap things up with a declaration. "It's getting late, and I don't want to hold you."

She looked away. "You're not holding me," she said, ambiguously.

"Yea...well...I need to find a job or I'm not going to be worth much to anyone," he said, putting himself out farther, but feeling he might need to repair his last remark.

"Jobs and snobs and butterbobs!" she sneered.

"Butterbobs?"

"It's nonsense," she said, waving a hand dismissively.

"I have to eat."

Upon hearing this, she paused, expanded her breath, and asked, "Does God not provide things to eat? I'm sure you'll be fed. I'll work on it. No, on second thought, I'll not. But you recently made a new acquaintance, yes? His name is Richard? I might help you in a broader way, but he might help you in the immediate term."

He nodded slowly, understanding she meant Richard the street hustler. "How do you know about him? You spying on me?"

"Yes. From above. And your other needs? Your shipwrecked romance with that cursed shrew?" she said, her voice darkening. "I think I can help," she said, a wisp of doubt in her otherwise strident voice. Her eyes clouded over. "I have ways of approaching this that are, shall we say, unorthodox? There's always a way to find someone interested. I'll start to think about this. Perhaps I'll bring you lasses. We shall see."

Carl felt startled. "That would be selfless of you."

She sighed. "It is, but you see, *mon chere*," she replied with a reluctant sigh,

> "Although it's quite sudden and
> really quite scary
> Fear not, my dear Marik, for
> I'm your love faerie."

With this, she lifted the wand above her head, swirled it once, then twice, then with a placid expression and a flicker in her eyes, she brought the wand down, crashing, onto her opposite shoulder, and as fast as she had appeared, suddenly—

Bing!

She disappeared.

CHAPTER FIVE

He picked up the receiver, hesitating.

Standing at a pay phone in Penn Station, his cell phone dead and tucked away in his backpack, Carl felt awkward and on display. Several people made hurried, emphatic calls around the bank of four telephones, but despite plugging their free ears with their spare hands, the callers could easily eavesdrop on his predicament, he thought, ashamed of himself. He also lacked the coins he would need, and since his credit card was near the limit, he'd need to dial collect. Another worry, because his parents explicitly warned him: no more collect calls after you graduate. Period.

With the collapse of his job hunt and a sullied reputation, he considered the situation increasingly grim. He had to call. It was an exceptional predicament, but he would need to navigate his parents' well-constructed barriers to tell them why, in fact, they should accept the charges. They were funny that way, he mused. On the one hand, they spent money like drunken sailors on things they felt they needed—another sweater, a case of zinfandel, the SUV, another charge card to shuffle balances and interest rates, a gift for an uncle—but on the other hand, they were stingy to the point of ridiculous. They laid down strict rules about ordering desserts in restaurants—only once a month—and when it came to matters such as electricity, they rarely read after dark. They even unplugged appliances when not in use because they drew minute amounts of current. As for telephones, they once hung up on an aunt who was having a seizure, although they didn't know it at the time, because the allotted minute had expired.

Aunt Rita survived, but she was on meds.

Tapping the phone, Carl dug inside himself, finding the pride and optimism he needed to deliver the news, and dialed the operator, who immediately patched him through. The phone rang three times, then Barbara Moretti picked up.

"Collect call from Carl. Will you accept the charges?"

His mother hesitated. "Tell him to call us on his cell phone."

Click.

Carl frowned. The request was impossible; the only other option was his credit card, which stood near the limit. Where exactly, he wasn't sure, but he thought he recalled the last bill stating that he had $132 and change to go out of a limit of $12,500. This was one of three credit cards he used to get through the last year of school and the initial expenses of starting his career. The other two were tapped out.

"But it's an *investment*," everyone at school assured him.

Holding the phone gingerly to his ear, not trusting its cleanliness, he dialed the operator again. Fortunately, he didn't need to pay rent anymore, having moved into the so-called Park Hotel, but the pangs of hunger, thirst, and self-deprivation had arrived in force. The company's paychecks would hit his bank account for two pay cycles. Unemployment insurance, after taxes and negotiation, might cover his credit card obligations, but eating was now an issue.

"Credit card call, please."

His mother answered immediately, sounding concerned and perplexed. "Hi, honey, we heard through Lisa about the news. We happened to call and she told us. I'm so sorry. We didn't want this to happen to you so soon after the last layoff.

Can you tell me what happened? Did you do something wrong?" she asked, suspicious.

The accusation caught a lump in his throat. "Mom. I didn't do anything wrong. It was another," he sighed again, pausing to collect his thoughts, "you know. They wanted to save money, I guess, you—"

"Honey, companies don't do that! We want to be supportive. But you at least have to be honest with us. There must be something you're not telling me. Your poor mother needs to know. Did you not deliver an assignment? Did you have conflicts with your boss? I know at my job we just—"

"No," was his curt response.

"Where are you living? What are you eating?"

Not wanting her to worry unnecessarily, he lied. "I've crashed with a friend."

They paused for a moment, searching for a way out of their conversational imbroglio. Carl ran a hand through his tangled mane, staring into the bottom of the phone stall, while his mother audibly fidgeted on the other end. He already had a bad feeling about his request for money, since they'd balked so many times during the last year of graduate school and beyond—hence the credit card debt. At least he had his degree, he thought in a flash, noting the irony.

Her voice sounded bewildered. "I don't understand. Why would they let a bright young man like you go? There must be something else. When your father was your age, Bell Telephone snapped him up right out of school, and pretty soon they whisked him right up to vice president. Oh, they loved him. They said they were going to lay a career out ahead of him, and he worked hard for them, you know, but sure enough, they did. That's what you need to do. Maybe those computer skills…maybe your father was right. You should have gotten a law degree."

"Mom," he replied tensely, "two of my lawyer friends couldn't even find jobs in their field. They wasted $120,000 for nothing but some letters they can attach to their names. I picked computer science, and combined it with business, and got all the hard skills. Lawyers can't do what I do."

"But your cousin, and—"

"Mom! That's enough! Do you know how I feel right now? I don't need to be lectured about my stupid career decisions."

"Now wait a minute! I'm only trying to be helpful. You have to be positive."

"I am positive. I'm positive that the people running Frontier Reinsurance are idiots, and what they need more than anything else is to hire me back before their customers start bailing on them and their projects get stuck in no-man's land."

His mother's voice began to sound strained. "They're successful for a reason. You need to look up to supervisors and learn from them, not be so proud. You're just starting out in your career."

Carl began to feel dejected. "Funny, but it feels like I'm finishing." He paused, gathering strength. "And I need money."

"Carl," came the piercing response, "we cannot support more of your…your habits. You know that. You need to…well, straighten yourself out, that's all."

"Mom, things are bad. Really bad. I don't know how long I can survive on what I have." He listened carefully for a note of sympathy, but to his dismay, she seemed stuck in a mindset.

Her voice became standoffish and even cracked. "We can't help you. We need to save for retirement, and we've already paid for your college education and even paid a little toward your graduate education, don't forget," she continued, searching her thoughts.

His voice became faint. "I know. I know. But—"

"Here, Carl, your father wants to speak to you. I love you."

"I love you, too," he said in obligatory, although sincere, fashion.

A rough cough appeared on the other end of the line. "Son? What is this?" came the abrupt voice.

Stalling for time, Carl tried to soothe the situation. "Did Mom get my birthday card?"

"Don't know. Let me ask her. You did? Okay. Yes, says she got it. Now what's this I'm hearing about you losing another job? And your apartment, too? What, you want to live the rest of your life on handouts?"

The words pierced Carl's soul. "Dad, you know how hard I worked in school. Come on. They canned me for no good reason."

"School? This isn't school. It's real life. Son, they don't just fire good, talented workers for no reason. Doesn't happen that way in the real world. When I was your age, you worked hard, showed them you were committed to the company, and they moved you up. That's what they're all looking for. The only guys who ever flunked out were the losers. Skipped work. Insulted the boss. Is that what you did? You were always lazy around the house. Never picked up the trash when your mother and I asked you. It's time you grew up, young man. Time to take responsibility. Companies don't do this sort of thing to the good apples. That's not how the world works. Don't try to put one over on your father. The main thing is…and you'd better learn your lesson here…you have to work. Have to work for every dollar you make."

"Yea," came the muted response, "and even in real life I work hard."

His father paused, then replied with a vexed and authoritative tone. "Apparently not hard enough. Carl, what happened? First, it's the one job, then it's another. What's the matter? Can't you get along with anyone? When I was at Bell—"

"Dad, that was thirty years ago! With all due respect, father. You're dreaming if you think these companies care about running their businesses anymore. It's all about grabbing the cash...a quick bonus...then leaving the mess for the next guy. It's not all input-output, you know. It's not all get a degree, learn valuable skills, work hard, get rewarded."

The elder Moretti became more gruff. "Don't tell me about respect! You think things have changed so much? It's all about money. Don't get idealistic on me. You need to show them commitment, work hard, keep your nose clean, then they get to see what you're made of. They're always evaluating the fresh recruits, picking the winners and the losers for promotions right from the start."

Carl sighed. "Money. Dad, you're not sounding rational. I said they're in it for the money, but...Dad, listen. Now they say the junior ranks are nothing but slackers. We can't read and write. We don't have the hot skills. We're lazy, spoiled. Meanwhile, the management of this place rapes the company blind! It's not just me, Dad! They let three out of four of us go. Kept one on...he's the worst they have, too, but he's in with the boss. That's the real world, Dad. What, you think the real world doesn't exist anymore?"

"That's a fine attitude to have. Don't be so negative! Think positive, or you'll never get anywhere. Now what are you going to do? You looking for something else, or just calling your Mommy and Daddy for help? I know why you're calling."

"Dad, that's uncalled for!" Carl banged his hand on the phone.

"Your sister called in yesterday," Carl's father said, voice tensing further. "She says they've already moved her into management. She's a star! They can't say enough good things about her. That's the way you need to be. Call your sister. Ask her how she does it."

Incensed at the comparison, Carl clenched his fist against the receiver. "Sounds like she's getting some breaks I'm not getting. That's all."

"No, that's what you don't get. You *make* your own breaks."

Carl couldn't stand the way his father kept assaulting him, over and over, with the same refrain. "Someone has to pay you, Dad. You can't—"

"You've got to give them a reason to pay you. Money doesn't fall out of trees."

The young man wanted to hurl the phone against a wall, but wanting to stay rational and in control, he maintained his cool. "They had a reason to pay me. As a matter…hey, Dad… they asked me to train my replacements. They want the three of us to stay on until that's done. How does that sound? Huh? Am I getting through?"

Carl's father paused. "I've never heard of that before. When you're fired, you're fired. They fire you because you can't perform…not when you have the knowledge. Doesn't make sense. What are you not telling me? That's disrespectful. An insult."

"An insult. Like anyone cares, Dad. This is business. Modern style. It's the same all over the place."

Uncomfortable, his father stammered, "I don't…I don't understand the situation there. It sounds like you've run into some tough characters. Reminds me of a cousin in the mafia. Forget I said that! But all that doesn't change one thing: you're out of work, and it's your job to find a job. Period. Look…ah, I don't know anyone anymore. They're all retired. So you need to get your career squared. You can't keep bouncing from job to job like this. It's not what a man ought to do."

Carl clenched his fists in frustration. *Oh, Chrissssstmas… there he goes again. Now it's about my manhood.* Not liking the insinuation one bit, he became emboldened. "Dad, you're living in the land of yesteryear. I'm telling you. It's different now. It's not a bunch of guys hanging out, raising their kids. You should see the resumes these days! Especially in New York. Nine months here, fourteen months there. It's a street brawl around here. Believe me."

"Your sister's doing fabulous. So's your cousin, Tony, the one with the law degree. Looking at them, I don't know what your problem is. What you need to do, son, is decide what you want to do. Decide who you want to be."

The words hurt, but Carl decided to gut it out, pressing for one, final shot. "I decided who I wanted to be freshman year in college. Now's it's been taken away. How can you suddenly pull the rug out from under me…and…and then tell me I don't know what I want to do? Huh?"

For the first time, his father remained silent.

"Look. Dad. I'm in a really tough spot here. I need your help. I don't know. Enough to put a roof over my head. Until I can find work again."

"No. We did that last year between jobs. Best thing we can do for you now…I mean it…is teach you to fend for yourself. And be positive. None of this negative attitude, for cryin' out loud. When I landed my first job at Bell Telephone, that's where I stayed. For thirty-five years. That's what you want.

Something solid. Don't settle for these fly-by-night outfits again. Choose a good company."

Exasperated, Carl threw up his free hand and spun around. *Can't take this man on like this,* he decided. He leaned back into the phone. "Dad. It's not that simple. Not when you need to keep on the treadmill or no one will hire you. Got to keep moving. That's the way it is around here. Around everywhere. Look, I…I really have to go." With that, dazed and exhausted, and moreover at a loss over how to proceed with his life, Carl said goodbye, hung up, then fell back against the phone.

Feeling defeated, he nevertheless felt compelled to strike on.

Somehow, somewhere, he'd pull out of this tailspin. He began to feel dizzy. He cupped his head in his hands, trying to focus. Having exhausted his best option for help, and not wanting to show up on their doorstep to receive another round of thrashings, he walked to the exit of the train station and into the redemptive sunlight. With head down and hands in his pockets, he crossed 8th Avenue, then headed uptown.

The air was hot; noxious fumes swirled around him.

The problem was, and he learned this after losing his previous job, most of the people he knew were in the same boat: young, right out of school, minimal influence, and in need of proving themselves, hence a need to minimize risk, even if it was simply recommending someone for a job. On top of this, his colleagues from graduate school were a competitive lot; when you were down, they didn't need you and you quickly become a non-person to anyone except the closest of classmates. After he lost his last job, not one so-called connection from school, despite the vaunted power of alumni networks, led to an interview. On top of this, promises of staying in touch and forming life-long networks evaporated right after graduation.

Already, many people had vanished.

His colleagues at Frontier Reinsurance would be no help, and after less than a year in New York, Carl had barely met anyone in software development—hardly the hottest field in Manhattan, anyway.

Suddenly, however, he remembered something. Angry at himself for forgetting, he recalled the recruiter who called several weeks prior to the layoff...but he couldn't remember her name. All the programmers, including himself, had brushed her off, dismissing her as a pest. *Rizzo? Piso?* He thought for a moment. "No, Sue Pizzo—" Anxiously, he fumbled through his pockets, producing enough coins for a phone call, then found a public phone and dialed information. Along 8th Avenue, he felt the raw energy of traffic and rush-rush attitude of passersby; he could lob in a few calls, though, even here and on the run.

He called information, received the number for Pizzo Associates, and pressed one to dial. The phone rang twice before a crisp voice appeared. "Tech Solutions. This is Sue." He could hear her against the traffic, but it was difficult. Drawing a long breath, he expressed as best he could, uncertain of what to say, that the two had spoken several months ago and agreed to reconnect if an opportunity arose.

"Yes," came the abrupt reply, "I remember."

An awkward silence ensued as Carl realized the conversation wouldn't flow smoothly. "At the time," he said, forcing himself to sound upbeat, despite her initially cool reception, "you recommended I call back if the right situation presented itself."

"I remember. How can I help you?"

Again, he sensed this would not be easy.

"Maybe I can help you," he replied clumsily.

There was no response.

"What's happened is," he continued, "the company... Frontier Re, you recall...recently decided to replace its junior developers...the ones they hired last August...including myself...with fresh recruits. They're letting their hardest-working, more experienced go in the name of cutting costs... now they'll have to train a whole batch of newcomers. So now I'm officially out looking for new opportunities."

At first, she failed to respond, but after an excruciating pause, she responded in a shrill, even demeaning tone. "I know Kerry very well. We started our careers together at another firm. She's one of my favorite people in HR. Real smart, dedicated, and she knows her staffing business. So your evaluative statement regarding their reasoning—cutting costs—won't quite cut it. Like I said, she's good at what she does, and I'm sure she has a comprehensive strategy in mind."

Carl gripped the phone tighter.

"And it's not that I don't have any sympathy," she continued, apparently munching on a carrot now, "but this isn't Iowa. This is New York, and you have to add value where you are, or—"

Exasperated, he tensed his stomach muscles and groaned. "I worked weekends there. Delivered code on time and bug-free. Plus developed good relations with their customers, recommended improvements to their system—"

"That's all well and good. It adds to your skill set and resume, but that doesn't mean, in the realm of perception of adding value, they were so impressed," she said, her attitude turning even tougher. "I actually spoke to Kerry yesterday. I don't recall her mentioning you specifically."

Liar. He gripped the phone tightly in anger.

"But I do recall her mentioning having three qualified programmers out there on the market soon—she didn't mention your name, I would remember—but they wouldn't be available until after they trained the replacements. And to be perfectly honest, I'm going to have trouble placing you guys...because the job market for programmers, I hate to say it, is soft. There aren't enough slots to go around anymore... and that's for several reasons. On that part, I'm in complete sympathy with you. Believe me, I am. But, in terms of placing you in this market when I'm not getting a certain comfort level yet, well, it's going to be tough. I'll call her and double-check. Is this the number where I can reach you?"

"No. I'll call you."

"Fine. Call me next week. Oh, it's ringing on another line. Goodbye."

The call ended.

Carl drew in a long breath, certain White had retaliated against him for balking at the idea of training replacements. Dejected, he pressed the receiver back on its hook, grimaced softly, then proceeded toward the park at a quickened pace. Upset, angry, and needing to blow off steam, he looked around him, saw the bustling activity of the Port Authority— its blinking neon culture shouting down at him from all around—and trudged forward with defiance, pressing his toes hard against the firm, cement path.

He walked this way for another thirty blocks, making it to the quiet thicket of trees some forty minutes later, having stopped for water along the way. Then once he was back to his comfortable, makeshift bed sheets, he propped his head in his hands, which he clasped behind him, closed his eyes, and attempted to sleep.

CHAPTER SIX

Still in his afternoon reverie and weary from trudging through the July swill, he only managed slits for eyes when Dasha leaned over him, tugging his hand.

"Come on, sleepy! Get up! Your time for napping is up!" she said.

"I'm tired. Go away!" he groaned, not fully meaning it.

"No!" she snapped, smacking his leg. "I have exactly one hour...and nowhere to go, besides! If you want to be standoffish, that's fine...I'll sit here anyway and, oh...I don't know...count your blessings. You might still have some," she said, intending to rib him.

They bantered this way for several minutes until Carl, with a sudden jolt, bolted upright, confronting her. "My parents ditched me," he said, not knowing why he said it.

"And this is new? Tell me something I've never heard," she replied, unmoved.

"You think this is normal?" he asked, realization and loss creeping in. "Is it possible that the two people who brought you into this world will...when you're tossed into the gutter... give you that extra kick in the ribs to finish you off! I say that because, look...I know you're a sweet person, so I'll put it in terms you understand. Like a baby seal, I'm getting clubbed to death."

"Ha!" she crowed. "You poor baby, you." She pouted in jest. "You find me entertaining, I see. Yes, here...I'll prop your head and perhaps serve you a kiss." With that, she pecked him on the forehead. "There! Better?"

Carl felt new life stirring in his soul. He laughed, "You stole one from me."

She looked away, mischievously. "I am a thief! Today, I steal your kiss, and tomorrow your heart. But once you stole mine."

Baffled, he propped himself up on his elbows and stared into her eyes, his own crinkling with uncertainty. "How did I do that? That's not possible. Is it?"

"Suit yourself," she said, suddenly cooler.

"I still don't believe this is all possible. What do you know about my past that I don't know? Tell me. Please. You make my past sound so much better than my today."

She rapped him on the chin with her wand. "Please, please, please! Enough! I don't want to hear this kind of defeat from my handsome, regimental officer, Marik Kuzmin Andropov. What's the bother? You are useless now? You think your past was so great? Perhaps you're paying for it. You don't know yourself. You're a man of dashing wit who attracts all the ladies, who you hold in the palm of your hand. You...my dear Marik...even possess taste for song and dance! Now, now...this lump of lard on the ground? This is not the Marik I know. I've heard legends of you...surrounded by Cossacks and renegade bandits, you raised your sword in defiance and sent the order to fire, cutting them down with torrents of musket fire. If ever there were a real man, it was Marik. This is you."

He searched her face, wondering, *What on earth are you talking about?*

"Your parents," she continued, ignoring his expression, "were most unfortunate. I pitied your predicament, but perhaps they'll come about. They were unkind to you and you ran off to war, in desperation...this gave you honor in their eyes, but you were miserable. You hated war, but at the same time you hated the way the rebels burned their way through the countryside and you loved Russia. You joined the service at seventeen, but were immediately given an officer's commission. You served for seven years."

"Until I was twenty-four. But at twenty-four I was getting ready to attend Carnegie Mellon. Your time line's off by...oh, 175 years, if I'm to go along with this wild tale."

"Call it what you will," she said, tossing her chin in the air. "But I'll continue with my story." Resolute and proud, she drew a long breath and continued. "So as I was saying, this man Marik...lived in the Orenburg region at a manor estate owned by his paternal uncle, whose health was failing with this and that ailment. Perhaps he exaggerated a few things here and there, but for the most part, your uncle was counting down the heartbeats he'd been allotted at birth. This man, Marik, as I say, was of the utmost honor and respectability, and in the year 1828, the Tsar Nicholas personally commended him for valor. Are you not impressed? Yes? Are you not proud of him for this already? Then I met him while he was in St. Petersburg, right after he earned these honors, and he stood so tall. Oh, he was a dashing soldier! But this man Marik, because he was of such indubitable honor and decency, could not bear his brother's sudden dissolution in St. Petersburg when word of his brother's antics quickly spread and caused a scandal, especially when his brother was found *in extremis* with the wife of Marik's commanding general...a beloved wife of ten years."

"Did his brother die in a duel?"

"No, it did not go as you would expect. In fact, the general embraced the young man who, by any sensible stretch of imagination, might have been placed before a firing squad for some trumped up charge or perhaps sent alone to the frontier with a bow and three arrows to have it out with the rebels. Instead, the general embraced the man the next time he saw him at the fete, poured him a stiff drink, and thanked him for giving his lovely wife such pleasure because, truth be told, his frequent jaunts to war had him worried that her loneliness might lead her to self-harm. This was the general's true concern. Can you imagine that? So the general immediately promoted our poor Marik, bewildered as he could be, in the Tsar's cavalry."

"Amazing."

She shrugged. *"Faber est suae quisque fortunae."*[vii]

Carl studied her closely, amused and intrigued by her outlandish assertions. Her tales were preposterous, bold, and indeed, abjectly absurd, yet somehow through her dancing feet, her casual smiles, the feints, and the barbs, he gained the distinct impression she was, on some level, entirely sincere, and even embarrassed to unload this heap of apparent nonsense on his troubled soul. She may have spoken with forked tongue or even, for all he knew, enjoyed toying with downtrodden men eager for a woman's affections, but this possibility didn't gibe with the modesty, shame, and, dare he say, grace of her affectations. It was not the unreal that made her so interesting to him, in this state of rejection and isolation; instead, her appeal—her charm, her pretty smile, her radiant locks of brunette—was precisely the connection she seemed to feel with him, which, in turn, made him feel connected, too.

"I think what's most peculiar of all," she said, ruefully, "is something overheard at the burial when Marik's brother died. Word spread quickly that, as the pall bearers raised the coffin to lower it into the ground, the general turned toward his wife, and wiping a tear from his eye, stated clearly and without hesitation, "I feel as if I'm losing a son."

The lines around Carl's mouth drew downward as he struggled to understand this reaction at this time in this context, but he held his tongue, wanting to hear the rest of her story and, to be certain, relishing the panegyrics of her face as she recounted it.

"News of this comment spread like wildfire, naturally. All over town, people speculated on the meaning of this utterance. Was it said to assuage his wife's feelings? To patch over a rift in their marriage by granting her an emotional concession? Was it sarcastic, perhaps? And if so, did she know it? Was this one of those many digs and barbs meted out by long-married couples, one that, when piled one on top of another, can burst forth at the most inappropriate times and still, in the end, not damage the fiber...the essence...of the relationship a whit?" She blushed, remembering something and apparently feeling quite foolish. "Or was the general sincere? Had he begun to love this egg-snatching weasel as if like a son? Could it be, everyone wondered, he actually, and I say this with some emotion myself, loved this woman so much, and indeed with such compassion and affection, that he would sacrifice his own pride simply to honor her happiness? Was he saying in this, in fact, that he would cuckold himself during the long days of sacrifice and war—turn askance, if you will—in order to make her feel loved and, in turn, ensure he will come home to a smiling wife when on furlough? The infidelity of it all! Oh, how this racked the poor clergyman's' brains! And the dissolution and primacy of flesh behind it! That could fill book after book, I'm sure! But think," she said, peering into Carl's eyes with sudden openness and courage, "that when they were betrothed, he vowed to stay with her 'til death do us part. Is this not a covenant of the body? Does this not say that flesh-unto-flesh, we will live this life together to our fullest abilities, but, in the end, when breath and spirit last depart from our lungs, we're free to move on and, if still living in this life, still free to forge new relationships without the dreaded pall of sin? So this commitment they had was not to feel shackled, or feel as if this is the one and only true love in your life, and therefore life is meaningless without the other. This is important to me, you see. To disrupt their vows would at once be to live in sin, yet to accept the earthly boundaries under which such oaths are made," she said, imploring him. "Do you think that in my distraught state of losing Marik, I would not think in such terms?"

Carl shifted uncomfortably on the grass, increasingly sore, but also intrigued. Light filtered through the trees, dabbling her cheeks and forehead with soft shades of color.

"And sometimes these oaths are not made," she continued, her voice suddenly sad, "for many reasons. Perhaps they live without commitment. Maybe," she said, tugging a blade of grass from its roots and tossing it to the air, "it's a casual fling. Like some romance at sea. Or," she said, eyes brightening again, "it can be more uplifting. Perhaps they burn with love, only to extinguish this fuel later and, with mutual affections and no regret, part their ways on different paths—both the better for it. And then there's another possibility, and this is saddest and most dear to me of all, that, although love is true, and moreover meant to be, forces beyond the control of mere mortals intervene and love breaks, as grapes without rain cannot make wine." Having said what she needed to say, she bowed her head.

Carl watched her, empathizing with her sense of dejection and loss, wanting to know more about her, but at the same time struggling to grasp the import of her words. Reaching into his own experience, he recalled his own shattered life: once so promising, it now lay in ruins. He sighed, admitting, "There's love and there's infinite love. They're not the same beast. Whereas one has beauty then withers to nothing, the other beats beauty from the start and grows from there. But where it goes after we do…I don't know."

She suddenly giggled. "Eternal love's an agony. Sometimes it contradicts itself, and often it hurts. Yet, it's a thing of infinite beauty and wonder. I could talk about this forever and it would still fascinate me."

He scratched his temple, thinking. "Yes, well…everlasting love's not in the cards for me now. I'm a broken man. I've been tossed into the street to die, and no one cares. Can't find decent work. It's out there, people say, but if you're the guy actually looking for it, it's a whole different ball of wax. And without good work, a man's not too appealing to the opposite sex. And without appeal, my chance of finding love is somewhere between slim and none." After he finished, he added a self-deprecating chuckle.

"Yes, yes, here you go again. You're in a rut. Excuse me," she said, feigning annoyance, "but are you not speaking with a rather…interesting…lady?"

"Interesting? Maybe, but until I get my life straightened out, stand clear of me. I'm a repair job now."

She giggled. "Women love to repair. This is true, because,

"The more broken his wing,
The more joy we will sing!"

Delighted, she pressed her lips together and squeaked.

For several minutes, they didn't say a word. It was getting late now, and the park seethed with activity as harried workers donned their rollerblades and running shoes for a last chance to work off frustration and take in a needed dose of greenery, fountains, and exercise. Inside their grove of trees and bushes, where summer's heat surrendered to merciful, frosty-cool shade, Carl and Dasha enjoyed a moment of peace and respite, happy to have the company and, it seemed, utterly without feelings of pressure to entertain his or her companion.

Carl's mind drifted toward rustling trees, quiet ponds, and lodges: the peaceful spots where he used to camp. The park, with its landscaped beauty and arcing spines of bridges and stage, was a portal into his past where, at an earlier time of life, urgencies of work and pay, and even thoughts of the future, were not part of his reality. The distant sounds of blades scraping pavement, a sudden shout, and bicycles whishing by were drowned out by gentle memories of waves against shore, where fingers dangled over hulls of rowboat and canoes and lingering in placid waters of darkness. As his mind drifted into this dreamlike state, he reminisced over shouts and snickers, which beyond the distance of time resonated against the din of the park. Now, in evening's early glow, everything faded. Soon his face became serene and content, if not also sad.

She placed a hand on his knee. "Tell me," she whispered. "Of what are you dreaming?"

He looked into her soft, caring eyes and smiled. "The past. But not the distant past, as you do."

She smiled. "This is a start. Try to remember more in your dreams. Here. I'll sprinkle some dust on your eyes...if not for magic, then to awaken your imagination."

"No offense, really. It's just, right now, I'm not feeling open towards—"

"Ha! Tsk, tsk! What is this nonsense you're talking now? This is not about me and you! Oh, you're thinking this is... urghhh...men, they are so vain! As soon as a pretty woman smiles in their direction...it's so typical. Typical!" she huffed.

With her last words, he couldn't help but chortle. "I'm sorry."

"You should be. Shame, shame, I say!" she continued, working herself into a faux frenzy. "Young Marik Andropov thinks my energies are devoted to winning his love, like some archer hitting his mark, when I must confess, in all sincerity, this is not the purpose of my visit and lamentations. Nothing of the sort! Hm," she sniffed. "If this were so simple, I'd sweep you up with my magic spell. Don't get the wrong idea about me...I'm no floozy. This is something different altogether, although I'm not disposed to explain."

Gathering she truly had something to conceal, and feeling certain he wouldn't pry it out of her, at least today, he resigned himself to playing along. "Fair enough. Not that I need to know. Right now, I need to get my life straightened out. You say you can help. Okay, I'm going to look for a job. Any job. Drawing unemployment isn't an option...it's not enough to stay solvent. And you say you're a love faerie? Well, love faerie, how about finding me some love? Find me this elusive prize right here, in my condition, and I'll believe anything's possible. I might even believe your wild tales of magic and mystery."

She clasped her hands together. "Excellent! He's a live one, yes? Can I do this? Will this not be fun? No, no...finding him love, what am I thinking? Will I succeed? What would that...ugh. Yes, I need to find him love. Excuse me while I reason this out. Yes, I said this, and I'm here, and I must follow through."

Feeling ill at ease, he glanced at her, quizzically.

Seeing his reaction, she responded with a more deliberate tone. "It's a long story of how I got here. The things I had to do: the layers of approvals, the paperwork, the inquiries, the appearing before the magistrate. Heaven! It's hard to explain. I'm doing my best to relate this...I had to jump through countless hoops to come here, but it was all for a mission to," she said, even more sincere, "answer your cry for help."

"Huh? What cry for help?"

"We knew you were in trouble."

"What, do you have ESP?"

"Not exactly," she said. "Never mind. I need to go. You stay here and I'll...I promise. I'll return on the third day, midnight at the new moon, meet you right here, and we shall discuss my plan for you. In the meantime, stay put, sleep well, stay warm, and, oh, speak to this Richard about finding a job. Right now, he's your best choice. Good luck, and ta, ta!" she exclaimed, chipper and bright. She waved her wand in the air and,

Bing!

CHAPTER SEVEN

(1)

"Here," Richard said, flopping Sunday's *New York Times* next to Carl's outstretched arm, "you need to check out the job classifieds."

Carl rubbed his bloodshot and weary eyes. Indeed, Sue Pizzo had failed to take his call. "Aren't I better off looking online?"

Grimacing, Richard waved a hand dismissively. "Not now. Man, you're in a crisis. You need cash fast. Check this out first. Trust me. Then, if you can't find anything you like here, I have something else up my sleeve."

"What, is it legal?"

"What are you talking about? Of course, it's legal! I'm not pointing you down the wrong road. Wouldn't do that to—"

"Wouldn't take that advice, anyway," Carl said, feeling a need to lay down the ground rules, despite Richard's helpful tone.

Carl gathered an extra ounce of strength, propped himself up, and rolled over onto his left side, holding himself up with an outstretched hand. He began flipping through the sections. "I'm embarrassed you're doing this for me. It's not that I can't figure out to look in the want ads." Richard shrugged. Carl continued searching, tossing sections aside, until he came upon the classified section, then he immediately turned to the programmer ads. He tore them out, but before he could stuff the page in his pocket and head for the nearest FedEx Kinko's, his eyes caught an ad on the front page:

His interest piqued, Carl carefully ripped the ad from the page and stuffed it into his pocket, then tossed the remainder of the paper beside his backpack. "Thanks," he muttered. "Some lady at a museum. I needed someone to prod me. It's better than hanging out like a freaking vagabond."

"Hey, man, I've been there," Richard replied, sympathetically. "That's why I'm helping you out. I know exactly where you're at right now, and if you don't get moving forward pretty soon… I've seen it many times…your mind starts to go, you lose your spark, and pretty soon you're sitting around, staring out the window at the rain pouring down. Or one guy I ran into once, he ended up jumping right off the George Washington Bridge. Yea, I know. But the thing is, you see this wad of cash in my pocket? That's an example of what a man on a mission can do when he has to pick himself up by the bootstraps and no one in this whole world's going to help him. You know what I'm getting at?"

Carl nodded.

"What you need to do now, my friend, is to not let those little voices inside start telling you you're a failure or not worth a damn. You know? They may say all kinds of things about you...you're this and that...but you can't listen to them. Wipe them right, clear out of your mind. When they condemn you, you need to know you have that inner light. Anything short of that, and like I say, you'll soon be standing there on the edge of the bridge looking down."

"We don't want that, do we?" Carl quipped.

"Heck, no. C'moooon...you know how many friends of mine I've heard talk that way? I've seen it all: guys on crack, guys whose parents left them to fend for themselves and next thing you know, they're up against federal charges...even guys with minor records who nobody will hire...so back on the street they go. Man, this city's all messed up. All I can say is you have to not let the powers you feel hanging over your head let you down. You've got to reach down inside and find out what you're made of and learn not to live for other people. You know what I'm saying? Because if you live for them...you live for the man. And you see yourself through their eyes instead of your own. Then the whole world is one bad trip on acid. You know what I'm saying?"

Pondering, Carl pursed his lips. He nodded his head.

"I know you do. I know you're tracking with me. That's one reason why I like you so much. Man, I can see a little of myself in you. I remember the first day I lived on the street. There was nothing like it. Nothing but your tattered clothes between you and some crazy mother's cold, steel blade. Lying out there in the street...no one in the world could care less except you, and even you are hanging on by a thread in terms of how much you're caring, and then you stare your face into that dark, ominous tunnel and ask yourself why in heaven's name you are even alive at all...to live like vermin that's rummaging through the trash for a scrap of food."

Upset now, Carl sighed. "Yea, yea. Whatever. I—"

"Don't tell me whatever. I don't want to hear that kind of talk. Carl my man, you're my student now. Now you listen up. I know you're still hanging in there and plugging along, but from here forward I want to see some joy in your face. It isn't enough to scrape along in the street...guts churning over where the next meal's coming from. That is beneath you. This is what I tell my friends, too. You stand tall, and you don't let them get you down, no matter what. And you go call on that lady at that museum."

Carl agreed the suggestion made sense, then promised to apply in the morning.

(2)

The sign outside her door read, "Applicants Form Line Here," with a big, red arrow pointing to the left. Already, a small queue had formed, although the scheduled interviews would not begin for another forty-five minutes. It was 7:15 AM, and the muffled sounds of young men shuffling in place—there were no women present—muted the otherwise hollow echoes of the tiled and bare hallway. "Bonastre, Toni—Supervisor" read the name plate on her door; the office remained silent and locked. Carl held his bag in one hand and a half-finished bottle of Tropicana orange juice, some pulp, in the other. The interviewees kept to themselves, despite the close quarters, neither speaking nor making direct eye contact. Each was in his own world for his own reasons and respected the quiet truce they had tacitly formed.

At 6:00 AM, Carl had dashed to the gym, where he showered, shaved, and threw on a respectable oxford cloth shirt, a tie, and a blue blazer he had tried his best to unwrinkle. From there, he walked briskly to 42nd Street, jumped onto the cross-town shuttle, and proceeded to the museum via Grand Central Station. The whole trip took him close to fifty minutes, and the whole time he felt anxious about arriving on time, having inadvertently left his watch in his backpack.

The sad lot waited, scuffling their feet, with eyes fixed on the walls or downcast, for a while longer, but at precisely 7:58 AM and with a flurry of noise, jangling keys, and rapid-fire greetings, Toni Bonastre arrived. She had jet-black hair, curled and wandering, as if she were both fastidious and independent-minded, and her tanned skin, both youthful yet rough, belied her otherwise big-boned frame, which seemed strong as stone and quite athletic. She moved at a frenzied pace, and in the dim, fluorescent lights of the corridor, she gave the impression of an aged coach who, through unpredictable life circumstances, suddenly found herself managing the staff of a modern museum. "So many eager faces," she announced in spirited fashion. "People, people...I need people!"

She cast a fleeting smile at no one in particular, then with frenetic energy, she jangled her keys in one hand, slid the correct key among dozens into the slot, and popped open the door, through which she slid and disappeared in an instant, clicking the door shut behind her. Then the applicants could hear banging and creaks, drawers opening and closing, and other signs of intense activity, which encouraged several amused glances.

One-by-one, she called them, screaming each name from her desk. As the first left her office, some ten minutes after he was called in, she was standing behind her desk, pointing a finger toward the exit, which was fifty feet down the hall. "Out! I'll have no car thieves in my museum!" The poor sap, despite the public humiliation, seemed amused by her antics, waved a sardonic gesture in her direction, and disappeared down the hall, making certain his laugh was loud enough for her to hear it. "Unbelievable," she said, waving the next man in.

Third in line, Carl waited another twenty minutes before entering the room, where he found her scribbling furiously on a notepad, her mottled hair bouncing with every jerk and snick of her arm. He closed the door, an action that seemed to unsettle her, then waited in nervous silence.

He scanned the surroundings. Her office was jam-packed with memorabilia: photos of children, family members, old school portraits, small trophies, awards, and inspirational knickknacks covered the walls, desk, and cabinetry. Her desk was littered with papers, forms, trade magazines, newspapers, and other detritus, although the volume of material was not enough to obscure his view of the woman, who remained, despite the clutter clearly, and even imperiously, at ease, confident, and in charge.

"Excuse me," she said, suddenly squaring off with him. "The last gentleman...he was a good candidate...I had to record some information. I think I'll hire him," she said with a wink, as to tell Carl she already liked him and might hire him, too. But her face instantly turned cross. "So what brings you here? Why aren't you working?"

He cleared his throat, taken aback by her abruptness. "Well, two weeks ago I lost my job as a Java programmer, and I—"

She threw her hands into the air, smiling broadly. "Oh! Out of work for two weeks and you're already looking? Bravo! Well done. Continue, continue."

Taken back by her forthright mannerisms, he took a moment to wind up, then responded with as clear a diction as possible. "I was there...Frontier Reinsurance of Madison Avenue, for almost a year." She frowned, nodding. "And they decided to downsize their programmers in order to make room for a batch of indentured servants."

"The fools!" she sneered. "Replacing their experience with greenhorns? To save money...I know why they did it. Okay, continue," she said, her voice growing impatient.

Feeling she might be on his side, Carl tried to breathe more easily. "So they didn't make adequate provisions for us, going forward, so to speak, and I'm in a situation where I need to start as soon as possible. I really don't want to draw unemployment, and it's not enough to cover my expenses and health care, anyway."

She gasped, tisk-tisking with a slow shake of her head. "Oh, you poor young man, not having health care. Inadequate savings, too, I imagine. Yes, yes, continue."

"But the big attraction here, and the reason why I picked your ad from the *Times* classified section—"

"Oh, you found me in the *Times*. I'll make a note of that. Continue," she interjected.

"Yes, the big attraction was that I, and for many years really...have been a frustrated artist myself. Painting: watercolors, oils, still lifes, even a few portraits."

"Nude, I hope," she jostled, blushing.

"Um—"

"Sorry," she apologized, although half-sincere as she clearly relished her bawdy excursion. "We like to have a sense of humor around here. What's a little nudity to a museum, eh?" she continued, facetiously.

Carl tried his best to grin, hoping he could alight a sense of humor at a time when he felt constricted by a need for good behavior. "No, no...What do you think attracts artists to painting?" he blurted out, before turning pale with a feeling he sounded hopelessly stupid.

Dasha

Noticing his discomfort, she pressed her lips together and showed him an open palm, as if to beg forgiveness. "No need. I know. So what's your name?"

"Carl Moretti."

"Oh, you're Italllllliannnnn!"

He nodded politely. "Half."

She raised her elbows and hands to the ceiling. "It's an appariiiiition! I was thinking about Columbus Day last week," she continued, motioning toward him quickly. "Of course, the marauder's been dead for 500 years and moreover was a colonialist, of course," she barbed in conspiratorial fashion, and somewhat sincere, "but he was Latin. A romantic, no doubt! We need more romantics...oh how I know it," she confessed, blushing in remembrance. "This Columbus. Could it possibly have all been for gold? Unless he had a lover to support! He must have had one or two bouncing around in Spain, Italy... But you look Irish, too. Are you Irish? I'm Bolivian, you know. Never mind, you don't care. I'll let you slide. No matter!" she exclaimed, winking again.

Again, he attempted to engage her with a laugh, but it wouldn't burst forth; instead, his forced response came out as a sudden hack. He covered his mouth, trying to maintain decorum.

"Anyway," she said, leaning toward him, eyes shining now, "we have a slot left. I think you can fill one," she continued, face turning violet again. "Never mind. Hmm...I'm thinking right now...security, maybe some off-hours bussing, waiting tables...no, maitre'd, at special events. We have lots of dinners and conferences here, you know. And the exhibits! You'll love the exhibits! Oh, and some of them are so irrrrreverent! They're really very funny. It's a party here half the time! Consider yourself on vacation. Wait, do you have any felonies? No,

96

no, of course you don't. What am I saying? We'll need your social security number, though. And you'll get to meet lots of interesting people. Plenty of room for growth here! And you're in computers, right? Computers! They're everywhere, can't avoid them!" she huffed, pointing toward an antiquated, soil-tarred box on a side table. "It isn't even plugged in anymore. Thing must have blown a fuse. But we can use a programmer around here. Don't think this is a whistle stop on your career," she admonished. "Oh, if only our turnover weren't so high. Keep losing people left and right. They fly outta here like angry I-don't-know-whos, some of them. People, they're so unpredictable. Just like my ex-husband," she shuddered.

"I'm looking for something steady," he assured her, now thoroughly amused.

"Steady! Hold me down! Now we're going steady!" she flirted, shamelessly. "I'm kidding! Don't look at me that way! Listen, we have a training program starting next Monday at 9:00 AM sharp. Come ready to work...you don't need a tie, we have uniforms...take a test, fill out some forms. If you make the cut, you'll start the following week. I'm thinking the following Wednesday. It'll depend on my calendar. Do you know my calendar is such a mess?" Then, with an erratic flurry of effort, she looked down, peeled through a stack of papers, jotting rapid-fire thoughts on an adjoining notepad along the way, then shouted at the top of her lungs, "Neeeeext! Hurry up, hurry up! I don't have all day, you bastards!"

Carl shrank back with this outburst, then with utmost haste, he said a quick goodbye, bowed slightly for no particular reason, and left in a flash, brushing the next applicant with his shoulder as he left. Finding the whole experience stimulating, if not downright hilarious, he whisked himself toward the exit, resolving to return the following Monday.

As he ran for the outside door, images flashed though his mind: the old employers who had been so nasty toward him, and Bonastre, who could be his salvation or something much worse, for all he knew, and tossed within the mix of swirling thoughts was Dasha, whose gentle face and mysterious disappearances felt like ballast, albeit a wavering one. Who were all these people in his life, he wondered. Where was this all taking him? It all seemed unsettled, unresolved and unknowable.

But apparently he had work, and that was meaningful. He had a place to go in the morning, something to do, and the chance for a paycheck.

Upon reaching the exit, he threw open the door, sighed with relief, and stepped into a brightness that, for a moment, helped him forget his troubles. He took in the energy of the city and it felt invigorating.

At least for now, he thought, the search might be over.

CHAPTER EIGHT

(1)

Bubbly and high-spirited, she arrived at midnight. Carl was fast asleep and dreaming of faraway lands when she woke him by tugging on his outstretched toes. He faded into the waking world slowly, reluctantly, despite the sudden pull from an unknown person. He was, by this time, perfectly comfortable in his makeshift home.

"Wake up! Wake up!" she exclaimed.

He turned over on his side.

"Look at you. Rumpelstiltskin! What a beard you'll grow lying there like that! Come to, arise, you lazy boob! We need you here in the land of the living, where I can talk to you."

Wiping his eyes, he gradually brought her lithe figure into focus. "What are you doing?"

She heaved a quick breath. "I arrived precisely at midnight. You cannot say I dally aimlessly. I heard the news! I heard you've already found a job. Congratulations!"

"Yep," he mustered, "it's a job, alright. But a good job?"

"Spoiled rotten," she replied, rolling her eyes. "They are so spoiled, these people, expecting this and that. If you want to see a rotten life, I can tell you all about it. But don't worry... that's not what I want for you. I want you to be happy. So here's what I have for you. You have a job, and now I will introduce you to some ladies. Are you interested, my sweet Marik?" she teased, eyeing him salaciously.

He continued to wake up. "Always," he admitted. "But I say that having fallen off the love wagon several weeks ago, and in my condition…let's face it, around here, the cutoff's a hundred grand per."

"Nonsense!" she scolded. "I'll have none of that self-defeat! Listen to me, I have some names, addresses, phone numbers, emails." She stopped, studying him closely, then leaned closer. He could feel her warm breath on the edge of his lips. "Listen," she whispered, brushing against him. "I've known men, as friends, of course, who had nothing but the uniform on their backs, a few sacks of rations, a government-issued rifle, and a pair of boots. Sometimes they were lucky if they had their boots. Yet, they were the most glorious men I ever knew: proud, and the ladies loved them for their courage and the way they carried themselves. There was no helping it. When you're afraid, and the enemy's cannons are near, and you hear explosions, and see smoke, and hear the rumble of armies, and you huddle in fragile little homes, the windows rattling with war…then when the men return, triumphant, having beaten your foes back in humiliating defeat, then you know what it is to respect a man who takes a shot and keeps fighting. Suddenly, this kind of man is worth more than all the gentle fops with gleaming swords who, as soon as they smell gunpowder, turn and flee." She placed a hand on his chest.

"So you're telling me I still have a lot to offer," he said, turning away.

She tugged his arm. "Yes, yes, yes! And you should feel fortunate you have someone who will take care of you. Like Florence Nightingale. You see, I've come here to help you," she said, her voice caring and concerned.

"From where?"

"There."

"Where's there?"

"Up there," she said, pointing to the sky. "Believe me."

"You're saying I don't believe. I guess I don't…I don't believe. How can I believe what my eyes are telling me when it's so unbelievable?"

"You'll see, you'll see. Anyway, here," she said, unfolding a scrap of paper and handing it to him. "I've pulled together a list of people who can help you. They're fun…with them you can explore many things that may surprise you."

He eyed her suspiciously. "Do you believe in God?" he asked, not knowing why.

"Yes! Of course! How can you look around and not believe? Do you not believe the eyes can see so clearly? Do you not believe the heart can beat its thousands of beats on its own, without your prodding? Do you believe the sun and the moon and the stars suddenly popped into little orbits on some random chance, and nature's celestial spheres are in harmony simply because they are?"

"Could be," he said, ruefully.

She tapped him on the nose with her wand. "And if this were true, on what grounds would we bother to get up in the morning? Simply because we are, and therefore we do? Or is there some sense of purpose?"

He turned his head back toward her, his mood lifting somewhat.

"You see," she said, undaunted. "There's much mystery in the universe when you're trapped in this shell. But the wonder of it all! You should see what I have seen, my little Marik. If you could see the beauty…the one that does not wither and fade, but keeps on forever and ever. Then you would know. Then you would believe."

As she finished her sentence, they heard a bell chime, its pitch delicate and light.

"Oh, there's my bell," she said, softly.

"Better answer it," he said.

"One doesn't answer it," she replied, crinkling her nose and cheeks sardonically, "one only responds."

Bing!

(2)

When Dawn arose with her morning paint, Manhattan was a pyrotechnic glow of pastel hues and shaded nooks.

Carl woke with a start. Stuffing belongings into his bags and plastic bags, he wet his fingers with the remains of a water bottle, dabbed down strands of errant hair, and without hesitating further, headed to the nearest payphone.

Today he had much to accomplish. His to-do list, a notebook page filled with tasks such as call the bank, check his balance, find out when the 401k could be disbursed, find out how long it takes for the check to arrive, then how long it takes to clear and so on, seemed oppressive and onerous. He also needed to reconcile this information against the due dates of his credit cards, the cell phone—he might need to cancel that account—and the student loans, then compare this short-term budget against his paycheck, minus taxes...and food.

The situation was entirely stressful and grave.

He ran to the ATM, praying there would be money. Fortunately, the machine whizzed out a crisp twenty dollar bill. Also on the agenda were scores of phone calls, faxes, and emails, all of which he needed to do from a FedEx Kinko's, where he'd need to rent the computer by the minute. Already, thinking about the stress of the day and feeling the noxious fumes of

(8)

traffic in the air, he began to feel a sore throat coming on. He had nowhere to cool and relax for free—none he could think of—so he resolved to do the best he could and tried to budget his cash accordingly, focusing more on liquids than food.

There were fifty job search-related calls to make, and he needed far more leads to do a proper search. This, on top of a new job at the museum. The question of finding suitable work in his field was moot, he realized, if he went broke in the process. Imagining the challenges he faced, his blood pressure rose: at this cash burn rate and in Manhattan, he couldn't last long before going broke. He had already paid for the gym up front, so that was not an issue, but he would likely need to tighten his belt. Literally, he would need to lose weight. Having not eaten well for several days, he was already starting to feel like a skeleton.

Walking briskly and with determination, he reached the subway station at 72nd Street, ducked inside, and with an urgent sense of mission, rummaged through his pants pockets for a coin, only to tap himself on the forehead when he realized it was a toll-free number. He called the credit card company, fumbling his plastic in a trembling hand.

"This is Carl Moretti, credit card number 2320001634561," he said. After a brief conversation, he got to the point. "Two weeks ago I lost my job. What? I can't hear you clearly. No, no. I don't have credit insurance. It was expensive," he said, heaping himself against the wall for support. "But my student loan companies…they've deferred my loans with accrued interest. Can we make any provisions, interest only I mean, until—"

Around him, the roar of traffic and clip-clap of feet, along with honking horns and the flicking of turnstiles, made the environment too noisy to converse naturally. The hot air seeped over his body, which began to sweat, sticking his shirt against

103

his body. His breath was forced and laborious. He pressed the phone closely against his ear, trying to hear.

"You can?" he asked, incredulous.

"Yes, I can waive this payment, but you'll need to make one next month."

"Really? That's great, thanks. Yea, I can get back on track by then. For one thing, my 401k funds will be freed up by then."

"No problem. If there's anything else we can do to assist you, please don't hesitate to call us."

They ended the call abruptly. Feeling relieved, he sauntered casually back to the street, turned uptown, and headed for the gym. He was two blocks away when out of the left corner of his eye, he saw an acquaintance approaching. Tabitha Murphy was someone he knew from a recent software conference he'd attended. Since her path would intersect with his at the next corner, despite the humiliation he felt vis-à-vis former colleagues in his unemployed state, he stepped up his pace, began crossing the street, and put on his most positive smile.

He called out to her.

"Wow, hey! What a surprise," she sang in a chipper voice, wheeling toward him at the crosswalk light. "How are things at, where…Frontier Re? Oh, wait, that's right. They're having some problems, I hear. Downsizing programmers. Ew, you weren't caught up in that, were you?" she asked.

He frowned, then nodded. "'Fraid so. They axed me and three other guys. We were all hired as a team, they groomed us, and now they're dumping us *as a team*. Funny how that works."

"Mmm-hmmm. You know it. It's not just you. I'm hearing this all over. Yesterday, I was talking to a Cobalt developer in Seattle. He says his whole group was outsourced three months ago…and not to worry you, I just want you to know you're not alone…he says they haven't been able to find anything. They're all right there on the cutting edge with their skills, but what the hay? Who cares, I guess? A lot of them have houses… kids…now. Didn't matter. Now one of them, apparently, and I know this sounds silly, he's working the lines in a car wash at twenty dollars an hour. Another one moved back with his parents at forty-nine. I don't ever want that to happen to me when I'm that age," she said, shuddering. Carl noticed her eyes were dazzling, and underneath her attractive expression, she had a certain, solid sense of who she was and a determination not to be pushed around. "Wow…guys like you are joining the Programmer's Guild…for good reason. Did they take care of you, at least?" she asked.

Reminded of their stingy package, he let out a quick snort. "Oh, sure. They offered us a few weeks' pay if we stayed on to train our replacements. I gave that the big negatory."

"You're kidding me? That took guts! I haven't heard that one yet!" she exclaimed. "And where are they getting those replacements?" she asked, suddenly connecting with him again.

"No idea. Not the foggiest. But I basically told them to stick it. I mean, I'd rather teach them a lesson about throwing experience out the proverbial 10th floor window. Let them see how easy it is to train replacements when the people who know the code all skedaddled. Sometimes they only see value if we rub it in their faces."

"Yeaaaaa…and good for youuuuu," she commended, poking his chest.

He laughed. "Right now, they're probably wondering whether they have to rehire me. But knowing that cheap SOB who let me go, his pride'll stand in the way. He'll get some kid right out of college to write acres of spaghetti code, then pay some kids from a consulting firm another half-million to a mill to fix the mess. All that to cut my $95,000 salary in half."

She grinned broadly. "After he loses his job, they can come begging for you to come back. So hang in there. Oh!" she added, snapping her fingers. "There's a good networking opportunity coming up. I mean, not great, but it's a party. Lots of members of the opposite sex will be there," she added, a knowing twinkle in her eye, her voice purring.

"Oh yea?" he responded.

"Yea."

"So where is it? And when?"

She smiled demurely. "A week from Sunday. Here, let me write it down for you. She pulled out a pen and a business card, which she turned onto its back, then leaning softly against him, she began to write. "It's at 76th and Fifth. The Wintermore. Apartment PH-2. Yea…it's a penthouse. There's a doorman. Say you're there to see Suzanne Thomas. It'll be a good time. Seven PM for drinks until…I don't know. Until they drag us out, I guess?" she added slyly.

"Suzanne Thomas. Wait, I know her. Isn't she Frank Thomas's sister? The one who married the oil guy before he croaked, then started dabbling in real estate?"

"You got it. One and the same. And she's siiiiingleeee now," she said, wagging a finger in mock reprimand.

"What would she want with an unemployed tech worker three years her junior?"

"You never knowwww," she baited, beginning on her way. "Maybe she just has a thing for boys." Then, with a casual toss of her hair and a pinch of her nose, she turned away, crossed the street, and disappeared. Carl watched her admiringly for a moment, then turned away himself and headed for the gym.

The usual routine of changing into shorts, cross-trainers, and a grey t-shirt, then stretching for five minutes, running for thirty, and lifting for fifteen, his workout was uneventful, but during his sweat and toiling, his thoughts returned to his predicament. The incessant bills, the sordid job market, the strange living conditions, and the sense of utter disenfranchisement and abandonment were taking their toll. Whereas when he lost his previous job, he was fresh out of school and filled with optimism and had, despite the tough spat at home, found a new job in short order, he feared this time would be different. He couldn't put his finger on the reason, exactly, other than a creeping sense of dread: as if he felt this coming, and coming for some time, and now the forces of the universe were aligned against him.

Mercury was rising, and with the top of his resume now scorching in flames, creditors poised to beat on his door, his previous headhunter suffering as much as he due to the cutbacks in tech employment, and new recruiters apparently unwilling to talk to him, Carl's name was mud. He felt lost on what to do.

Other than accept the job from Bonastre.

Thoughts like this continued to churn through his mind as he walked out the door, but with his body refreshed and his brain flooded with endorphins, for the moment, at least, he could appreciate the sunshine and even, to be sure, a moment of living.

CHAPTER NINE

After lumbering through the week without event, and having continually evaded park officials and police officers alike, Carl settled into this clearing in the bushes that was, like the ceiling of his bedroom in upstate New York, painted with stars. By Monday morning, he had nearly lost track of the days; indeed, he was certain the week had begun only because he walked to a newspaper stand and checked the front page of the *Daily News*.

It was 6:12 AM, and the sun had begun to poke its head over the long horizon, radiating the air with quiet energy. The training class at the museum started at 8:30 and, to be safe, he thought it would be prudent to shower at the gym immediately, hop on the downtown 2 or 3, and get himself there a good forty-five minutes to an hour early. He would wait in a nearby coffee shop.

He gathered his belongings, stuffed them into his duffle bag, and with determined eyes and a rushing sensation, slid through the opening in the bushes. His thoughts raced ahead: how the job might go, how long he could survive on their pay scale, what this gap on his resume would mean to future employers, and so on. On top of these worldly concerns, he felt a gnawing, even jarring, emptiness. Living alone after sharing an apartment left him dangling in space, answerable to no one and, by extension, feeling unconcerned about anyone's questions.

He had none to ask, either, and he sat quietly as Bonastre read off the names at the start of training, over two hours later. Training began with these usual formalities and introductions, and all seemed quite easy and straightforward, but by twelve o'clock, the recruits were clear: Ms. Bonastre, although charming, effervescent, and undeniably hip, took no prisoners. At 9:15, only fourteen minutes after her introduction started, a hapless recruit had straggled in.

"Sorry. Delay on the A," he said.

"Subways? Do I care? You're still late!" she barked. "I'll let it slide, but don't think this will be acceptable in the future."

"I had a follow-up with the doctor this morning. Post-surgery."

"Do I look like a surgeon? Out!" she screamed, pointing to the door. "No need to waste your time when you're already wasting mine. See? I'm fair and balanced." The outburst eviscerated the crowd of young, downtrodden men.

No doubt, Carl realized, she planned to weed out most of the lot. Churning through their ranks, evaluating and discarding with discriminating efficiency, she would select and weigh as a housewife from Queens peruses the meat section at the supermarket. Five-foot-six, vibrant and even sprightly, she wore a black-flecked shirt, tan pants, low-heeled pumps, and a dazzling array of costume jewelry. Yet she seemed completely unconcerned with pretense or appearance, as if she threw on these duds simply because it was the quickest getup she could snag from her closet.

She laid down the law in no uncertain terms: the sentence for infractions was two-tiered: first infraction, a warning, second infraction, a pink slip. But after impressing them with the seriousness of her rules and her will to enforce them—and when many were wondering why this babbling supervisor had transformed herself into a hydrogen bomb—she suddenly broke into the most infectious mood. In fact, her shift in tone was so abrupt, so utterly convincing, and so unexpected, that at first the men, some of whom were nudging each other and drawing effigies of her on their notebooks by now, felt shocked to the point of concern. Was this woman in her right state of mind they wondered, glancing at each other. How could someone turn on a dime so adroitly, hardly breaking a sweat as she dispatched, fired, cajoled, beseeched, and enlightened in the sweep of a few minutes' time—company time at that. One remarked on the possibilities. Another asked whether they should stuff her in a broom closet. Still another asked whether she kept a broom for transportation. This incited snickers in her audience.

Snickers she immediately heard. "Yes, question," she minced, her words sharp enough to slice a carrot. "Please share your question with the rest of us." The men stopped laughing, hoping she'd move on to other targets. Her mind moved so quickly, surely another thought would enter her mind, rescuing them. But she didn't budge: after so many minutes of incessant jawboning, shuffling, leaping, and gyrations, she had became as placid as a mountain lake. As serene and unmovable as a deer. As inert as a forest pine.

The tension lasted several moments.

But again, to their chagrin and to everyone's surprise, she broke the spell with the most sincere, and indeed warm and inviting, gesture of the day. Her eyes, bespeaking affection, compassion, and even a hint of depth, began to sparkle and shine, and her cheeks, once taut and cold, began to turn red, coloring her face with enthusiasm, freshness and life. She dropped her wild arm movements, replacing them with grace.

"We work hard here," she said, "and our demands might be high. But we're also family. If you ever have any concerns, my office is always open." She glanced in the direction of two laughing hyenas, who smiled in embarrassed fashion, and she let it go.

They would begin on Wednesday, and before the strike of one, she thanked them, dismissed them, and departed the room.

Soon they heard a door clasp shut at the end of the hall.

CHAPTER TEN

That night, Carl fell into a dream. The whole day had been dreamlike, from the sudden start, to the steady pulse of shower water, to Bonastre's torrid affectations and his subsequent walk home to his bushes. All day, he had a sense of day passing and a night emerging: everything was a dream because he didn't expect it and because it unfolded, randomly, before his eyes.

His dream began with a stampede.

A herd of cows had broken loose, splintering the gate, and they were charging full force toward the road. He leaped into his father's harvester, trying to chase them, but realized quickly the vehicle was no match for their speed. The young man chugged at a furious pace, trying in vain to save his family's fortune; his parents couldn't maintain their lifestyle on his father's pension alone.

No use, he thought. *They're getting away.*

Trembling, Carl shut down the engine, leaped off the vehicle, and with britches rustling and hands flailing, and hoping to alert the household, he grabbed a horse's bridle with his left hand and the saddle horn with his right, slid his left shoe into the stirrup, and lifted himself into the saddle. He rode off at furious speed.

He began to gain on them as he whipped his horse's rump with the loose reins. The runaway animals, for their part, continued charging ahead, speechless and empty-eyed, yet surely determined. "Giddy-up!" he cried, digging in his heels.

The horse lurched forward. Dust spewed ahead of him, filling the air with choking bits of dirt, leaves, and sticks.

Suddenly a shot rang out. He heard metal whiz above his head. Another projectile grazed the ground ahead, spitting debris into the air. A third shot off his hat. A forth went by his arm. His heart leaped and pounded in his chest, traumatizing him to the point of drying his mouth.

Beginning to perspire, he felt clammy and cold.

By his side was a sword. He was wearing a uniform. And up ahead the cows, he saw, had turned into cavalrymen and horses. They were no longer running away, however. They were charging forward. The men ahead drew their swords and he drew his. Then ahead Carl saw ramparts, then cannons interspersed at regular intervals along a line of defense. The air ran thick with smoke, and one after another, the opposing batteries roared, flashing angry fire and roaring leaden projectiles into his rank. Cannonballs exploded in brilliant arrays of twisted arms, rearing horses, and flashes of red.

A warrior stood on the fort, flag whipping in the stiff wind, raising a pistol at Carl. With his horse galloping ahead and the rush of adrenaline intense, Carl felt an urgent sense of doom. Immediately, he ducked. The enemy soldier fired, and the ball whizzed over Carl's head before ripping through trees on the far side of the field. Carl pressed on, sword smacking his side. In his right hand, he held a single-shot musket. Needing to take action, he slipped his finger onto the trigger, raised it toward the battlements ahead, found his target, and fired. The weapon cracked, recoiled in his hand, and sent a hot musket ball toward the melee ahead.

The other soldier dropped.

All around, horses rode by, angry men fired at will as they interspersed their shots with the kicking of boots and grunts, and burning stench filled the air. The noise level rose to a roar. Carl's ears stung from the whipping of wind and his face pressed against him. His jaws tensed, he grabbed a rifle from its sheath on his side, then aimed it with one arm, and he fired like a madman.

He returned the weapon to his side, burrowed into his saddle, holding his head behind his horse's dazzling mane, and raced ahead. Walls loomed ahead. The herd of cavalry charged, the fort roared, blazing with fire, and angry batteries pounded the field.

"Marik, take the battery on the right, I'll take the left!" cracked the voice of his immediate superior, who was ranked cornet.[viii] Remembering Dasha's name for him, Carl realized he'd been given an order in the fever-pitch of battle, and without second-guessing a decision at such a time, shouted his compliance. At this moment, Marik felt warmth, too. The comrade was a friend, he felt assured, and Dasha's presence somehow rose in his heart. Marik spurred his horse through the haze of battle, leaping ahead, while the senior officer lurched to his left.

An artillery crew was upon him, and as Marik approached, their worried eyes and their desperate efforts to defend themselves deeply disturbed him. It was as if no horror so great as this could possibly happen. To pit himself against these defenders, risking a musket ball through the spleen, great blood loss, the swirling confusion of clouds and trees circling as he fell onto the tumultuous earth, seemed impossible. Surreal. And galloping blindly ahead, his horse seemed detached, too, as if it were acting out a dreamlike existence. Grapeshot flew over Marik's head, cannons thundered both ahead and behind, explosions sent eruptions of soil in all directions, pinging his clothing and face with debris, and the open field where they had charged seemed suspended in another place and time.

Marik's eyes watered as he fought the images back from his soul, and his stomach soured as another cannonball exploded into the fort, sending swords and splinters and faces in every which direction. The horse steamed forward, undaunted, and Marik felt this was fortunate; his charging horse was his only salvation from charges of treason and cowardice because he hated this fight.

But he found his inner resolve.

A rebel stood up, pulled back the flintlock, raised his musket, and aimed directly at Marik's forehead. The man squeezed the trigger, Marik ducked, and lead whistled overhead. Furious now, Marik raised his sword overhead, galloping at full speed, and noting the terror in his opponent's face. The trench in front of the fort rushed to the foreground, his horse leaped, and Marik let out a blood-curling cry.

Slashing his sword across the chest of the defender, Marik rode past the wall and into the square, where he found a dozen or so rebels waiting, hands up in surrender.

Carl pulled back the reins of his steed and inspected their catch. Men and women stood on porches and in the square, helpless and in full surrender, as the imperial troops marched in. He pitied the sight, and at the same time wondered why on earth they would rise up against His Imperial Majesty, burning and slashing their way through the countryside like animals.

He pointed to their tallest one, apparently a leader, and ordered him to lie on the ground, hands over his head. Pathetic with their ragged clothes and sallow cheeks, it was clear his enemy hadn't eaten well. Marik studied them for a moment, then realizing the situation was too urgent for any considerations of feeding them, he nudged his horse and trotted over to his commanding officer.

"Marik, brave work. There'll be a medal in this for you."

Honored, Marik accepted the compliment with a nod and salute.

"Now give them twenty minutes to identify their leaders for us. We'll make summary judgments. And have your men build a gallows."

Reluctant to carry out these grim orders, Marik nevertheless saluted and rode off to his men, who built the required structure while women wailed and men watched in pure horror. Marik felt guilty, but at the same time, felt certain they were criminals in every sense of the word.

The judgments were made quickly and without emotion, and they hanged the rebel leaders as planned. While women sobbed in the doorways and enemy soldiers watched helplessly in shackles, the convicted were marched in single file to the waiting noose. Each died in weary silence, maintaining whatever honor and defiance they could muster amidst abject defeat. Marik watched the condemned walk with bravery to their deaths, granting them a begrudging respect, even admiration, and hoping the ugly business of executions would be over quickly.

But one rebel more than any other caught his eye.

The man, perhaps 50 years old and with lively, almost humorous eyes, returned his gaze, as if calling out to him. Marik turned away, then looked back. The vanquished man made it clear he liked his opponent, and even seemed to call out to him, as if in greeting. This friendly gesture shook Carl's soul, and for a moment, he was sorry the roles were not reversed.

Marik lived to regret the moment when the rebel walked stoically to his execution, accepted the rope, then dropped violently through the trap. As the body swung from the dangling hemp, Marik felt a horrible chill, then became short of breath. Terrified, he reached for his throat, feeling himself choking, then turned toward his commanding officer in terror. The officer responded with a sinister laugh. "Choke all you wish! No heaven for you!" The man pointed to the gallows.

Then Carl bolted upright, clawing a bush with iron-tight fists.

CHAPTER ELEVEN

(1)

"If you don't believe me, take a look yourself. They set it up in Exhibit Hall Two...the crew arrived last night and worked until 5:00 this morning. Would I kid you?" Bonastre insisted, sipping her morning java and tossing Carl a key. "Wait until the patrons come. This kind of art is much better appreciated when you have a crowd," she said, becoming elated. "So you can see their faces! That's the real art, you know. The art of tugging and pulling on these people who glom on to any chance to be disgusted, outraged, titillated...to stand back and relish the venom...pure venom...that spews from critics in certain quarters. Hm, hm! Then we count the dough!"

Carl snickered with her, laughing more at her animation than her words. "I'm on security for the exhibit?"

Gulping a big shot of coffee, she nodded. "Yip. And you'll take tickets from each group. But I thought you were good for this job because it seems nothing fazes you much. We'll need someone calm and composed in there." Then she began to cackle. "To drag out everyone who faints! Paramedic! Help! Excuse me, it's early in the morning. Maybe I'm not myself today."

After leaving her office, Carl decided she was *quite* herself today. *In fine form*, he thought, heading toward the elevators, which were, incidentally, modern, silken, and eerily silent. One hardly knew they were moving. On his way upstairs, all the while staring at the blink-blink-blink of the numbers from Basement Level 2, where Bonastre kept her office, to the second floor, which consisted of nothing but a formidable room with atriums, steel scaffolding, glassy-waxed floors, and picture windows that adorned long, rectangular walls, Carl began to think about Dasha.

Even this early in the morning, with a mind of oozing sludge, less than a cup's worth of caffeine in his system, and a foggy, vague sensation of remaining asleep, he could barely focus on the institutional surroundings. His passion lay elsewhere. Why couldn't they visit museums together? Walk in the park? Share a carriage ride? Roller blade near Sheep Meadow? Why did she have to keep popping in and out so quickly? She possessed so much: her delicate face, her soul-stirring words, the way she glanced at him with timid cheeks and fluttering eyelids, the ripples in her skirt as she danced and pressed her toes into the earth, and the way sunlight sparkled on the tip of her wand. He sighed, realizing he longed to touch her right now and to seize whatever fleeting laugh or kiss she might offer.

The elevator stopped, although he couldn't feel it. The light behind the number two glowed violet, then the door slid open. With thoughts of romance dangling in his heart, he stepped into the enormous room, his footsteps first echoing, then pinging, to oblivion. Up ahead, and close to the center of the room, stood a case on a pedestal; his heart palpitated, not through anticipation of the strange, looming object, but through the images of Dasha that raged within him—images of unspeakable beauty. His shoes clicked, one after another, on the tile floor. The room felt stale, the air conditioning not yet on, and his breath felt short and labored.

He approached, stopped, and stared quietly into the case. Then his stomach churned.

There before him stood a morbid sight. The inscription beneath the case, printed on glossy-white paper and shielded behind transparent plastic, read, "The Rotting Body–Humankind's Naked Truth, B. Alois (2006)." Brooklyn-born Alois, fresh out of the Brooklyn Academy of Arts, was a new artist on the scene and had, apparently, made waves in New York's cultural circles. Moretti knew of the man through an article in the *Village Voice*, which had praised his daring, iconoclastic style. Others in the urban sophisticate community, including an avant-garde deconstructionist who recently moved to New York from LA—apparently helping to design new office buildings "for a new New York—" also praised Alois as, if not the next Picasso, at least "nearly as impactful."

Apparently, Alois had garnered even more attention in London, where critics had said everything from "riveting and provocative...a must for the Tate Modern" to "while the rest of us struggle to adopt iPods and fad diets, Alois reveals a sordid future...London will never recover from the onslaught" to "after premature celebrations, Britain will be modern once again" to "a self-indulgent slime of poor taste."

A critic in Madrid, noting Alois's affinity for the deconstructionist movement, praised him in unqualified terms, suggesting the American *"artista extraordinario"* overcame base effrontery with a *"sentido delicado de la muerte y del decaimiento,"*[ix] although a lone, dissenting voice suggested they add an Alois wing to the local museum *"en la forma de una sardina poder."*[x] Alois brushed off all critics, both positive and negative, having achieved "pure art," and instead emphasized the love and affection of his adoring fans and boosters who, without fail, insisted that geniuses such as Da Vinci, Rembrandt, and other agents of the West's evolving culture were misunderstood in their day, too.

The artist gained no accolades in Paris, however, which raised Alois's stature throughout the English-speaking world, earning him instant cult status. The French either chose to ignore Alois, sparking rumors in New York that Alois was, as one gallery owner slyly opined, "sticking it back to France," or they heaped unfiltered abuse. Critics in New York dismissed this is "your typical, Parisian stubbornness," while in London critics were more circumspect, suggesting their French counterparts were "perhaps more interested in Cannes." Many French were not amused by the slights, and a magazine, after making a passing reference to Alois's sensations abroad, duly panned the American artist as *"un imbécile qui a le chic pour fouillant les bennes."*[xi] Another, wryly noting Alois's recent definition of French cuisine as "tongues, livers, and creams… how appetizing," suggested Alois may have an *"inspiration trouvee en sa propre bile,"*[xii] which upon reaching the ears of Alois, according to the *Village Voice* article, was received as "a backhanded compliment."

Whether good or bad, Alois relished the attention.

This leads to the nature of the exhibit, which begs a description. The box, resting in the center of a table of the kind used for caskets in family viewings, hovered four feet off the ground with a black, velvet curtain draped around it; the curtain dangled all the way to the glistening-white, tiled floor. Made of Plexiglas, the box was glued together but lacked a bottom, and light reflected softly through the plastic, which was mildly opaque. Inside the box, at the precise center as measured from all corners, lay a porcelain dish. Oval and decorated with blue-and-white paintings of Chinese origin, this dish demonstrated how Alois incorporated neo-Eastern themes in his self-described "pan-syncretistic denunciation of culture." In other words, explained the Western phenomenon and maestro, the world must join together to annihilate all cultures and return to "humankind's amoebic predilections."

But on top of the plate sat the prize...the point of it all: in raw, decaying display, festered two rib cages of uncertain origin and, between them, on a burnished, silver pedestal, sat a double hamburger with cheese, ketchup, pickles, lettuce, tomatoes, and mayonnaise. Swarms of flies, and apparently maggots, too, flew and crawled around the infested cage.

Appalled, Carl looked away, when suddenly, "Aha!" cried a voice behind him. The outburst came completely without warning. "You see the truth, but refuse to look! Does one choose to be blind?" A sinister laugh ensued. Carl wheeled around, facing his accuser, and to his shock and surprise, found himself face-to-face with the great artist himself.

Alois.

"Hoo-ha! You're shocked to see me here? I see...I see. Where do you think I went? The North Pole? Ha, ha! Hi ho, cheerio! The ice is melting up there. Wouldn't want to slip into the sea! Don't look so puzzled...it'll be here soon enough. The whole planet's warming up, you know! Soon we'll all be fried to a golden brown! Do me medium rare! Uh-oh! Just spoke the truth again! Hi ho! Better wait here to die, my friend, where at least we have air conditioning. Don't have brownouts around here ... oh wait, yes we do! I forgot! Right on, ol' fella? Hey, you look like a sensible chimp. And we're all chimps sometimes, aren't we? Yes, sir! You think we're more than that? Good luck, stupid duck. Mother Nature has her way of priming the sump pump every 400 million years or so and piping life's crapola right out of this planet. Goodness knows, we're overdue! The big one knocked out 90 percent of all life; this time, let's shoot for 100! Whoa, Lucy!"

Lucy? Carl wondered where this man could possibly be coming from.

The artist, some thirty-five years old, was dressed in black from head-to-toe, with ebony-laced, canvas shoes and a jade medallion hanging from his neck. His eyes were afire and his face, traversed by a fluid mustache, was crinkled and creased, as if at an earlier age he had spent too much time in sun and spirit. His eyebrows, thick and obsidian, cast a deathly pall over his stocky frame, which belied his identity as an artist. He was so stout, he could easily pass for a bouncer or a construction worker, if it weren't for the affected way he swished his arms in the air and his guttural laugh, which seemed to shake his body like waves, as tremors ripple a shoreline. His beltline, lacking a belt, bulged around him like a tire, although in every respect he seemed agile, indeed quick on his feet. And his hair, matted tightly against his scalp, trailed around and behind him, where it tied into a pony tail.

Nonplussed, Carl froze and stared.

"Don't stop breathing, my friend! Then it's all over for sure! The TV show's over...time for bed!" Alois said, walking toward the frightened young man. "We all know this now. Your brain conks out, then, whammo, you're a heap of carbon! These wild stories about out-of-body experiences...a life after. That's the brain losing oxygen! That's all! Give it up! We're all rotting flesh, but is that so bad? We can still make something of this illusion, can we not? I see you're troubled. Did my hamburger display crack through your illusions? A doctor friend told me...he said they take bodies down to the morgue all the time and freeze 'em. Now there are art galleries that throw up the corpses for full display! Show death, I say! Death's a beautiful thing, am I not right, young man? There's something so...so *honest* about it. Art is truth...but today it's harder, more brutal.

In all its Darwinian coldness I give it to you, my son!" By this time, the artist stood face-to-face with his prey. "Don't tell me Dante was brutal, either. He still believed in heaven! Well, I believe in the tooth fairy! Hi-ho! Cheerio! Aha...I see cat's got your tongue! Can't have that. Maybe we should, mmm," he sneered, smashing a foot into the floor, "stomp on your toes. Hi-ho, the dairy-o, eat with a spoon!" Alois's eyes grew wild and his mouth trembled.

"You startled me, that's all," Carl muttered, sincerely, not wanting to make enemies with this apparent foe.

In mocking fashion, Alois opened his eyes wide. "Like that? Ha, ha! Gotcha! Now if you really want a surprise, check out my exhibit. Look well, because that's where you're heading! Oh...You think I'm kidding. Ever visit a graveyard? What do you think people are doing there, sleeping? Not! I know...I know...you don't want to see," he continued, pointing both index fingers at Carl's flustered-looking eyes. "Here's the thing, kid. You might call me crude, you might call me lewd...and generally rude...but ya doesn't have to call me Johnson. Hi-ho! That is, as some of my critics say, but pff-yea-right! Do they know what my art is saying?"

"Nope."

"Aha! Insightful," Alois responded, throwing down his arms in satisfaction. "I'll explain. Yes, siree...there's art...and then there's the awesome Alois. That's alliteration, please note. Oops, a moment of formalism! Three lashings! Hey...listen... my father used to speak in rhymed iambic pentameter, although he was also a butcher. See his influence anywhere? Apples don't fall far from the tree, do they? Anyway, you keeping up with me, chumpy-whumpy? Listen...and I'll only tell you this in strictest confidence. Wouldn't want to spoil the public image...they love the macabre, you know? I'm a big-hearted optimist. Maybe my heart's big because I eat too much...hoo-ha!...but it's also because I see humanity's ship's sailing over the horizon. It'll tumble over like a twig over Niagara, but that's neither here nor there. Hm, postmodernist thought, wasn't it? Listen, dearie, as I enlighten your mind. Look at that exhibit over there. Brilliant! It's brilliant, isn't it?" As he said this, he grabbed Carl's left bicep with a tight fist. Carl shook him off. "A feisty one! Look...where you see maggots and flies over there, I see rebirth! Where you smell stink and decay, I smell nature's engine a-churnin'. You see, my dear, when one life is taken away, another can form anew. It's a natural cycle! Like a dishwasher or a car wash! And who cares how hot it's gettin' in that ol' dishwasher when nature's cleanin' her plate? Imagine if Da Vinci were still alive? Wouldn't have our own chance to lead the stinking mess, would we? But there's more. The hamburger. That's a poke at our mass, consumerist culture. It turns back on ourselves: we eat meat, but we're in the grinder ourselves! Get it? High-ho, high-ho, it's off to rot we go!"

"You're mad," said Carl, testily.

"You think I'm mad, eh? You're damned right I'm mad! Mad as hell about this rotten deal we have, but what can we do about it? I'm just another pile of minerals and water like everyone else. Best we can say is who cares! That's the way to get even." Laughing at himself, the great artist began wheezing uncontrollably. "Sure, we can complain, protest! But then...and here's the thing, kid, and the reason why the flock flies to these exhibits...we have to face it. If life's so stinkin' rotten, then better off to know it so when your body starts turning to bedrock and you're stuck in your rocker all day, at least you know the gig's coming up. A bad joke can only last so long! Hi ho!"

"If that's the case," Carl interjected, wanting to probe this man's wit, "then why get up in the morning? Why not lie there and rot, so to speak?"

Alois flipped a finger in the air. "A philosopher. Good question. That's what philosophers do...always asking questions but no answers! That makes me the enlightened one. Hi ho! Cheerio! Yes, yes...how could I know? Let me ask you something, Mr. Meaning and Existence: you ever wake up on a bad day and have some angel land on your shoulder, telling you it's all going to be alright? Huh, that ever happen to you?"

Carl squinted his eyes, defiantly. "Yes."

Startled, Alois choked on a cough. "Excuse me, but did I hear an affirmative? Does this man mince words with tomfoolery? Tell you what, if you can summon angels on little butterfly wings at the drop of a hat, then bring me one right here. Right now, and show me the fun. Let me believe!"

The young man shook his head. "Can't do it myself. She's in control."

"She? Ha, ha, you silly maroon! Everyone knows angels are pudgy cherubs flying around and displaying their little...hey, you ever go to the Met? You can see them there. No women allowed. Not in those sexist days. Whoa, Lucy! No, it was an all-male club, except for the Virgin, who wasn't even allowed to fornicate. How about that? Sure, the other Magdalene, the other Mary, might have been a bit loose in the frock...shall we say...but a king is entitled to some perks, right young fellow?"

Carl wanted to slug him, but held himself in check.

"Excuse me if you think I'm crude. I mean no offense. I'm a teller of truth, that's all. And truth is, this world's stink-o. The whole, greasy, sordid lot of it, so it's no wonder those Renaissance artists talked so much about hell. That's where we are, and artists do nothing if not observe, you know what I mean? Heaven…that's dope for stupid people with plastic covers on their sofas, pink flamingos in their lawns. Hell… that I can believe in! But heaven, you can stick it where the sun don't shine!" Now breathless, Alois finished with a grunt.

"Actually, I'm Christian."

"Aha…an existentialist, are we? Who knew? Only you! Ha ha! That's a philosophy joke. Lotta good that faith'll do ya when your corpse begins to rot. Oooo…please…come help me! I'm Christian! Just kidding, mate. Don't look so glum. Hi ho! Cheerio!" Having exhausted himself, Alois's demeanor suddenly turned for the worse. The artist began traipsing around the case, right hand flitting into the air. "Look where Kierkegaard is now, genius! Deader than a doornail in the Mojave sun! Yessirrr, nothing left of him but a couple of dusty, old books. Ought to throw those on the ol' bonfire, too, as good'a use as they are to you now. Along with a lot of other ones I can think of," he grumbled, cheeks turning pink.

Studying the fellow in jaw-drooping wonderment, Carl judged there was no use in argument. It was clear the man harbored calcified views; and besides, watching over the exhibit was his job, and while it didn't fit his description of the ideal one, it was better than reneging on his debt obligations. "I'll be watching over the exhibit today."

"Yea, yea." Alois waved a hand dismissively, transfixed by his creation.

So Carl, hoping to steal away for another cup of coffee before the exhibit opened, started moving toward the elevators, all three of which remained motionless along the southern wall. His shoes clip-clopped against the hard tiles as he walked, as stealthy as possible, away from the macabre sight and its gesticulating creator. Then, hearing Alois's piercing voice, Carl's heart froze.

"Oh, my my!" said Alois, still facing his masterpiece. "Is this all? What time is it?"

It was a strange query, the way it was asked. Carl paused to gather himself, then glanced at his watch. "Show starts in 35 minutes."

"It's already over!" suggested Alois, sounding distraught.

"No, it's starting in 35 minutes," Carl replied, feeling nervous.

"Aha!" the effervescent man interjected, turning around. "You've entered the Rubicon! There's hope for you now! Hoo-ha, my boy! Like your watch, you take a lickin' and keep on tickin'. Aren't we feeling ambiguous today? You've passed the test. Go...go. Have your break," he exclaimed, grinning.

Carl drew a short breath, then held it. "Now I'll leave," he said, softly. With that, he continued toward the elevator, pressed the button, and proceeded to leave the exhibit.

(2)

The exhibit started with the pushing and jostling of a modest-sized group—Carl counted a dozen—several of whom wore press badges. The exhibit hall, still empty and vast, was brightly lit now: halogen lamps beamed from the rafters, steel beams and vaulted ceiling. Air-conditioning hummed in the background. Although it was not clear to Carl where the vents were located, he could feel cold air settling on his shoulders, arms, and the back of his neck. He stood to the right of the elevators, walkie-talkie clipped to his belt, hands folded in front of him, and facing the exhibit. Over to his left, Roberto Rodriguez, whom Carl met at the training class, stood in his usual, regal way: six feet tall, stalwart, broad-shouldered, and dignified. Rodriguez took the visitors' tickets, one-by-one, quietly thanking them.

In the two hours since Carl first spoke to Alois, the exhibit had changed. A placard that explained the purpose of this *oeuvre d'art* had been erected on an easel, presumably by Alois himself. A man and a woman, both dressed in trench coats and staring blankly ahead like mimes or robots stood on pedestals to the carcass's left and at forty-five degree angles to the crowd. Alois stood on the right and held a remote control device, a grey, rectangular box with several switches, LEDs, and an antenna; from the way he crutched it, Carl felt this object must be part of the exhibit. And most peculiar of all, far up in the rafters, thick ropes arced in semi-circles from one set of beams to another. A platform, surrounded by a metal railing like a trapeze, had been set up at one end; Carl heard someone, or something, stirring up there.

"May I have your attention, please!" Alois announced as the guests settled down, standing between them and the case. "Ladies and germs," he continued with a nasty smirk, "welcome to my latest offering to the world of art. I'm delighted, even humbled, by the opportunity to be here today, in this hallowed hall of humanity. And yes! We are, indeed, here to leaaaarn… to see, and most important, to feel, what it is to be alive. Until we aren't! Hoo-ha…got you there!" he chortled, facetiously.

Awkward laughter bubbled through the crowd, but the two, statuesque models on the left, still expressionless and silent, failed to budge. Carl sneered mildly, trying his best to be polite and respectful, while Roberto, ever the paragon of class, remained dignified and silent.

Alois waved his arms. "Please. Please! Gather 'round. We need to view the body…well, all the bodies, but you know what I mean...*in situ* where you'll see the purpose of my art most clearly. Come, come, quickly! We don't have all day. Actually, we have as much time as we like, but that's another matter." Then the maestro, miffed by their slow and hesitant pace, snapped a foot impatiently on the floor. The stone-cold statues to his side remained motionless, even to the point of Carl's admiring their professionalism.

The crowd stared in awe, whispering amongst themselves.

"Aha! I see you're surprised by this scene before you. Many are, but if you think I'm depraved by thinking this way, try Sandro Botticelli! Or not. But I see we're also feeling squeamish, aren't we, my sniveling snits. Well, well, what a surprise. I guess no one will feel that way in the morgue!"

Unable to contain himself any longer, Carl belted out a laugh. Roberto, in kind, pressed his quivering lips together, refusing to glance in his colleague's direction.

"Oh, I see we have humor entering the room. And was he invited?" asked Alois, a sardonic twist in his smile. Several patrons, eager to glean all they could from the great visitor's generous speech, shot incensed glances in Carl's direction. Clearly, these people considered this employee a rube. "I see I've ruffled some feathers," said the artist, noticing the buzz. "But enough! Where were we, oh yes, the body. We all are trapped in these withering wrecks, destined to melt over time into sordid, fetid lumps...and best we can do then is thank Mother Earth for providing this earthly ride, then exit stage left, so to speak. Learn to appreciate ugliness and decay! It's your truest friend...it will stay with you forever! Hi ho! Cheerio!"

Many in the audience murmured their agreement.

"But if you think this is shocking, wait'll you see what's next!" he taunted, affecting his best stage whisper.

The crowd grew still.

"Because while it's true that life begets death, which begets life again. And while we know it's a cycle as natural as time, and we have proven beyond all human doubt that sentience...consciousness my friends...is nothing more than a bunch of neurons firing in your brain, and when that goes, it's on to Toledo! Well, my friends, there's still plenty of hope! For, you see, we are nothing but information. Liiiiife information in DNA, and when we pass, we leave our digital bits for new life to arise! And with this, life can spring anew! So the secret of this world is to, dare I say it? Procreate, procreate, procreate! Fornication! In the name of rebirth!" he roared. "But you better not get stuck on beauty when you do it. Any port in the storm will do! Hi ho!"

This brought thunderous applause from all but two in the crowd, who, becoming incensed, did nothing but frown, their arms folded defiantly against their chests.

"Because," he continued, in a whisper that silenced the crowd, "that's all there is. There's no hocus-pocus, no Santa Claus, and no Easter Bunny. And there's certainly no tooth faerie. Right, you say. We know this. These are all, how to do you say, dope for the dopes!" he exclaimed, relishing his wit. "And who needs that when there's plenty of dope to go around?"

Again, many applauded the great genius Alois. Some were beginning to tear, while others became mesmerized, as if in a trance.

"Aaaaand," the artist chuckled, beginning to settle down, "there are only so many of us who get it. As for the rest, as the Romans used to say, *dictum sapienti sat est.*"[xiii] Clearly admiring his erudition, Alois emphasized his thought with a moment of silence. Then, drawing a long breath, he announced in a high-pitched roar, "Now your attention is required for a most unusual coda to my song! Everyone, please, stand back! Further,

further, I say. Make plenty of room. A few more feet. That's better, right there. Attention, patrons! All eyes to the rafters where, as you will see if you look, a man will appear on the platform. His name is…bugle, please—"

The statuesque figure closest to Alois, suddenly alive, face filled with expression and eyes gleaming, removed a bugle from underneath his robe and, with alacrity and skill, proceeded to belt out a bugle call.

Enraptured and with wild pleasure, one man in the crowd shouted, "Bravo! Bravo!"

This pleased the artist immensely.

Carl couldn't help snickering again, but feeling trepidation, he covered his mouth.

"Ladies and gentleman, and germs, too…the great, the only…representative of humankind's superman prowess, the diminutive, yet sublime, a man who's powers exceed his diminished size…an übermensch if you ever saw one…ladies and gentlemen welcome the Great…Suuuuumanooooo!"

Immediately and on queue, a tiny man, no more than four feet tall, dressed in a polyester Superman outfit, and complete with crimson shoes and flowing cape, high-stepped his way onto the platform, grabbed the dangling end of a rope in his hands, and waved to the thunderous crowd. The audience cheered wildly, now bursting with tears. Then the trapeze artist of sorts took a proud, exaggerated bow.

Alois glanced up, then in self-satisfied manner, turned to his fans, who remained blessedly happy. "We may be small," he said, pointing toward the ceiling, "but don't say that to a dwarf!" Then the maestro, who until now had held his greatest passions in check, sallied as loud a voice as he possibly could, "Rapunzel, let down thine hair!" Once again, his cleverness turned him giddy.

The diminutive man, who had turned motionless, then sprang into action: he reached across his body, drew a shiny, plastic dagger from his belt, and, without further ado—and waving his knife wildly in the air—leaped off the platform, holding the rope in one hand, and flew, as fast as physics would take him, toward the case. "Oooooooahhhooooahhhhh!" he wailed.

The crowd was stunned, and moreover horrified, to see this man hurling toward the festering meat without a safety net. What would he do? Crash into it? Would he hurt himself? Worse, would he die right here in front of them? Horrified, they reared back, jaws clenched and bracing themselves for a catastrophe. Carl shot a glance at Roberto, who looked as terrified as everyone else.

All except Alois, who seemed in beatific bliss. Alois knew, evidenced by his fiendish grin, the performer was heading straight for the case, and nothing could stop him. It was all part of the plan.

"Stand back! Prepare for a crash!" Alois exclaimed. "And is this not how the dinosaurs went? A missile from the sky?" With that, the racing projectile, arms contorted and flailing and now only yards from the case, let go of the rope, tossed his weapon aside, and proceeded to ram, feet first, straight into the Plexiglas, throwing it, the meat and the swarming insects, right off the table.

Flies flew into the air.

Miraculously, the man was unharmed.

"Freedom!" Alois sang. "The flies will outlast all of us!"

The crowd stood in stocked silence as the pests buzzed high into the air. Carl shot his friend Roberto an incredulous look, and his friend returned an equally stunned expression.

For his part, The Great Sumano leaped up and danced a jig, delighted he was okay, and the ringmaster, beaming with pride and relishing the reaction of his captive audience, threw an arm toward the mimes. "Do you get it now?" he asked, puffing his chest. "But that's not all," he said, releasing his fingers toward the statues. "If you thought that was shocking, wait'l you see *this*!"

And on queue, the two performers dropped their robes.

They were buck naked.

The crowd gasped. Carl winced. Only Roberto, refined as ever, maintained his cool. The dwarf feigned surprise, but Carl surmised this was rehearsed.

And emblazoned, indeed tattooed, across the chests of the two statues-turned-actors were the words, one on each body: "Religion Sux."

With the image complete and his patrons entranced, the triumphant artist, the one and only man on the planet who could conjure this feat, raised his chin into the air and cried, "Fear not, my flock! If it's not real, how can it hurt?"

This brought down the house.

CHAPTER TWELVE

Standing for eight hours in a climate-controlled room with little more responsibility than showing up had proven taxing, so rather than grabbing some Chinese food on the way home "to the nest," as he had planned to do, Carl headed straight for bed and fell asleep. The hours passed like years as he nestled into his dream world, which entertained and soothed an otherwise torpid young man.

He dreamed of Dasha and battles, heroics and grit, and as one scene shifted to another in his mind, the possibilities of breaking—indeed fighting—his way out of this youthful demise seemed attainable. Most of all, he dreamed of Dasha, although not as a lover or even someone he madly loved, although he felt the possibility arising in his soul, but instead as a wellspring of faith. Not faith in her, per se, but her faith in him.

This gave him a sense of needing her in order to achieve something himself.

In a vision, he opened a door.

It was tall and heavy, with iron rods bolted across it. Dasha appeared in the doorway, fires flickering in the background and tapestries hanging on granite walls. The air was crisp and breezy, an apparent summer's night, and sensing her invitation, he placed one foot inside.

"Stop, no further...please," she admonished, more concerned than commanding. "You're not permitted here."

"By whose laws?" he scoffed. "Tell me everything. I need to know."

She turned away, upset. "I'm afraid I can't. Go! You must discover this in your own dreams!" She flew into tears.

And Carl awoke in a feverish state.

Early in the morning now, 1:35 AM according to his watch, he felt himself wide awake, so rather than attempt to sleep, and moreover feeling a rumble in his stomach, he pressed himself off the grass, grabbed his wallet, and headed to an all-night eatery. It took fifteen minutes to get there. He walked inside, choosing a booth along the far wall.

The man who took his order looked stoned.

The memories of his dream lingered, making the stark surroundings—stainless steel coffee makers, cheaply-framed pictures, Formica countertops—seem unimportant in the larger scheme of things. Along the bar, which stood on the opposite side of the restaurant, sat a man and a woman, one on each end, and behind the bar, a middle-aged, portly figure scurried back and forth, fixing dishes and wiping counters in his spare time. Late nights always brought out the oddness in people, Carl mused, noting their tiredness, muddled thoughts, and general sense of detachment.

The food arrived quickly: a chicken parmigiana, a baked potato stacked high with butter, and a few generous sprigs of broccoli. They also served him a house salad dressed in blue cheese, a towering glass of apple juice, and a basket of rolls. Carl salted his food and dug in, losing sight of the time, the place, and even the mood. Then when he finished, he tipped the waiter, who had disappeared in the kitchen, and walked back to his bushes, where he slept the rest of the night.

He arrived at work early the following morning, relishing the chance to take a warm shower, which the museum provided in the men's locker room. He also donned a fresh, dry uniform. But even in the pale, yellow light of the locker room, where nothing but the buzz of distant boilers disturbed the morning calm, thoughts of Dasha enveloped him and his dreams couldn't escape.

A young woman this striking, who arrived amidst his most shameful moments yet seemed non-judgmental, and even sympathetic, would haunt the thoughts of any red-blooded man, he thought. Haunt was the word, too. While Carl felt their chemistry and knew he'd see her again soon in the park, she hadn't visited the night before and he suddenly scolded himself for wanting something he couldn't have.

Again.

She was elusive, ephemeral, and more than anything else, it was all too ridiculous. Living his lifestyle, no matter how well Carl kept an air of pride about himself, weighed on his self-esteem. The museum staff didn't know he lived in Central Park; he gave them his old address. So daydreams of Dasha— her sparkling, curved lips, and engaging smile—seemed more torture than fantasy, and he tried to suppress them accordingly.

Carl dusted himself off with a towel and sat on a bench, staring near-blankly at a locker. He thought of her snuggling next to him, her taffeta hair dangling onto his shoulder, her chypre scent musty and sensual, her soul intimate and warm.

The door swung open and in walked Roberto, rescuing him from these wicked thoughts. They walked together to the office.

Slowly, the casual hum of work turned Carl's mind to more immediate concerns. Although the building looked modern and new, it was more spit-and-polish than substance. Yet life at the museum was refreshing. Although Bonastre maintained a strict, formal atmosphere for work, it seemed this was not an easy place to get fired. She seemed more than capable of creative thinking. Up front she was a tyrant, but once you were in here, you were in, not least because she expected so many people to quit on their own. Any place where flashing a group of museum goers was part of the product, well, Carl reasoned, a manager could only expect so much loyalty. Bonastre remained the martinet, in a sense, barking missives in this direction or that and citing rules of one form or another in seeming haphazard fashion, yet she maintaining an astonishing, inner sense of balance—as if her extremes all converged on a delicate, immutable middle. Her only vice was her schedule: it was one pet peeve, and no one dared violate her calendar. They said you could set the atomic clock by her punctuality. She never walked the floors, instead biding her time on Basement Level 2, on the same floor as the boiler room.

At 11:00 when they met in her office, where he routinely checked in, Carl found Toni in a heightened state. "Alois, Alois!" she cried, pacing behind her desk and throwing up her arms in despair. "We pay this man $100,000 for three days of lecturing and an exhibit, and now he's demanding $50,000 out of my budget for more stunts! As if he doesn't have enough. He's brilliant, yes, but he says the shock's wearing off! Now we have to up the budget and shock 'em even harder! How ungracious…the louse! The fiend! What more can I give him? A deal's a deal, and we had a deal! Should I go off and rip up every piece of paper I sign after I sign it? Oh, excuse me while I rant. Do you know this man was nothing until I showed his art here two years ago? Hm…hm. The nerve. I guess he knows how to shock someone, doesn't he? Of course he does. He's the king of the shockers! That's why I hired him. You heard it right here; excuse me while I scream. No, never mind, I won't do that. I'm not intemperate, my dear Carl. They'll never hear me over the boiler room, but pfahh! Enough! Great place to get murdered down here, I tell you. Remember that. If you ever want to knock someone off, you know where to go," she said, breathless and dazzled.

Carl sounded sympathetic. "Maybe *you* should shock *him* and cancel his exhibit."

"Ha, ha! Great minds think alike! I've thought of that... you don't think I wouldn't think of that, do you?" she inquired, pointing at and eyeing him askance. She turned and faced him. "Don't forget, I don't only work in the museum, I *am* the museum." She said this with a wink. "Nobody, and I mean nobody, messes with Boiler Room Bonastre! That's what they call me, you know. Call me whatever they want, I say. They don't know that I know it, or I'd have to...oh, shut up. I don't usually talk to myself this way. So, how did you like the exhibit?" she asked, shifting direction and tone on a dime.

"Fascinating," he said, finding truth and a lie in one word.

She stopped and grimaced. "No. It's pure schlock. Pure, unadulterated garbage. That's why I love it! Where else can you go to get a frontal lobotomy than right here, at my museum. I told you it's my museum, right? Yes, I did...that's right," she said, now pointing to his forehead. "Anyway, I couldn't care less about the $50,000."

"Why not?"

"Because! We can pack 'em in here like canned tuna, that's why. If they'll come to see this monstrosity I've foisted on them, it's like setting up a wishing well. They just throw in their quarters hoping for a miracle! You tell me that one? No, that was Anthony. Great recruit. I have only one critic so far. One! And she's from the Jewish World Perspective, a web site. A web site! Said it's disgusting, immoral, crass, and on and on.

Who cares? It's nothing. When I pay 50, 100, 150 thousand dollars, I want heat! Raw, passionate energy that makes my heart go aflutter! We're not getting started yet. I want half of Omaha protesting us 24/7 with press coverage, shots ringing out in the halls...despair, mayhem! Not this...this nothing." Getting weary, she stopped and heaved a heavy sigh. "No, this business isn't the same anymore. Ten years ago, oh sure, half the armed forces would have been sent in here to root us out. They'd arrest me, handcuff me, some big, rock-hard sergeant with Ray-Bans draggin' my quivering body off to the pokey! We'd be selling tickets faster than you could say retire at thirty-five. But now? Nobody cares anymore. It's all smut, filth, and slime anymore...it's all the same to them. We need something new. An invasion from Venus."

"That could be a long wait."

"I know, I know, and I don't have the time. Instead, I need to grab whatever stash I can from this joint, excuse my French, before I cut and run. You know what I mean. Time's a'ticking here, and I've got a few dozen rabid fans, a budget popping at the seams, and a renegade artist who doesn't even have the good sense, or decency. Decency! To give me some controversy. I mean, at least offend the Catholic Church! Where are the nuns when I need them? There are some Catholics left here in New York! Sheez, I mean, really," she said, ending with a sour sneer.

Carl tried to assuage her concerns. "I'm Catholic. And if it's any consolation, I found him mildly offensive, he–"

"You did?" she interjected, face brightening. "Well, that's something, isn't it? Good, good, good. I got under your skin, eh? Can't always get what you want, they say, but at least he's pressing someone's buttons! I like you now. But you don't like him, do you?"

He shrugged. "He's okay, in spurts."

She lip-synched his words, as if chewing them over. "That's okay. That's good, actually. At least I've accomplished something here. Tell you what," she said, sounding authoritative again. "I'll bump you up. Reassign you. I know...I know...you already have the perfect job. Stand around and be shocked for pay. But hey, it'll be much better than that gig. There's a seminar coming up this Friday night, and it'll last through Sunday afternoon. Lots of important guests, dinners, speeches, yada yada. I'll let you be server. Like a catering thing. It's a good job. You stand there in your uniform and look handsome."

"What's the topic of the seminar?"

"Books," she replied, distractedly. "Something about books...modern literature I think. I'll be working this one, too. They're paying lots of money, so Boiler Room Bonastre will be there!"

"That sounds extra-fun," he said. He immediately wished he'd kept his silence, but she paid no attention to the sarcastic remark. As he left the office, wondering where the jab had come from, a fleeting thought of Dasha flashed in his mind. But he pressed it out, thanked Bonastre as if to repair his last remark, then followed along to the break room for a moment of quietude.

CHAPTER THIRTEEN

The sign stated in bold, large-block letters: "21st Century Fiction—A Professional Inquiry." Carl stepped toward the easel, where the cardboard sign rested in prominent view, studying the attending newspaper and magazine clippings that were scattered around and behind it. There were articles such as "Fiction Sales Tanking Says Insider," "Insider Decries E-Book Revolution," "The Shotgun Approach: Why Bull's-Eyes are Passé," and "Proven Author's Latest Called Beacon of Sales Hope."

The door to the main ballroom, where hundreds of conference attendees would endure a grueling, three-day self-flagellation, was open, and inside stood a podium, behind which a large screen had been lowered. The room was filled with an array of round tables, around which sat narrow, metal-framed chairs.

Furthermore, the room was arranged like a political convention, with signs over each table. Examples included: "Mystery-Thriller," "Chick Lit," "Gay-Lesbian-Bi," "Literary Art: Psychology and Style for Niche Markets," "Modern Satire: Pulling Your Punches for Cash" and so on. People would congregate in the groups to which they had been pre-assigned.

Alone at 5:30 AM, Carl stepped inside this large, empty space where he would act as food and beverage coordinator over the next few days. The air was stale and the lighting soft, and at this wee hour he could scarcely imagine the activity ahead. Indeed, diminished by the grandeur of this room, with its vaulted ceilings and divider-opened space, he felt almost like the last soul on earth. He spent the next fifteen minutes preparing for the day, which included unloading his cart with the basic necessities of sugar, Splendid, a non-dairy creamer, straws, napkins, and other non-perishables. Later, he would wheel in the coffee, doughnuts, pastries, bottled water, assorted teas, and plenty of alcoholic beverages—all at 8:15 according to Bonastre's strict regimen.

He wondered about her order for champagne and Bloody Marys, considering them passé, but the event sponsor had insisted, and who were they to refuse customer requests, she scolded. He finished his task in numbed silence, then returned to the kitchen, realizing he needed to get to work before the monster came breathing down his neck. Languid and with weary movement, he pushed the cart to the corner by the freezers. The wheels of the vehicle squealed softly, once on every rotation, as he brought the cart to a rest.

The pastry chef, who had ordered most of the conference foods from an outside vendor in order to focus on the night's dinner, told Carl to prepare for a big day: there was not enough counter space in the food preparation work space, so the pastries, which would be arrayed on steel trays and covered in Saran Wrap, would need to be moved quickly once they were removed from the refrigerator. Chewing on a blueberry muffin, Carl said it would not be a problem.

At this moment Bonastre stormed into the kitchen, fussing over details of many sorts and barking pointless orders that she immediately retracted, then reiterated, in rapid fire. Seeing her staff was on top of its game, she nodded with a satisfied humph and proceeded to her office, where she had phone messages waiting. Today, she seemed unusually anxious, yet not entirely unpleasant, Carl thought to himself. This would be the third conference of its kind, and the potential profit stream from this new service of the museum had put much pressure from the Board of Directors onto her shoulders, yet it also represented a golden opportunity.

And the morning's preparations were going well.

The customers arrived three hours later.

Carl watched them pass through the hall and into the main conference room. The throng was a jostling, bustling, proud array of back-slapping cronies, complete with bold suits, pants, and polished shoes, and although some wore an odd assortment of colors, patterns, and styles, they looked, in aggregate, professional and ready to work. Most were literary agents. It was clear from the cordial greetings and spontaneous conversations that many were on familiar terms and, in fact, each knew each other well.

This was a reunion as much as a working conference.

The conference chairman, Herb Seligman, arrived with his own entourage, which carried a different energy: one of gravitas, reserve, and quiet authority. Although this industry might be on the skids, as evidenced by their placards, Carl judged they were not suffering personally. Standing there, his tasks done for the moment, Carl watched as the conferees chomped on refreshments that were, after all, quite delicious and free. With a long, three-day slog ahead, it was wise to fill their stomachs with fuel.

Suddenly, Bonastre appeared, snapping her fingers and shooing him further into the room. "Away from the door! Come on, get moving...get moving," she exhorted, "there are people to serve! Stomachs to fill! Find something to do. Here, they're thirsty! Where's the cocktail tray? There...there! Give 'em their booze! Quickly...before they turn on us!" Not wanting to argue, Carl snapped into action, pretending to work by scurrying around the room and trying to look useful.

In truth, there was nothing to do yet, but he made a good show.

At precisely 9:00 AM, with the ring of a bell and clinking of glasses—the liquor flowed at a furious pace—the conference began. Seligman stepped to the microphone, quiet and grave, and with his regal, somewhat smug, presence at the podium, the incessant din and revelry of the crowd quickly turned to ice, and within fifteen seconds, the affair became nothing but business.

Seligman cleared his throat, tapped on the microphone, then began. "Welcome to the First Annual New World Publishing Conference." His measured phrase hushed the crowd...not a whisper. "For the past several years, as you know, there has been a rising desire for an integrative approach to our industry's, one would say, mounting challenges...and this conference has been carefully, and *wisely*...we hope...incubated through many hours of thought and planning in order to have... a bit of analysis, as it were, and to address the financial...and cultural...challenges...we, as an industry, face."

Carl noticed he would enunciate certain words, as if for emphasis, while letting his voice trail off or soften at other points, lending himself a musicality, as it were, that further enhanced the presentation.

Seligman drew himself up ever-so slightly, then surveyed the crowd with deliberate, subtle bobs of his head, as if a hinge on his back were touching a spring. "But first...before we discuss the array of issues we have at hand...one might call this a bit of a diversion, but as we will see, it's a diversion we must take...we need to gaze beyond the grandeur of this room, and our wonderful colleagues and friends, to the wondrous, great beyond. Where many people, places, and things we might call, for want of a unifying phrase, externalities, lurk, waiting for us to fill their lives with a certain need that only we can define." The audience leaned closer. "Outside this conference, where we're blessed with the greatest industry in the world, and this museum, where I hope we'll all take the opportunity to prance the halls of great, contemporary art, and be inspired—"

Toni motioned toward Carl, beaming with satisfaction.

"—because outside our world, we are faceless and unknown. It's the impact we have that is, shall we allow ourselves this thought, so sublime. Or, at least, one hopes so. We must remain modest. Has everyone seen the Alois exhibit, by the way?"

Some in the crowd murmured "yes."

"Excellent exhibit. And thought-provoking." Seligman straightened his back and sipped his water. "But if we take away one *golden nugget*, if you will, from this conference, it will be an awakening of the mind into at least, I offer to you, some gentle prodding in the manner of steward, rather than master, and into an imaginative approach to understanding who...out there in the vast wilderness beyond the sanctity of the Hudson and East Rivers...dwells in that English-speaking, and it still is largely English-speaking...place called America. It still exists. And to do that, I have a surprise."

The audience grew excited.

"Yes...today, we've invited a distinguished guest, a member of one of those fine organizations where our wares are displayed and sold, to speak about his thoughts, from an esteemed institution's perspective, of the fiction buyer today. That is, that nameless, faceless soul in search of nourishment out there beyond the island of Manhattan...and let's see whether we can glean something useful that might help us in our more pressing, and practical task...of lifting our sales and profits to

the heights we often achieve in our books. May I introduce
to you, the Senior Vice President of Marketing at Roundtop
Booksellers, Incorporated...Henry (Hank) C. Thatcher. Mr.
Thatcher." With this, Seligman swung his left arm toward a
side wall, where Thatcher, a tall, crisp, and elegant man, who
glistened in a $4,000 Savile Row suit, leaned casually.

The crowd applauded with a rapturous spirit, pleasing
Seligman, who applauded himself. The drinks continued to
flow.

Pleased by the introduction, Thatcher sashayed to the
podium. "Thank you, my friend," he said, graciously nodding
toward Seligman, who beamed at the recognition. "But
Houston," he began, leaning into the podium and pointing
to the crowd, "we have a problem. And the problem we have,
at the bookseller level, lies in the steady decline of book
sales, especially in the area of fiction! I wanted to address
you today, then, not as an advocate, but as an ally in a war
of technology and culture that threatens the vibrancy of our
empire! Threatens our entire way of life and existence! This
great industry of books we have, in which I've been immersed
for over thirty years, is undergoing radical change. And I have
a pressing mission: find out what it will take to get hot best-
sellers back onto my shelves."

Some murmured and stirred, not least because this message
spoiled the atmosphere of revelry. "That's why, and I thank
my long-time and good friend over here for his stewardship
on this...we gave you your assignment in advance." Seligman's
eyes suddenly darkened, revealing his complicity. "On the
subject of New Fiction for a New World, what better way to
contextualize the old ways than a revisit of a book many of us
were forced to read in school? Yes, we asked you to re-read, or
simply read for the first time, that old-time whaling novel and

bane of high school existence, *Moby-Dick*. How many of you read this for the first time?"

Hesitantly, many raised their hands.

"A long slog, isn't it? We sent you the unabridged version. Now tell me, you've all been asked to critique this novel… and we'll be generous in calling it that when it's packed with so much non-fiction commentary on the nuts and bolts of harvesting whales…in order to gain an assessment of a so-called classic as if it were submitted to you today. So we can assess where American literature went wrong and how to fix it, then go forward from here. Make sense?"

At this point, many nodded in agreement, but in the back of the room, disgusted with the format and tone of the breakfast, but having too much decorum to make a scene, several literary agents abruptly stood up, said a few pleasant goodbyes, and proceeded to leave the premises.

Carl began to lose track of his assignment, having been hooked by the topic.

"Always a few dissenters," Thatcher sighed, his tone mildly supercilious. "But it's expected. Let's continue…okay? You've all put together evaluation sheets on the book, and I'll ask you to turn them in afterwards. But for now, let's go across the room to those who volunteer, and see what your reaction would have been if this manuscript suddenly landed on your desk. Go ahead, yes, you."

A man in the front, the most loudly-dressed in the room and nearly falling off his chair with eagerness to speak, shot up. His pink shirt with red stripes—Egyptian cotton, however, and exquisitely tailored—and brightly-polished shoes, long, scraggly hair, and a diamond-studded Rolex, bespoke wealth and individualized taste in one, fell swoop. His voice was strident, as if he owned the museum. And he was a contributing member. "Harry Slinkmeiser here. Run my own agency. You all know me," he preened, albeit bored. "Of course I read this in high school and I've been waiting thirty years to say this, but what a heap of excrement."

"Excrement," Thatcher pinged, his demeanor stoic. "Interesting. Continue."

Sensing he should proffer new insight to this snappy-dressed suburbanite, Slinkmeiser's tone grew even more authoritative and shrill. "There's nothing right with it, of course. Where do I start? Beside mixing genres of fiction and non-fiction, all in an uneven and haphazard style I might add, Melville's writing simply doesn't ring true. I mean really, a captain with a peg leg, three native bum cakes, and a green kid out chasing a white blob of blubber around the ocean? What kind of fantasy is that? And Ahab and his obsession...what ship captain, responsible to his investors and needing to attend to a business enterprise...would chase a whale around the open sea like some kind of lunatic? Again, it doesn't ring true. It's not appropriate for his type. Then the relationship with Ishmael starting out clinging to Queequeg like a Today's Man suit. Please. I think not. Again, it doesn't *ring true*. Can we say Ahab's a wooden character? Not only the leg, but I mean his dialogue. Aye this and ahoy that. Please, who speaks like this? And who wants to read about a bunch of whale blubber? Not the people in Melville's time, and certainly not me. Then the changes in point of view! So haphazard. Where was this writer's editor? But they're all overdramatic, too. Over-the-top as Shakespeare! Pig's tripe...all of it."

"I disagree. The characters, the whole narrative, is far from overdone. It's flat. He skips along and never gives me the meat...the man never gives me depth in his characters. Why is Ahab this way? Since when is an animal the villain of a novel?

What's the whale's motive? And what's the nature of this relationship between Ishmael and Queequeg? This novel…it's all surface," a woman said from the back of the room as she stood up. "Sorry. Barb Woodson here."

"Whatever, Barbara," Slinkmeiser huffed, rolling his eyes in disgust. "I say vanilla and you say chocolate. Like I was saying, though…Melville starts with that ridiculous call me Ishmael, then switches points of view all over the place. Ishmael. Hel-loooo…this isn't the Bible, people! Why doesn't Melville stick with the character? It's isn't enough to know the poor sap wants to sail off and seek his fortune. What a cliché! Haven't we heard this story a thousand…a million times before? I want to know his *motivations*. Who's his mother? Do we know anything about his childhood? Was he beaten senseless by his stepfather? They used to do that a lot back then, you know. Come on, o' Victorian author, show me the smut. Give me the dirt. Get into that kid's brain and rip it out! Put it under a microscope. You think I don't know why Melville didn't do it? Are you taking me for a buffoon? I know. It's because no one cares about Ishmael, and deep down, Melville knew it." The man pressed backwards on his heels, almost swaying now. "Yea, I read the whole book anyway. Palm Beach gets old after a few months. My second home's there, you all should know."

"We know!" shouted one man at Slinkmeiser's table. This brought several snickers from around the world.

"Good. Anyway," Slinkmeiser continued, hardly noticing anyone now, "the guy…and by the way he was the dark sheep of the Melville family and had lived at home…of course he died in obscurity. I suppose we should be impressed? A loser in his own time, and a loser in my book."

Carl laughed quietly, wondering whether he could respect anyone in a decision-making position again. He did like Thatcher and Seligman somewhat, though, because they seemed to be trying.

Slinkmeiser's eyes bored into Thatcher's. "What agent in his right mind would want to shill that slop? Not I! Oh, sure, it has its intellectual moments. He makes a few points, okay? He might even scare out a laugh or two. He's old-fashioned. But all that outrageous, overdone elegance. No one wants that anymore. They want slop! Blood and guts, so give it to the SOBs I say!" He stopped to observe the nods of agreement, then continued, even more strident this time. "By comparison, take the best author with my agency: David Bree. Bree's prose is consistent, mature, refined. He can describe something in intimate detail for pages, entire chapters...and there's so much research behind it. I like the way he adds culture to his brew...no one does it better. Oh sure, his characters have problems...but they cope so well by caring about little, and Bree layers into his bleak writing a humorless outlook...so wise an approach...that makes his characters all the more artful and gritty. Oh, it's all so serious! And real. Like furniture. Or garden hoes. Bree meets all my selection criteria. He can write 600 pages of exposition, with occasional dialogue tossed in but nothing that leaps out as too bright...and it's all so detailed to the point that, let's say, a few less-alert readers I've stumbled across tell me reading the guy's hard work. Au contraire! This stylistic choice is a sure sign of quality. Give me a long slog, and I'll feel I've accomplished something! One reader even called the overall effect so arduous she wanted to hang herself on the spot. Bitch. But Bree's great...and oh-so-truthful. Truth is what we're after, even when truth says we're all empty, shallow vessels floating in a cold, dark sea. Ha! I used a Melville metaphor. There's some use for the fellow. Anyway, wonderful stuff, Bree. People gushed over him at a cocktail party last Wednesday, telling me oh, isn't this Bree fabulous! They're all readers, you know."

Thatcher raised an eyebrow. "Fascinating. Tell us more about your selection...rejection...criteria."

"Easy. And it's okay you don't know. You, as the bookseller, are merely the mover of product, and I say this with all due respect," Slinkmeiser insisted, feeling an ounce of compassion and not wanting to offend someone who could deny his titles access to the market. "To answer your question? It's not about finding a gem. It's all about rejection. Process of elimination, because it's much more efficient to determine what's wrong than to try to imagine what's good. Because what's good, exactly? Set up your criteria, such as needs a good plot, an inviting setting...like Ireland or the Caribbean...give it prose on an eighth grade level, to keep the market as wide as possible, and throw us characters with gaping flaws so we can relate to them. And no poetry...oh, the rabble hates poetry! I also think an author has to do his homework. Show me the expertise. The platform. If you can lift out entire passages and post them on Wikipedia...like we can with Bree...you know the author's done some homework. And while we're at it, pop onto a trend! Memorable characters are always a plus: drug dealers, hookers, con men. Then of course you need a good cover, but that's not the author's job."

"I get you. So you're saying Melville broke these rules?"

"All of them," Slinkmeiser snapped. "The book's extremely poorly written. He introduces characters then tosses them overboard. He develops no one. Ishmael is flat...forgettable... an insipid choice for a protagonist and hardly unique. What I'm looking for in him is some flaw and I never see it. He's a nice kid, no vices. That's it. Most of the crew are just there: sailing a ship. A few quirks here and there, but the central character driving the action is a whale we don't see. Unacceptable. The ship sets sail but the narrative doesn't get going for me. It's endless hours of nothing important. Sure, Ahab's peg leg's an interesting prop, but the book just rattles on blah blah blah because, what, Ishmael's so great? In society? I don't know. What are their motives? The whole thing's too...there in your face. It jumps out at you. Too lyrical, too. I don't like eloquence jumping out at me like that. All that drama! I mean...look...take Dostoevsky. He had the same problem, always so damned funny and profound and in your face about it. Never did understand his...or the Bard's...appeal. There will always be a horde of stinkards to entertain, but I say give 'em action heroes at the box office. Leave the book world to me. Frankly, if I personally like it, I pitch it, and I like books to be more polished, dry, if you will. In a literary novel, give me the style but faint, almost not there at all. And don't try to say something to me. I resent any hint of commentary from the author."

Thatcher looked around the room, nodding. "Melville needed an editor, didn't he?"

"Pfwyea, Moses, he needed editing! He could have cut most of it! Maybe make a short story, say ten pages long. Pull something out and make something of it. He could focus on the relationship between Ishmael and Queequeg. It had interesting aspects, but he needed to develop it. What happened to the couple? Show me. He could have done something with this; he could have built the novel around it. Then spice it up, for cryin' out loud! Make it raunchy! Nobody bats an eye today unless you disgust them."

"The only criteria he knows are the ones hardwired in his brain," came the voice of Robin Swift, some sixty years old and dressed to the hilt in Armani, who stood up defiantly, huffing at Slinkmeiser.

"Oh, no, no, no, no, no!" Slinkmeiser responded, fielding her volley. "How wrong you are! Bree takes liberties with the English sentence! Sure...he abandons punctuation and his sentences run for pages. Who says what's right? I'm not rigid. No, I'm more a connoisseur...like you, Robin...and I don't mean that in any derogatory way."

This incited a murmur of whispers.

Chuck Frères, a slender man in his mid-twenties, sporting a tie of green-and-blue leather, dropped his hand and darted up, two tables away. "Fine, if we all can shout out of turn, it's my turn on the stage. But don't get me wrong. This discussion's a liberation," he announced with crisp confidence, holding a drink in the air. "To our elder, Harry Slinkmeiser, who should have rescued me when I was a freshman English major! Three cheers!" He said this softly, but with utter joy and goodwill, and also with a sarcastic inflection in his voice due to the affected style in which he spoke.

Carl shook his head, wondering how he could be in the same room, let alone generation, as Frères. *Frontier Re'd love a suck-up like that*, Carl sneered to himself. His thoughts drifted toward Dasha. Her shining lips, her fragile expressions, her availability, her humility and spirit...they all made her alluring, yet stronger. He longed for her face, a smile...something to waken his heart and help him endure this parade.

Then the noise of the conference picked up as Slinkmeiser spoke again. "Let's let 'em have it now! Enough kid's gloves. This bygone, Victorian writer was clearly biased against African-Americans...just look at Daggoo—"

"Daggoo wasn't American," Swift chided, looking cross.

"Shut up, Robin," Slinkmeiser hissed. "He was damned black enough."

"Was it not a white whale chased by a white captain?" asked Thatcher, mischievously, conveying a certain defense of Melville. "And the whiteness of the whale was not entirely flattering. How smart does white Christendom look in this book?"

"Whatever," Slinkmeiser scoffed.

"And what about the title...Moby...is there not something licentious going on here?" Thatcher asked, raising his eyebrows in subtle and conspiratorial fashion. Many noted he seemed to have sympathy for the book and kept quiet.

"Oh, please! The Victorians didn't have sex! That's why they aren't around anymore," Slinkmeiser said, considering his remark self-evident.

"Interesting. Yes, you."

"Drake Mansfield here." A gentleman in his sixties, well-dressed, gruff, and rather stocky with a deep, gravelly voice, had raised his hand halfway. "Nothing about this novel leaped out at me. I'm afraid there's no market for it. I'd have to send Mr. Melville a quick letter saying look, I'm sorry, kid...maybe you should work on another vocation. Learn a trade. Writing's not going to be there for you, I'm afraid. Your work...it doesn't meet the standards of a professionally published book. I wouldn't want to say it. I mean, the guy's famous now. Dead, but famous. I even thoroughly enjoyed many aspects of the book, but I'm ultimately opposed to the subject matter. Too religious, for one thing. I also wish he'd used a pen name because his name grates me, somehow. And if anything crossed my desk attacking a major industry, when most of my friends are well-ensconced in businesses and career by now, I'd feel compelled to say no, right off the bat. You all understand. I admit, his style's lovely, but style isn't enough in the New York publishing world. It's tough around here. We need something with more substance. Explore the crack houses, for God's sake. America's been an oppressor for over two hundred years and it's time for change. Tell Melville his day has come and gone. I'd try to be constructive, but it's hard with this book."

Suddenly having an idea, Frères snapped his fingers. "Constructive! You know what I'm thinking? Okay, maybe we could rescue the novel. Like, say one of these dudes on the Pequod is carrying a virus. Some South Pacific strain that mutates, and one day he starts hacking and yuking and heaving all over the deck. He's barfing overboard and it's all chunky and crap and smells like jungle rot. So they're looking at all this slime and are like, dude, you're heaving your cookies on our nice, clean deck! The next thing you know, they're all yakking away and Melville describes it all in great detail. He could even describe the color of their vomit. Now, that would be interesting! What better way to steal the attention of brain-dead zombies who don't read anymore because they're glued to video games and TV? Hm? It's so like a new author I've found—"

"Brat!" Swift cracked, her voice sour and cynical.

Frères jumped back a step, waving his arms in the air. "Excuse me...I was the one tossing my cookies here. Please. So they all get this nasty virus, and they're racing to get an antidote in the ship's bio-hazard lab. It would have given this old doorstop a contemporary vibe. Maybe rescue Melville's career. Give it a new title, too, like "A Nice Day at the Beach." Then readers would be like, hey, I'm going to the beach! I'll buy that! He'd score big. I mean, he's funny sometimes. He's not all bad. It's a thought, anyway."

"They didn't have bio-hazard labs on whaling ships, idiot," a man in the back shouted.

"All the *more* reason why it's pap," Frères responded, insolently showing his teeth. He sarcastically lashed his jaws in the man's direction, then with a triumphant air and nothing more to contribute, he sat down quietly.

The crowd grew silent for a moment.

Incredulous, Carl watched what he felt was turning into a circus with wide eyes. As a young man, he'd never seen the inside of an industry quite this vividly before, and he found it an eye-opening experience. *Can't believe they're bashing Moby-Dick. I love that book.*

Thatcher broke the silence by clearing his throat. "This is good. Let's keep it open. Let's keep this flowing."

Hearing this, Carl wanted to weigh in his opinion, at least, but after glancing at Bonastre and seeing her scowl, he checked his tongue.

Barb Woodson raised her hand half-way. "I have more to say. To be truthful, when he started out he grabbed me. I was hooked from the first sentence. He really wrapped me up in his world of Nantucket...I love Nantucket because I go there on vacation, lovely place...and I was enthralled, but then, and this is where he lost me, he goes on this sea voyage. As soon as he'd taken me out of this charming setting that I love and puts me on a whaling ship...I mean, what do I care about whaling ships? Frankly, I lost interest. Sorry, but that was my hard, cold assessment."

Slinkmeiser, his entire table of friends, the young man, and a few others grumbled with contempt.

"Thank you. Any others?" asked Thatcher, scratching his chin in thought. "Sounds like this guy isn't getting anywhere. I don't want to be judgmental, by the way. Any takers?" Thatcher pointed. "Yes, you."

Svelte and in her late twenties, a woman stood up. "I have to say…and no I'm not a taker…no one here has mentioned it yet…and I'm *quite* disappointed by that. We haven't even addressed the issue of professionalism. Can you imagine how this manuscript would have been submitted? Think for a second. If I get one more improperly formatted submission…and I don't even do art fiction. He would be rejected immediately."

Eyes ablaze, Frères threw up his arms again, as if in rapture. "I agree! I agree! If a manuscript about whales and God with all that poetic mumbo-jumbo landed in my in box, I'd go berserk! I'd throw it on the floor and stomp on it a hundred times! There's no market for it! Stop sending me this crap! There's art, and that's a niche for agents who hate money, and there's the books for those of us who have rent to pay! I mean, come on! I hate it when I get solicitations of stuff I won't even pitch. I say so on my web site. Stupid authors."

Feeling upstaged now, Slinkmeiser charged back into the discussion with a vengeance. "Oh, I'm sick of the artists, too! Can we say it? I don't bother with the art end, either, unless, of course, it's my latest find: Jeff Plummer. He has a contemporary hook, though: he plasters quotes from artists and intellects all over his work. That way people reading it will say wow, I learned something today. Then they don't have to go read the stuff. Literally, he puts the intellectual into bold, neon lights! That's marketing for you. That's what they want out in Peoria, people. Sure pays my bills…although he's not selling as well as I'd like."

A man at Slinkmeiser's table heckled, "Shut up, Slink! You own six cars and four houses! Only bills you need to pay are maintenance!"

Swift, indignant and fed up, laughed in agreement. "You have more money salted away than the Pope! Too bad, Harry, you won't spend it on your ex-wife and kids, whom you never call!"

"The brats aren't my problem when the woman wouldn't use contraception!" Slinkmeiser confided, his tone nasty but with utterly sincere. "Besides, the bills are killing me. I need a hit soon or I'll go broke!" Then, realizing he'd exposed himself too much, he blushed.

"Serves you right, sleaze bucket!" Swift fired back. "And I liked *Moby-Dick*. There. It's a good read, and it's a damned shame no one here would represent him. I would. So maybe I go swirling down to the bottom of the ocean with the Pequod. At least I lived! Sometimes I even get lucky. There might be an editor left who likes these old classics."

Thatcher smiled. "That, Ms. Swift, is half the question. The other is: where are the readers? I don't know. Maybe you should represent Melville. He's unique."

Slinkmeiser guffawed. "Take it, he's yours. No one would publish that slobber anyway. Melville. Give me something fresh...new...there's so much talent out there. Then if it's still not selling, it's only because the country's getting dumber by the day."

Hearing this, Carl couldn't help chuckling aloud, earning an instant and hot glare from Bonastre. Bonastre mouthed something to him, but he couldn't read her lips from across the room. No doubt, from the sour expression on her face, it was something unpleasant.

Thatcher and Seligman looked at each other, annoyed over Carl's outburst, but before any backlash could develop, Slinkmeiser, now in a fury and not noticing Carl's interjection, reared up, swigged down the rest of his drink, and boomed, "The novel's a stinking fish! You heard it here first and last."

The room grew still.

No one had anything left to say and the mood was turning dark. Then sensing the atmosphere, everyone who had been standing slowly began to sit down—even Slinkmeiser, who seated himself last.

Thatcher narrowed his eyes and shuffled his feet behind the podium. People stopped eating, sensing a conclusion was near. "Wonderful. A lively discussion. Well. Some differences of opinion, but a general consensus. This book had it's day... and now it's time to move on to a New World. Our world, not Melville's. And the title of this conference says that in giant, bold letters."

Most in the crowd smiled and nodded.

"Looking at your faces, and hearing Ms. Swift here," Thatcher continued, "a tiny minority of you might disagree. That's okay. I'm not trying to pass judgment or tell you what's right, although I was clever here, you might have noticed. While I pretended to wink and nod in favor of the positive comments, I wanted to draw out the...shall we say...outlying opinions."

Swift reared up, but most of the room shared Thatcher's conspiratorial smile, feeling they were on the inside of the joke.

"You see, friends, I thought there was nothing left of old literature. Sadly, there is. But books aren't selling out there, and we need to move out with this old and up to the new! Of course I'd be interested in hearing what a general reader might say. Just for a different perspective...not that we have to listen to one person. We don't lead by anecdotes. We lead by focus groups at Roundtop Books."

Many smiled. Then the mood became brighter, almost exultant. Everyone began to feel the conversation had come full circle. Bonastre glowed from across the room, no doubt considering her banquet an unmitigated success. They would promote her for certain.

But all this time Thatcher spoke these closing remarks, Carl fidgeted. He simply couldn't stand it anymore, as he disagreed not only with the opinions on the book, but also on the way in which they arrived at the same conclusion so easily. *Whole thing reminds me of Frontier Re*, he complained to himself. Finally, seeing the meeting coming to an end, and wanting to get in a word before everyone departed, he raised his hand, truly only wanting to help and contribute and without an ounce of spite. "Um, excuse me. Mr. Thatcher. With all due respect."

Thatcher looked shocked, but in front of so many people, he knew he must remain polite and in control. "Yes? A question from the...caterer...I take it?" Bonastre shot a menacing look across the room, and Carl felt it, but it was too late. He'd already made the leap.

"Yes, um...thank you. Sir. You said you wanted to hear from a reader. Hey, I read. Um...I even read *Moby-Dick* once for a ninth grade assignment. Abridged edition. Got an A. Anyway, I'm an ornery sort, I guess...but I...I confess I loved *Moby-Dick*. It's...it's a treasure. Don't know how anyone can dis it."

Immediately, the room erupted.

The situation now seemed in danger of turning into chaos.

Desperate to save his conference from disaster, Thatcher waved his arms in wild fashion. "People! People! Please. Have some order. This is a democracy! Maybe not in this room... that's a different matter. But we are a democracy and he has his right to speak his mind. He's a customer. We all should remember that. Customer preference is something we take into consideration at Roundtop Books. How fortunate we've stumbled on one during a time of critical importance for our industry. Yes, young man. Please continue. I'm listening."

Carl shuffled in place, heart pounding and palms dripping with sweat. "Yes, *Moby-Dick*. It's provocative...funny...elegant. And that's all well and good. But what I really love about it is something no one even discussed: I love myth."

"Myth!" Thatcher shouted. "Yes, we have a fantasy section in our stores."

"No," Carl countered, warming to the crowd. "I mean myth. All these outlandish, over-the-top characters chasing down a majestic white whale in the open sea, but not for mere profit. This is an exaggeration of the human condition...magnified so we can see it. And it's great fun! Absolutely wild, but deep. They chase this whale...who's at once God, both complex and mighty, and that which we chase. For what? You're asking for motives? You tell me why you get up in the morning and I'll give you a motive. Don't we all have our own motives? But this ship full of humanity...as you mentioned, different races, different creeds...are all joined together on a doomed mission. Ahab's mission. To hunt down this great leviathan Moby-Dick in the name of revenge. You call Ahab's peg leg a prop. I call it a motive. And he's a Christian who's angry at the God who created him for his human suffering. He lashes out like a madman instead of appreciating the awesome power of his life's experience. Only Ishmael appreciates life...and he's the one who's saved. There's redemption here. You say the islanders don't fit. I say how can you exclude them? You say Ishmael's not sufficiently flawed? I say the opposite. He's conjoined with mankind on this dark ship of destiny...a destiny of their own making. He's even...talk about prodding the sensibilities of the period...Melville throws him in bed with a black, heathen islander! Then Melville goes on to make Queequeg and the

other pagans more dignified, more brave, and more honorable...
heck, more human...than all the white Christians on the ship!
Don't you see it? If you're looking for more backstory, or more
development of the comic relationship between Ishmael and his
islander friend, then you're not playing in the big league. These
are archetypes! Forget them...Melville's talking about us! And
it's clear from this room that the book's more timely than ever.
You're looking on the surface. You're picking up pieces of the
puzzle but missing the entirety of God's art. What, are you the
gatekeepers of our culture? If so, that's more frightening than
Moby-Dick!"

Slinkmeiser shot up from his chair, pointing a finger at
Carl. "Ass! Who let this...this grubby...filth...into this room?
He's certifiably nuts! Delusional! I'm happy to call a spade a
spade when I see it."

No one else stirred, but they expected a quick denouement
for this brazen and idealistic youth.

To everyone's surprise, however, and even Carl's, Thatcher
motioned for Slinkmeiser to sit. "Yes...calm down people. The
lad may be crazy, but I wanted this to be an open forum. And
by golly, he's a member of the general public. That makes him
unique here. As I said, reader preference is something we take
into consideration at Roundtop Books. Continue, young man.
I'm finding this interesting. Sometimes I'm far removed from
the action."

Carl straightened up, less concerned about Bonastre's
tempestuous mood, and spoke with more authority. "Okay,
so Melville stands back. He takes in the whole picture. He
observes, with awe and wonder, the very whiteness of the
whale that so fascinates and blinds these hapless souls who're
tossing on endless miles of ocean. He's not driven to action.
No, that's Ahab. He's passive, sure, but he's the observer.

But that's precisely it. He's observing, and appreciating, this whole creation before us. And in wondering over the awe… the callousness…the anguish…and the sheer madness of it all…and in so appreciating the whale and the sharks who would feed on it…he transcends ourselves. This is Melville's art! Ishmael's a demigod! And dammit, if I don't want to be Ishmael, too! Don't you get it? Are you like the blind people of myth who describe an elephant after only touching a part of it? Myth, my friends, is reality…but magnified so we can see it. And the drama of it all! And the stakes! Look…. listening to you folks, I see now why I don't go to bookstores. It's simple: I personally don't like the books the gatekeepers personally like! I have a personal solution, though…I'm a tech-savvy customer…so I grab a book online now and then. You can find anything there these days. I don't need an agent or book chain to tell me what I want to read. Look, I'm a programmer…I know tech…and technology's changing the world. Heck, now you can publish a book directly…as an e-book. I can grab a book online, or catch a movie, or buy a video game, and I don't need all of you. So you better work real hard to win me back, and that all starts with the resonance of your offerings. I don't know much about business, but isn't that called building a brand? Make fiction enjoyable…and for me, not just for you. If you don't…you talk about the Victorians…you'll be the new ones! Sorry, but that's the God's honest truth. I'm only trying to be helpful."

Carl heaved a long sigh, finished, and stopped, then smiled with a wide, honest grin, having unloaded a burden from his soul.

The room was utterly shocked.

Bonastre mouthed, "My office. Now!" She steeled her eyes at Carl.

Stunned, Thatcher began applauding, forgetting he wasn't in the audience.

The crowd joined him, but without enthusiasm.

Then Thatcher cast a glance at Seligman, who replied with a thankful but reluctant nod. Thatcher shrugged, as if to say, "what can we do?" The pair exited the room.

Carl watched them go, feeling they might learn to be grateful for his candor. That is, if they took time to reflect on it.

CHAPTER FOURTEEN

Bonastre hustled him toward her office, fumbling for the right key.

She shut the door, muting the distant hum of the generator room, and sat behind her desk, delaying her speech, as if to hold him on edge. He rested his hands on his lap and stared at her desktop, not wanting to put her off initially. A tiny fan oscillated in the background; she ran it until the air-conditioning took full effect, which given her proximity to the boilers, was an all-day battle.

"Disappointed isn't the word! Outraged? I'd like to throw you across the room right now!" she fumed. "A trash compactor would be too good for you! Fortunately for you, the customers had scant complaint. They said you shook them up a bit, but the guys writing the checks...Seligman and Thatcher...they said you shook up the event, and that was all they were looking for. They said you're entirely forgettable."

"I only wanted to help."

"Let me do the talking here. Fortunately for you, I managed to grab Mr. Thatcher right after the meeting. So now the other side of my heightened emotion is this bit of good news: the meeting's a huge success! Our reputation's going to soar...my reputation's going to soar...and all that means more bookings and future events. They love the museum backdrop and guided tour; serving drinks and breakfast was icing on the cake. Seligman came up and personally thanked me for enlightening—he used that word—his attendees. And that's the biggest compliment we can get. That's the draw of our venue, you know," she added, didactically.

Carl nodded in full agreement.

She smiled. "But your behavior! I want to make this clear, it was unacceptable. I'm thinking about letting you go. That thought has been tossing in my mind. I caught you standing there listening instead of working numerous times and, despite my clear warnings, you continued like that. It wasn't you, it was everyone, but I consider you the leader, so I'll level this on you. And you can spread the word. I mean, I have to say it, you young people today do not know how to take orders! We pay you, we feed you, we clothe you, we give you health care benefits, and all we want in return is for you to take a little direction. A little! When I was in your shoes, you should have seen how I hustled. Still do today. You think Manhattan's an easy place to live? Huh? You know it isn't. It's a bloody war here, you know. My board's the most demanding, angry, insensitive group of men who ever walked the earth! You think I'm bad? You go meet them. Believe me, I'm here to protect you. Watch out for your interests. That's what I have at heart, you know."

Trying to, as she said, take orders, Carl remained respectful in the face of her onslaught.

"But listen, that's not all. You kids today knock off work as soon as the whistle blows, you wear tattoos, you lack basic hygiene, you all have big, spoiled attitudes, and what's an old lady like me supposed to do? I mean, this is what I have to work with! Tell me. Really, I'm listening. How do I get you little cretins motivated? We all were gung-ho for our careers from the start. What, do you expect Mommy and Daddy to take care of you forever? Do we have to throw the whole lot of you out in the street and, I don't know, just shut down this American Experiment altogether and call it a boondoggle?"

It was a lot to digest, and Carl, sliding down in his seat, more for a lack of sympathy rather than any desire to flee, struggled for words.

"The least you can do is answer me," she injected, impatiently.

Carl heaved a deep sigh, casting a wide, sweeping glance around the room. "Sorry. I thought you didn't want me to speak. What do you want me to say? I'm sorry? Sorry for disturbing the lecturer and taking something from the seminars myself? It was entertaining. I offered them something…I don't know. Shouldn't we all enjoy our jobs, too? Is that such a bad thing?"

"Insolence," she said. "Wrong answer." Nearly boiling with rage, she searched for words, and when nothing came to her, she spoke in a quiet, coiled fashion. "Okay. I get it," she said with a sigh. "I'm trying to speak to someone who just doesn't get it. We, in management, work hard to give you opportunities. The things we do behind the scenes while you're busy working, you have no idea. This is a great place to work. But you and your colleagues, and yes, I see you get along well with them, and that's admirable. You all need to learn how the hierarchy works. This is not a democracy we have here. There's a structure, a system, in place. And you need to respect your place within the process. Everything's a process. That's one of the first things they teach in school, isn't it? Business is all about processing information. I don't want to get too technical here but I say that for your edification. You see, I did not fall off the turnip truck yesterday, did I?"

He agreed with her quietly.

"Right. So now the question is, when we give you a cube, or an assignment, and a task to complete in a set amount of time, then your job is to take those data sets we give you and perform them with utmost efficiency. When we all do that as a team, then the whole enterprise is more efficient, and then we make more money. That's the name of the game. If it takes twelve hours a day, seven days a week, so be it. The war's waging out there and competition's fierce. But only after you've done your duties and given your pint of blood can you...should you even dare...think about fun. Or leisure, or any of the other things you're free to do on your own time. But not on my time. Right here, time belongs to me."

Not wanting to argue, but at the same time neither appreciating nor agreeing with her philosophy, which sounded like a 1930s way of thinking to him, Carl maintained his composure and tried, as best as possible, to figure out how to satisfy his boss without hitting one of her land mines. Finally, he stumbled, "Okay, I'm sorry if it seemed I wasn't listening. That's certainly not the case, I feel. But I hustled when I needed to hustle and took downtime when it seemed appropriate. I used to bus tables and understand that sometimes people want to talk and not be disturbed. That's when I stood and watched. Anyone can punch a clock and take orders. That's easy, really. I'd tried to work hard but make some decisions along the way."

She gulped and looked at him strangely.

"But let me tell you something, candidly," he continued. "Did you agree with anything I said? Because this museum... I'm not sure I agree with its mission."

Incensed and shocked by his arrogance, she became unnerved. "You think you're a wise guy, huh? That you can tell me what it is that makes you happy. I decide that around here. That somehow, in the thick of the jungle, we all need to get along. You think we all have a soul and this and that? Is that what I'm hearing from you, a mere caterer? You have a lot of nerve walking into my office and speaking to me this way. I ought to…do you know how quickly I can put you back out on the street again? Have you forgotten so quickly what it's like to be hungry? Oh, the nerve," she complained, shaking her head in despair, "someone find me workers I can trust. Listen. You don't need to lecture me about some kind of quality of life topic. I know all about it. I grew up on the edge of a rainforest. Used to run through the green brush, picking fresh papaya for my mother, who served everything so delicious for my family. I know what that's like. The warmth of the air, the ease of life, the way raindrops trickled down the Banyan trees at daybreak. But that's not what we have here. This is Manhattan, and if you want to work and succeed here, you've got to get out of that upstate New York mentality of yours…and get rolling! You know what I'm saying? Down here, the roses smell like that boiler room, not like your momma's garden. That's the real world. I'm telling you like a mother to a son. I have a son, you know."

She finished with a satisfied grunt.

Feeling flustered, again he sounded apologetic. "I don't know what to say. I didn't mean to say I have a soul…I mean. You got me. Yes, I'm dictating to you how I think things should be, and giving my own opinions here rather than taking the line as presented, and that's, I suppose you could say, insubordination. I…I don't know what got into me. But those words that flew out of my mouth, I guess it happened, and there's nothing I can do about it now except, I suppose, apologize."

Her face began to beam at last. "Yes, you could do that! You can apologize and old mother Bonastre can take that or leave it. It wouldn't change the situation of this morning, but it would be a correct and appropriate step."

Carl rested his chin on his hands, which he propped up on the arm rests. "But I'm thinking about it here. And I don't know why, and call me crazy if you want, but I can't do it," he said, watching her exasperation return. "I mean, life's too short, right? And why should I stay with a company, spend my blood, toil, and tears, in an environment with which I fundamentally disagree? I mean, what would that say about me? And for all I know, I stay with that company and watch it disintegrate before my eyes when, as it turns out, I was right and the management was wrong all along? What does that say about my career judgment? Companies and jobs come and go, but what we do have, and it's about all we have in this world, is our own sense of integrity and worth. If this is going to be nothing but a sweatshop, despite the salary, the benefits, and the admittedly nice surroundings, then am I living, or is my heart only beating a certain number of allotted strikes before I die? Like some clock running on batteries that will eventually run out of juice? I have to ask myself that right now, don't I? Right here and now. Tell me, Ms. Bonastre, why have so many others quit their jobs here?"

"I should fire you right now! That I haven't says wonders about your ability to charm. No one likes to retrain an employee, either. Don't get me wrong," she said, her face beginning to swell, "but you're in hot water. Make no mistake, Mr. Moretti, you set one foot out that door, and as the hot steam of July envelops you, you'll be scraping the alleyways for scraps of food. Wheeling your carts of recyclables to the center for your meager check. Sleeping on rags and yellow newspapers and living on rations. That's the life you face if you don't have me. Or someone like me. So take your pick. We don't all get what we want in this world. Sometimes enough is good enough… and the rest? Leave that to poets."

Carl's body was tensed. Facing termination, and having been through the humiliation twice already, he felt he needed to make a decision this time around and right on the spot. At the same time, however, he knew he needed the money, if only to keep himself off the street.

She was right in a way, too. Her face said she knew it, but the risk seemed unbearable. Show her he wanted the job, and she could cut him down an hour later, knowing she'd won.

Slumping toward her, he lamented the situation. *Why do I have to be so alone in the world? Why can't I have someone else on my side? To give me the courage to release this awful dependency on people like her?*

Bing!

Suddenly, and entirely by surprise, Carl found himself face-to-face with the one friend who fit this description. There on the bookshelf next to Bonastre, so close she could reach out and touch his boss and beaming widely, sat Dasha.

Dasha? Carl blinked in disbelief.

Bonastre frowned. "What are looking at? Now you see someone next to me? I don't dare look or I'll think one of us is crazy."

Carl's Central Park friend shrugged and silently giggled, then cast a cutting glance at Bonastre as if to say, "Go ahead. What do you need her for? There are other jobs out there." The message seemed clear: "Leave this place if you choose. I'll be there on the outside. I think you're great. If she doesn't agree, that's her problem."

Emboldened by her attitude, Carl relaxed, and with a face of measured calm, he looked at his boss, steeled his jaw, and with clear, moral resolve, responded under his breath, "You win. Here. But since that's the case, it's my duty to offer my resignation. Two weeks' notice, max. Then I'm out. I didn't refuse to train replacements for nothing, and I didn't move to New York for this. Thank you for the opportunity, but this gig's not for me."

Exhausted, her expression turned dour. "Out. Out. I'm disappointed it turned out like this, though, 'cause I tried…I really tried!"

Carl walked out, leaving his former boss in a tizzy.

CHAPTER FIFTEEN

Carl felt pangs of guilt that evening, having left a woman who seemed not entirely concerned with business, but he felt relieved at the same time. He'd bought himself a fresh start and now he felt compelled to enjoy it.

As night fell and the moon poked an orange cheek over the Empire City, he walked silently through Central Park. Along the western sky, rows of beautiful buildings jutted over whispering trees, standing like watch towers on glistening castles, and the sentries of Central Park South, standing guard over crystalline lawns, pressed from his back, spurring him toward venues uptown. Birds flickered in shaded nooks and moonlight, while more furry creatures of the dark scurried around, hesitated, or rested in wide cavalcades of stillness.

He dreaded the journey ahead, but as he walked, his arms began swinging carelessly: the longer he basked in the moon's tepid glow, the more calm he felt, and the more calm he felt, the less he needed anything he lacked, even companionship. Ahead of him lay twelve more blocks of walking, and at the point of his choosing, he realized, he could turn to his left and enter the brilliant throng of the west side nightlife, where restaurants and cafes were wide-open.

At 84th Street, he turned left, then proceeded to the café where he planned to meet Tabitha Murphy for a latte or two, which on his budget would be an achievable feat. He'd retrieved her email several days before at Kinko's.

He entered the establishment.

"Carl Moretti," her familiar voice called from a back table.

Recognizing her, he crossed the room to greet her.

She looked him up and down admiringly. "You're letting your hair grow out," she said, pointing to his scraggly mane, now close to his shoulders, and his scruffy face. "Don't look so dejected. It looks good on you," she said, warm smile across her face. "I think you should keep it that way. Here, have a seat! I already have you a coffee."

He felt embarrassed, having promised to pay, but swallowed his male pride and assented. "It's an accidental style," he responded. He sat down and grabbed his drink.

"Attractive, though. Reminds me of Johnny Depp," she continued. "Anyway, I'm glad I found you through Kim. Now what's this I hear about you and Lisa? Kim says...remember her from last year's Halloween party...she was the bathtub. She cracks me up. She knows someone who works with her and said you two'd broken up. And I thought you two were together tight," she said, searching his eyes.

He shrugged, blowing the steam over his coffee. "We were more like gum stuck on the bottom of your shoe," he quipped. She laughed, looking into his eyes further. "But, basically, I don't know how much you heard, but the company I worked for laid off all the American programmers," he said, rolling his eyes, "and the woman couldn't handle it. Started bossing me around, got short-tempered, began making demands and threats, told me I needed to pull my weight. The whole thing unraveled, and with it went my life."

Sympathetic but looking slightly put-off by his self-deprecation, she added with reassurance, "No, it wasn't meant to be. Move on."

"Don't mean to unload my troubles on you. But you asked."

She sipped her java. "No worries. I've heard my share of this lately. So what are you doing now?"

"Looking. I was doing a gig at a museum, but I left that this morning. Wasn't the right fit for me."

"Good for you! But listen, you're not going to believe this, but I know something about Lisa that'll make you die," she said, beseeching him.

His slurped. "Oh yea?" he asked, almost indifferent.

"Yea. You know that guy she was seeing? Raphael, I think his name was. Yea. Anyway, the two of them got a little out of hand with their hot and heaviness. They got careless, she panicked, had a quick test, and whammo…now she's pregnant."

A belt of air escaped his lungs. "What? Where'd you learn this?"

"She told me. I met her through a friend, then found out your situation with her. So I had to tell you. Oh yea, the bum knocked her up good. Then he took off with his girlfriend for Venezuela, and she was debating whether to abort, but, apparently, she's going to go ahead and have the baby. Now she's all like…it's okay, and all that…says it's a cool thing to do, having a baby now. Kind of like having an accessory. I guess she's bonded with it," she said, chuckling.

"You're kidding me. What a moron she is. Not that I'm judgmental. She can do whatever she wants now. Good for her, as a matter of fact; maybe it'll teach her how to love."

Tabitha blinked, sarcastically. "You think? Hey, listen, I have to run to see a friend. Thanks for emailing me. Hang in there. Oh, are you still going to Suzanne's Sunday night? There will be loads of babes there. You may be the only guy there."

His eyes twinkled. "Yep."

"Good. Oh...oooh...got to go. Take it easy, stud."

She left in a breeze, leaving him alone but feeling better. He watched her go, then as the door swung shut and she disappeared down the sidewalk, he decided he might return to the park and maybe, just maybe, catch a glimpse of Dasha. Daydreams of the mysterious woman were never far away from him.

They all come and go so quickly, he mused. *That's why I can't fall for them anymore.*

CHAPTER SIXTEEN

(1)

"Straighten up, straighten up!" she cried, tugging his leg insistently. "I don't have all night! They've given me less than an hour this time. Urgh, they're so strict! You would think at this point in my existence...never mind. What are you doing? You look pale."

Carl had been asleep for only two hours, and the sight of Dasha standing over his mottled nest of blankets and towels, in the wee hours of morning—despite her radiant face and arresting, bright eyes—failed to stir him. He would rather snooze. "Let me sleep. Please."

Feigning outrage, she smacked him on the knee. "Excuse me, but it's your one, true love visiting your lovely dreams! The least you can do is sit up straight and take notice!" she scolded.

In dutiful fashion, he raised himself on his elbows and faced her. "What? It's got to be, wait, what time is it?" he asked, truly flustered.

"It is time to meet your lover. I am your true love, yes? Say yes," she implored with a note of indignity. "You, if you only knew about our history. Huh! I would smack you even harder. So hard you might break into little pieces, Marik Andropov."

He squinted his eyes suspiciously. *She hasn't talked this way before.* "Aren't you forthright today? My one, true love? I think I'd rather sleep."

"The insolence! Look at you, lying there as if stricken by a mortal wound. I'll have none of it. Enough of your self-denial and regrets. If you think you know regrets, you should consider the whole picture. Do you not love me yet?"

Carl sounded innocent as a fawn. "I'm half-asleep. I don't even know my name and you suddenly ask me—"

Whack!

"Ow! Okay, okay…I'm awake. You've got me off-guard."

"Good," she said, rapping him again with her wand. "Perhaps I will teach you manners, too."

"With a club? Maybe I should throw you over my knee myself," he teased.

"Huh?" she exclaimed, feigning horror.

"Naw, it wouldn't be worth my time," he said. She responded with a smoky glance, apparently wanting to end the topic.

"You're a free man again."

"Yea. Thanks. I guess I owe you one."

"Thank me for what? It was your choice. Did I say a thing?"

"No. Look…leave me alone. I'm having trouble with all your appearances. Don't look so hurt. I mean…it's not that I don't have feelings for you. Really…ah…the thing is, it's exactly because I do. And all your comings and goings are driving me crazy. *Comprenez-vous?*"

She sat down beside him and sighed, searching for words. "Yes, of course I understand this. You have reason to feel this way. However, you must also see that I'm going through the same thing. Do you think these strictures we're under are easy for a woman so long in love and so short in time? But if you want, I'll leave you alone. I can leave you forever. Do you want that?"

Carl looked defeated. "No. No, I don't. No, you stay here with me right now...and...and go ahead and come around any time you want. My door's open. It's just that this is so mad."

She smiled warmly. "Wonderful. Love is this way. Tsk, tsk. But you left that poor lady in distress. I think she liked you."

He drew a short breath. "Yes. And I felt a little guilty leaving her there like that after she gave me a break. But I couldn't take it anymore."

"Was she beating you?"

"Yea. Three times a day."

"What if you find the woman who's your one and true love and you toss her out. Is that possible in your state? Do you break hearts and not even know it?"

"At least three times a day."

"Aha! Then we must change that. Men...they are so proud of themselves!" she replied, rolling her eyes in mock disgust. "They never want help, either. It is always no, no, leave me alone. Let me deal with this all myself and then the whole world comes crashing down on them."

"I did make a contact tonight. I'm getting out there again. Slowly, but yea."

"Yes, this is good. What else?"

"Um...I should look for another job?"

Her face showed agreement. "So do you love me yet?" she asked, brushing her hair.

"I don't know. But I have to admit, we have a bond. I can't place it. But I have this overwhelming feeling around you like we know each other. Maybe you're a long-lost sister."

She frowned, then turned her gaze upward. "A sister would not have these feelings for her brother, except in a Roman play. I think you need to dream. That will be where you find your answer. You've had dreams lately, yes? Dreams that stir your soul?"

"Somewhat," he admitted, cautiously.

"Excellent! Now I will," she continued, standing up then shifting about, "present you with my next offering, and it goes like this:

"Onto your crown, I'll sprinkle this dust
To arouse your soul with sparkle and lust
For ladies so fair, and feelings so true,
As mine's eternal...my gift unto you."

With this, she grabbed a sheath from a silken-green pouch, unraveled a string that tied it shut, and with a strange incantation and a whirl of her arms, she raised onto her toes, twinkled her eyes, and cast a pinch from the bag into the air, where it glistened, stopped, and cascaded toward his face, disappearing into his skin.

"Now what happens next?" he asked.

"You'll know soon enough. Here," she enjoined, handing him a scrap of paper. "It's the name of a gypsy lady. Contact her and see. Now I must go! Ta ta!"

Bing!

(2)

Weighed down by heartache, she hadn't gone far.

Sitting on a stone wall in Central Park but out of Carl's earshot, her chin resting on a hand, elbow against her shin, and casting a withered glance in the direction of Carl, who was entirely unaware of her presence, she sighed, then tossed a clover into the air. It danced and whirled, drifting down into the grass.

"I have a body again and now I feel this way. Does this not serve me right for coming here? Ohhhh…I didn't expect such torments," she groaned, tears rolling down her pallid cheeks. "These strictures I'm under! You would think I'm back in father's mansion! Pining away, again…Yes, you may go back to Earth, but you cannot kiss him they say. I cheated on this just once and it was only a peck. You cannot live in sin, they say. Huh! Then why make me endure this realm of the flesh when I could arrive as a ghost? Hm. You can flit and flitter wherever you may go…you may turn to spirit and fly to the moon for all we care they say…and so on and so forth. Hmph! Our ways quite departed when he landed in purgatory. Vexing, it is! And the whole affair is moreover offensive and indecent!"

Moonbeams shined on her face, illuminating her sadness; her eyes filled with tears. "How, oh how, will I ever have my Marik back? Am I here simply to be his servant? Yes, of course I love him and yes, I do want what's best for him and yes, I know circumstances are what they are. But…perhaps I should enter a petition. Perhaps there's a way. I'll have to think about it, then plead my case." She sat on her stone wall for a long while before gathering herself, then she directed her gaze at a lavender moon above. With a wistful cadence, she meandered aloud,

"Wicked moon on high, why taunt me with love?
Why circle this world and glide like a dove
When my heart's so deceived?
Why bathe in your
Rays of mockery? What else is in store?

Dasha

Marik and I, when he rode off to war
Shared conjugal thoughts,
but then I what...for
Months...became a wisp in his wind.
Shameful!
Bound by my duty, life became painful.

My love, he rode onward: long, far and wide,
Yet all to no end! Love's lost and denied,
My soul aches much now, and heart's
held at bay;
My heaven's part hell when love's torn away.

O, a just sentence it is to so pine
For a mortal, but what's his is not mine!
Our fates have diverged, and love is a crime
For which I must pay—that is, on God's time.

Or now's my chance. Or is something amiss?
Do blessings I crave, or love's fleeting kiss?"

Forlorn, her expression faded. She pressed her chin into her
hands and sank her shoulders toward her knees. Then with
pouting lips and a heavy sigh, she sank deep into thought.

CHAPTER SEVENTEEN

(1)

Sparrows chirped in a nearby tree, filling the otherwise hushed landscape with chatter. No cars swept by, there were no joggers yet, and the sun had not yet peeped over the grey towers of Manhattan's East Side, but Richard would not give Carl time to adjust. "Wake up, wake up! Man, can't anything rouse you? You look dead down there," he urged, shaking and standing over Carl, who remained prostate.

With a laborious groan, Carl pried open his eyes, lamenting the intrusion on his slumbers. He wanted to push Richard away, but the man wouldn't budge. "Go away! Why is everyone always waking me up? I'm trying to sleep!"

Richard frowned. "That's a fine attitude to have toward a friend, isn't it? I got up early to come find you. I suppose every friend who walks your way, you just shoo him off?"

"Let me be miserable," Carl replied, half-serious in tone. "I'm happier that way. Especially first thing in the morning."

"First thing in the morning?" Richard asked with a laugh. "Do you know it's Saturday and I've been up since 3:30... then had to take the A into Manhattan. That's my morning commute, you know."

Carl collapsed deeper into his sheets, which barely shielded him from the hard ground. "Go away. I was having a dream."

"Yea, you dreaming about some chick?"

"What of it?"

"Get a motel. You can't take women back here."

Carl straightened his back, then lifted himself on his feet, making him suddenly taller than his accuser. He looked down at Richard, who remained unruffled. "I'm feeling a bit sorry for myself. Okay? So don't rub salt into my wounds."

Raising his palms in the air, feigning surrender, Richard responded, "Okay, okay. What's the matter? You're edgy in the morning. Man, pick yourself up."

"I did. I'm standing."

"Alright. I'm hearing you. Listen, this is why I'm here anyway. To tell you about a job I've been saving up my sleeve for a moment like this when you might be more open to it. Remember we talked about that."

Carl covered his face with his hands, pressing hard. "Oh, no, what? Is it legal?"

"Hell, yea, it's legal. What do you think I am, a pusher?"

The question elicited no response.

"You," Richard said, poking a finger at Carl's shoulder, "need to chill out."

"Sleeping in public on two sheets and a towel, I've never felt so chilled."

"Okay, now that's funny. I like that in a guy. But listen up. It's an address and a number. It's a bar down in the Bowery. And I've written the guy's name on the back. Call him...or better yet, pay him a visit today. Place opens at six. Tell him Richard sent you. He'll know it's me...I've already told him about you... said you might pay him a call. Now here's the thing, my man. And you listen up good. You can make some serious cash at this joint if you play it right, know what I'm saying?"

Carl nodded, pensively.

"You call on this guy Terry. Tell him I sent you. He'll hook you up. You won't go bankrupt, at least. And you can get your life back together. I'm confident of that. Listen, I have to go. You take 'em easy, and I'll be back." With that, Richard extended a fist and popped it onto Carl's. "That's right, bro. We men have to stick together, because women," he said, suddenly winking, "you need a whole army to take on one."

That afternoon, Carl headed to the place.

As he approached the address, the neighborhood felt deserted. An occasional car or person happened by, but as Carl trudged along the sidewalk—he had walked the entire distance from Central Park—the multitudes of shops, now closed and grated shut, added to his feeling of solitude. So it was with relief and pleasure that he came upon the address Richard gave him. The bar was tucked among a string of faceless, low-rise buildings, with a neon-lit sign out front blandly stating, "Bar 26," an apparent reference to the cross street. An image of two men dancing adorned the outside wall, but the sign's lights remained off.

He blanched, realizing what kind of place it was, but having no particular disposition against it, he continued, more hesitant and anxious than before, but nevertheless determined to find out more about the position.

A bartender, he presumed.

Inside, he found a man rummaging through the kitchen, a cramped room with stainless steel sinks, an industrial-grade refrigerator, four gas burners with iron grates, and bland, milky-green walls of tile. The man, who held a spray bottle and yellow rag, was over six feet tall, with curly dark hair, hazel and sullen eyes, an earring in his left ear, several deep scars on his cheeks, and an athletic physique. He looked bored and distracted; off in one corner, Carl could see a mixed drink with lime in a plastic cup. The man noticed him, it seemed, but said nothing.

"My name's Carl Moretti. Your friend, Richard, sent me he—"

"Which Richard?" the man snapped, impatiently.

"Don't know his last name yet, actually. He works Central Pa—"

"Got it. Sure," he said, his voice warming up. "I've known him a long time. My wife and his...back when I had a wife... used to be friends. Yea, I still run into him now and then. Name's Terry. What's up?" he finished, abruptly.

Carl paused, reluctant to plow right into his request, although it seemed appropriate given the man's apparent interest in shooing him away. "Thought you might have work. Pronto. I need to get working again."

"Know how to fix a Manhattan?" Terry asked, continuing with his wiping and polishing and not looking directly at him.

"Two ounces rye or bourbon...half ounce sweet vermouth... bitters, if desired...ice...strain into a glass. Serve with a cherry."

"What kind of glass?"

"How about a Tosca wine glass? Or a cocktail glass will do."

Without acknowledgement, the man continued cleaning. "John Collins."

"Highball glass. Two ounces bourbon...juice of one lemon...one teaspoon sugar—"

"*Powdered* sugar."

"Powdered sugar. Mix with club soda over ice cubes... stir."

Terry kept moving, deliberately ignoring his applicant. "Okay. You've got it. We serve a ton of those drinks. Big money makers for us. Know how to serve a draft lager…with just enough head?"

"Yea, I—"

"Don't worry. I'm busting on you. You've done fine. Maybe you ruin a mug or two's worth while you're practicing. I don't care."

Carl felt his heart pounding in his chest. Clearly, the man was tough, he thought to himself, and he needed the job, and it seemed that if you satisfied this man's basic demands, he might otherwise leave you alone.

Finished, Terry dropped his rag, then turned casually toward Carl, who remained stiff and unsettled. "You're not queer, are you," he said flatly, as if stating a fact.

"No."

After eyeing Carl closely, Terry waved a hand. "Pssh, not important. You're a good-looking guy. They'll like you," he said, eyes twinkling with humor. Then he turned away, continuing with his work. "Hey, we don't discriminate. Have a lot of fun here, too. You'll like it. Remember this: this is my advice on how to work this crowd. When they ask you whether you're gay, tell them you're not sure yet. You have a vocation?"

"Computer programmer." Carl had to chuckle aloud.

"Right," Terry continued, not missing a beat, "I'm getting a lot of them."

"So you want me to lie?"

"Ever been with a man?"

"No."

"So how do you know you're not gay? It's not a lie, see?"

Embarrassed to be having this conversation, Carl shuffled in place, then dug his hands into his pockets. "I guess so. Anyway, so when do I start?"

"Come back at eight. Go grab yourself a shot of caffeine somewhere. Get yourself pumped up. It'll be crazy tonight. Saturday night always brings out the drunkest crowd. This is Manhattan. No one has to drive home. But listen, it's also a decent crowd here. Most are guys looking for a place to blow off some steam, under the radar where no one's checking out who's where. Just throwing on a pair of blue jeans, going out to listen to some music and hang out with the boys. A lot of them are couples, executives, guys with weekend homes stuck in the city with work. It's a sharp bunch. There are a few nuts here and there, but if anyone ever gives you too much trouble...you have to be able to give and take here, but you know what I mean... you let me know. We have a bouncer on staff. Stands by the door. You go to him directly...tell him what the disturbance is. That's the lay of the land. You stay high and dry, and I'll see you back here in a few hours."

"Dressed like this?"

"Pfff! You're fine."

(2)

Although the interior was dimly lit, at quarter-to-eight, with only a handful of patrons and a solitary bartender behind the bar, the place looked open and inviting. Standing in the doorway and surveying the scene, Carl could only imagine the throng of people he'd need to serve later in the evening. At least the money would hit his bottom line rather than fly out the window in the form of rent, he thought. The bouncer, an Abrams tank of a man in a sleeveless t-shirt, black shoes, and pants, waved him through, introducing himself as Dirk. Carl figured it was a stage name, but thanked him kindly.

A young woman named Isabelle Drake worked behind the bar. Her golden hair, both iridescent and silky, dangled in a straight, casual style over her frail shoulders, which seemed sturdy, as if she worked out and despite her narrow frame. She wore a blue dress, red, low-heeled shoes, and a black ribbon was seductively wrapped around her neck. Gliding around her workstation with a casual ease, she seemed warm, friendly, and easy to approach. In light of his persistent woes, he found her a refreshing change of circumstance.

"Name's Carl Moretti," he said, extending a hand.

"Oh." She smiled. "You must be the new guy. I'm Isabelle. They chant Isabelle, Isabelle, serve all you can…give me a drink and make me a man," she continued, ironic yet cheerful. "They're always teasing me. But they pay well. If you can take a little ribbing, you'll leave here with four-five hundred dollars tonight. Sometimes more. If you're entertaining someone with a wad of dough or an American Express Black, then there's no telling what kind of cash they'll drop on you. My best tip so far," she said, intentionally loud enough for customers to hear, "was five grand. That was a fluke, but the guy's charge was approved and he never called to contest it. So there it stood. Sold, five drinks for over five grand to the drunken millionaire with the neck scarf. That's how he was dressed that night. I'll never forget. Said my dear, you're one woman who would make me switch sides. He was cute. I wouldn't switch sides for him, though."

Carl's bubble popped. "Sorry to hear that. You're not half bad, I must say."

"I get by. Here, grab a towel. I'll show you how to ring the register in a minute. Things won't get cooking until ten."

Over the next two hours, the pace of business ebbed and flowed. Some early patrons had their two drinks and moved on, apparently to other venues or parties, albeit with an extra gloss over their eyes. Others filtered in, in threes or fours, found a table near the stage where the live music would start at nine, and started doing shots. Typically, one would designate himself as the bar runner because there were no waiters or waitresses in the joint. Over in the far corner, a group laughed and talked over God knows what; their constant cackles and bursts of hilarity added to the festive mood.

They made Carl feel instantly at home and he started serving drinks immediately.

Along the way, Isabelle showed Carl the ropes: where they stashed the extra liquor, how to break a sale, where to hide the hundred dollar bills, and so on. By the time 9:00 rolled around and the band broke into another set, the place was hopping, and Carl, who already felt as comfortable as someone could be on his first night, was busy covering the bar: mixing drinks, pouring drafts, and flying to and fro with money pouring out of his hands. He was making a fortune, and indeed he was having a blast insofar as getting his mind off worldly matters was concerned.

This was a good thing, he felt.

But at one point during the busy night, as the clock wound past 11:00, as his mind raced faster than his hands, which served drinks and exchanged cash with alacrity he never knew he possessed, his thoughts drifted to Dasha. He couldn't help it; she was the one aspect of the outside he could not, no matter how hard he worked, shake off. He imagined her smiling face at the bar, ordering a drink, laughing uproariously at his jokes, conversing, engaging his eyes with hers, however fleeting or insignificant her glances might be, and announcing to the world how wonderful was this man behind the bar. At one point during his montage, he stood stock-still, dumbfounded, lost in the question of how he ended up living in Central Park and meeting such an angel there, then working in this bar.

Isabelle snapped him back. "Come on, come on! No time to let up now. A few more hours and you're scot-free!"

He snapped out of it. "Um...I was just thinking—"

"Yea, yea. I used to do that. Join the fun! You're in a bar, for God's sake! Let loose. Goodbye, Allen! Joseph! Anyway, yea, Carl, I look into those eyes and I see a heart seeking to get out. But that alone won't pay the rent."

Carl went back to work, busily attending to shouts and requests.

A few minutes later, though, she caught him staring again. "I know. I see that look. You caught me," he said. "I have to shake her out of my mind. But look...all our customers are happy."

She brushed her hand across his back. "Don't be silly; I don't mind. Thing is, you remind me of an artist friend. A sculptor."

"Funny you mention that," he said, arcing over her to accept a ten dollar bill, "but I've been conjuring up all kinds of images lately. Trees, bridges, tiles...I see it all in Central Park and, I dunno, it gets my juices flowing. Wish I could do something more creative. I'm starting to think I need to use my imagination."

"Interesting. I'll remember that."

The crowd cheered and clapped as the band finished another set. After the noise quieted down, Carl handed her a dollar. "Here. Take this. I think you give sound advice."

She handed it back. "Keep it. There'll be a lot more where that came from."

Carl found her comment cryptic, but not wanting to pursue this discussion about himself, he nodded in perfunctory agreement, then headed back to work. After a wildly successful night, he left the bar before sunrise, exhausted but five hundred dollars richer.

He would definitely go back.

CHAPTER EIGHTEEN

The following night, Carl headed for the party. Tabitha was right, he mused as he stepped into the apartment: it was packed with eligible women, all dressed in cocktail dresses and sipping champagne or burgundy from long-stemmed glasses. Bone-white furniture adorned the living room while expansive picture windows held the fading skylight in relief against a warm, evening hue. The party had begun several hours before, which made sense for the guests because they had to work the following day.

Awash with buzz and laughter, the scene looked swanky yet fun.

Carl considered himself both where he should and should not be at the same time. He ought to get out and stay connected, he knew, but the all-female atmosphere was intimidating. What questions would they ask? How would he explain his situation, especially to the opposite sex? Then he saw a guy mixed in with the crowd and at the center of a splinter group. And a male rival...would this turn into a competition?

He hadn't taken time to think about his story; now he felt he should have.

Carl found a cushiony chair at the end of the coffee table, thanked a server for a glass of Veuve Clicquot, which the svelte young caterer removed from a silver tray, and turned his attention toward a nearby conversation. Enjoying themselves, the group prattled on aimlessly as they huddled and jockeyed beside the coffee table.

It took a few minutes before someone, the woman on his left, addressed him.

"So, what do you do?" she asked, swirling her drink with a seductive yet skeptical air. In her mid-thirties, slim and aggressively seductive, the woman leaned toward him, pinching her nose with feigned interest. In a row beside her sat three more women, all crammed against each other on the rectangular couch, rubbing shoulders and passed around food—Roquefort cheeses, rice crackers, peeled shrimps, all beautifully prepared and displayed in porcelain bowls. Opposite them, on a matching sofa, sat another group of partygoers, one of them the guy, whose name was Ben. On the other end of the coffee table sat Suzanne Thomas, the hostess, an imperious figure sporting an air of supreme authority, even to the point of turning her nose up at the others around her. She was impeccably dressed in satin lace, rubies, and long strands of pearls.

Suzanne held a cigar, but it wasn't lit.

Carl turned toward the woman who'd addressed him. "What do I do? Working on the bar," he equivocated.

"Oh, my father's a lawyer in Houston! He's the most amazing man," she exclaimed, seeming impressed with herself and needing to impress Carl. "My name's Priscilla Rogers, by the way."

"Nice to meet you."

She seemed not to notice his response. "My father recently handled the Shiff Oil merger. I'm sure you'll do something big someday," she added, insincerely and making him feel worse by comparison. "I'm thirty-one now and I've never been able to find a man quite like him...yet." She nuzzling against Carl's leg. "So, where do you live?"

"On the park."

"Impresssssssive," she said, mixing sarcasm with intrigue. "What? Studio, one bedroom?"

"Alcove. Lots of light."

"I love light! Ohmygod, that's so cool! We must be twins!" She sipped her champagne, considering a thought. "So what are you paying for that? It must be a fortune! Just curious."

Carl sipped his drink. "You'd have a cow if I told you. Why spoil the fun? Anyway, no JD next to your name?" he parried.

"Oh, please," she laughed. "My father got the brains. I don't know how he does it." She blushed, then paused. "But that doesn't matter," she continued, bearing down on Carl, her voice assuming a rough pitch. "I'm a VP with Williams Industries. We make bolts, screws, lots of industrial parts. Most of them are made offshore now. So you really live, like literally, on Central Park?"

He wanted to sidestep her questions, but she didn't seem the type to take a hint. "Really...right, directly on the park. You can't get any closer. I can almost touch the trees when I wake up in the morning."

"You're kidding me! That's amazing! I want to see your place. Wait, what's your last name?"

"Moretti. First name's Carl."

She searched her inner Rolodex. "Moretti. Nope, I don't know that name. Not that I know every millionaire in Manhattan. Tell me, Carl. How does someone, if you don't mind my asking...right out of law school...you do look so young...live right on Central Park?"

"Easy," he replied, enjoying the change in status he'd bought himself and having fun at her expense, although also feeling she deserved the ruse. "In my life I only have to show up and good things happen to me. Like Forrest Gump. Guess I was born to be in the center of it all," he added, obliquely.

"Obviously!" she said, taking a long drink. She drew a long breath, then studied his eyes.

The woman next to her, noticing her fixation on him, leaned over. "Whatcha talking about, you two?"

"Carl here lives on Central Park already and he hasn't even taken the New York bar yet!"

"Ooh," the second woman cooed, "party at Carl's house!"

Carl laughed.

Suddenly Suzanne, now with two drinks and the cigar in her hand, tapped her glass and shouted from across the coffee table. "Someone find me a husband! Is that one over there?" This produced howls of laughter from the sycophants next to her. "I mean really," she proceeded, nodding toward Carl and Ben, "find me one before I turn eighty! Give me strong shoulders. And make sure he's smart, handsome, and rich!" Loving her own joke, she exploded in side-splitting laughter while the women around her urged her on.

As she said this, a pretty woman, about Carl's age, who had remained silent on the couch's end spot to his right, smiled furtively in his direction. Clearly shy and embarrassed, she looked like she wanted him to speak first and her eyes enjoined him to do so.

Feeling bashful himself because she looked so charming, Carl nodded, but feeling disoriented and lacking a positive entrée—he was at least equally embarrassed in this situation, given the truth of his position in life—he averted himself from her glance.

The young woman looked disappointed.

Suzanne raised a drink glass. "But if we can't find hunks, there are other ways to get pickled!" Again, this produced howls of laughter. Ben nodded knowingly, while Carl's expression turned sheepish; his stomach fizzed with uncertain emotions. "Quick, Jill!" she said, snapping her fingers toward the woman on her left. "Tell me how to land a rich banker so we don't have to work! Who in her right mind would work if we could stay at home by the pool?" she inquired, sipping her drink. "Just kidding. I'm all career woman. Not!" she screamed, saucy and shrill.

This produced another uproar.

The woman on Carl's right seemed horrified, while the woman on his left also shook her head. "Disgusting," the latter said. "I love my work."

"Oh, Ben," Suzanne continued, clearly drunk, "maybe I should add you to my bachelor list. Everyone needs a backup." The woman's minions, and there were many although they were crowded on her side of the room, howled and hacked again. "Sure. Some of us might have belonged to LUG in college. Not me," she countered, teasingly. "But schmegging with other women was a college thing. Now the field is wide open!"

Suzanne glanced at Jill, enlisting support, and Jill nodded in return.

"See? We all agree," Suzanne continued. "Come on, let's get real, though. Who needs men, anyway?" Her tone turned cool and intimate.

One woman raised her hand.

"One out of eighteen. Not too good. Now I'll ask you," Suzanne said, lighting her cigar and taking a puff, "what if someday we don't need men to procreate. Would we still need a man at all?"

One dissenter gasped, shocked. "I'm engaged!" she hissed.

"You helpless wreck," Suzanne roared, entreating others to join her, "joining the slave galleys, are you?"

"You just said you're looking for a man with money," the woman responded.

Carl felt dismayed by the conversation and wondered how he ended up here. He glanced over at the woman to his right, who seemed deeply ashamed. Then he wondered whether he might find Dasha back in the bushes if he bolted this place.

"Sure, but not to *marry* him. Listen, listen, listen," Suzanne continued, suddenly excited. "There are only two reasons to have a man. What are they?" Expectantly and eyes blazing, she surveying the women around the table. This was followed by a moment of awkwardness.

"Companionship...and sex!" Jill chimed at last, triumphantly.

"Right!" Suzanne chuckled while drinking again, her lips escaping over the edge of her glass. "My disciple has spoken!"

A guest cackled.

The nice-seeming girl on Carl's right bumped his knee with hers, then turned and cleared her throat casually. "My apologies about them. I only came here because our parents are friendly. What's your name?"

The others failed to notice their conversation.

"Carl. Carl Moretti."

"My name's Valerie," she said, extending her hand. "I like your shirt."

Carl looked down but didn't believe her. "Oh. Thanks. They're just having a good time, as they say."

"I'm not. You live around here?"

"Yea," he said, his words subdued through unease and self-restraint.

The party continued. Others roared and cackled while the two, who were becoming oblivious to the rest, leaned closer to each other.

"Ben, Ben!" Suzanne announced from across the table. "What are you doing sitting there? Get your clothes off!" Flattered by the ruckus and attention, Ben laughed. Suzanne and her closest allies bored in on him.

Carl leaned closer to Valerie, trying to hear better. "Nice to meet you. Don't mind me, though. I can take a joke."

"It's not a joke," Valerie insisted. "They're serious."

"So was my ex, but that's a different story," he replied, sipping his champagne.

She moved yet closer, warming to him. "I was just saying to my mother the other day. She's my best friend and I tell her everything. I said it's so hard to meet anyone in this city. I mean, it hurts to say it, and then I hear them rattling on like that and I want to punch them."

Carl cracked a smile. "Yea," he said, searching for words. He felt an instant attraction, even bond with her, but *if she knew my whole story*. He couldn't commit himself to this conversation, he felt inside, and what's more, he felt too embarrassed to tell her why. So he fumbled with his drink and tried his best not to sigh, which seemed the easiest thing to do at the moment.

Then Suzanne noticed them. "Hey, what are you two doing down there? We'll have no fraternization here! We can't be making bangy-bang when we have to work tomorrow!"

"It didn't stop you from drinking," Valerie shot back, rolling her eyes.

"Whoooooa," came the chorus from the other side of the table.

Jill clapped her hands together. "Ooh, ooh! Listen to this! There's this new study out and they're saying some day we can make sperm out of our own bone marrow. Can you believe that? We could push men right to extinction…and never have to clean up toothpaste after the slobs again!"

This produced ferocious cheers.

"If the world were all women, they'd end up murdering each other," injected the engaged dissenter, who remained in a huff. "Personally, I've heard that someday they won't need women. They'll make eggs called artificial gametes from stem cells, then let them gestate in ovens like chocolate cupcakes."

The crowd quieted.

Several shot denigrating glances in the perpetrator's direction.

"This whole male-female thing is so passé, anyway," Suzanne continued, her face suddenly more relaxed. "I mean, don't we all know now that gender and sexual orientation is nothing but a socially-driven structure superimposed over an oblique organism? Huh?" She stopped, impressed by her own rhetoric. "What do you say, Jill? Come on, contribute to the cause," she snorted, leaning toward her ally. As Suzanne leaned left, Ben leaned toward them, hoping to win some favor.

Suzanne noted Ben's tactic and enjoyed it, but said nothing.

Jill lay down her drink, her tongue rolling seductively on her lips. "Yes, that's true, my dear. You see," she said, addressing the whole group, "they taught us in Women's Studies at Berkeley—I'm proud to say I've studied everything Judith Butler ever wrote—that, to tear a page from Foucault's *Discipline and Punish*, we're all oppressed and forced into society's perceptions and roles by regulative discourse. The way I read her, society tells us to think and behave in a certain way, then, like programmed robots we respond. So to free ourselves from this social structure, we need to unshackle ourselves from these...these games of rhetoric."

Suzanne threw down her hands. "Exactly!"

Jill responded with a knowing glance. "And if we're talking philosophy, weren't the ancient philosophers, our cultural ancestors, after all, swapping togas anyway? You know? I mean, we could hook up Ben and Carl over there and they wouldn't know the difference! If they would only get over a certain social mindset, they could have some fun. But leave us to rule the world," she said, tossing her hair aside and laughing, then glancing, as if secretively, toward Suzanne.

Considering this scenario inconceivable, Carl was repulsed by the thought, and moreover found the insult disgusting to the point of wondering whether he should excuse himself. Ben, on the other hand, smiled wanly, although he nudged himself closer to Jill's direction, again hoping to gain favor.

Carl felt this party had turned into a disaster and glanced toward the door.

But sensing his discomfort and wanting him to stay, Valerie shot a stare at Suzanne. "Actually, for the record," she said, sneering at the host, "I was graduated from Cornell, where I studied this issue in depth. You've read Martha Nussbaum's *Upheavals of Thought: The Intelligence of Emotions*, just maybe? I saw her speak on one occasion...oh my God, what a lady! She's a universalist, you know...in the tradition of Aristotle. She spoke of her perspective in terms of *capabilities,* which, by the way, is far more liberating than the nihilist approach that says there is no sexuality and gender...that it's all a mere social construct. Excuse me, but don't we have emotions? And don't we tap in to the essence of ourselves when we probe our feelings? Sexuality is not arrived at like a bus station. It's deeply personal, and through the struggle, it can also be moral. I'm a liberal, so I believe some people will probe inside themselves and find they might be gay or bisexual, or asexual and many identities. But I find your rhetoric that emotions and identity don't matter, such things are only whatever we say they are...deeply offensive."

Hot with indignance, Suzanne gasped. "Then get out of my apartment, will you?"

Jill shook her head in her comrade's direction.

"I'm kidding," Suzanne continued, taking the cue.

Valerie looked around the table, then satisfied they were listening, continued with confidence. "Don't you insult Ben and Carl's sexuality and identity in that way! If they say they're straight male heterosexuals, what's that to us? If we deny that is a unique and legitimate identity, then we devalue every other identity ipso facto, by saying there's no soul into which we all tap and by claiming we're all merely what...material matter with some rhetorically-based illusions. Don't you see? You're nihilists! The whole thing comes crashing down with your arguments! You destroy femininity, too, suggesting there's nothing special and nothing better about being a woman! I find that despicable as a liberal feminist! So don't you attack red-blooded straight guys because when you do, you insult me!"

Carl was impressed she would come out and defend his masculinity like that, and a feminist at that. It was downright jarring to him and he felt an immediate attachment to her. But he still felt uncomfortable...precisely because he felt insecure.

Suzanne and Jill whispered conspiratorial words to each other.

"If I want arguments," Valerie continued, wincing, "I can join a debate club! Nussbaum frees us from the notion that acquiring a male's income is a determinant of our happiness," she said, digging her claws into the women on the other end of the table. "She's also, if you read outside your own dogma, an advocate of emotional freedom…especially breaking away from restrictive emotions like anxiety. But what matters the most is what we feel in our own souls we are, and that's not a matter of the brain alone. You can't argue your way into an identity."

Suzanne remained cold, and her earlier ebullience was gone. "Oh, I'm speaking to The Professor of Parody," she barbed. "Yea, sure, I read the article in *The New Republic*. Still, I say you're a ditzy little housewife in need of a good bra burning," she continued, injecting her stinger.

"Oh! Oh, you bitch!" Valerie fumed in response.

Just as the mood turned this sour, Lisa Foley entered the apartment with Tabitha Murphy trailing behind. The conversation died down temporarily as they approached the gang who, crammed into a tiny space, had no seats for two more people. Several eyes stared at Carl, and feeling their gaze, his faced turned red. Valerie looked at him, understood immediately, then sizing up Lisa carefully, decided she hated her. As for Carl, he felt he'd rather slink into a corner and sulk, but he kept his chin up.

Lisa instantly noticed Carl, who had turned half-way around. She froze, looked him up and down, and with a sudden look of anger, waltzed to the other side of the room, found a chair, and brought it up as close as she could to Suzanne.

And now they have a new ally, Carl thought to himself as he watched his old flame take a seat. The sight of her made him ill and concerned. *What if she lights into me here? What will this girl next to me think?*

Then, feeling he needed to rescue Valerie and take charge of a difficult situation, he pointed in Suzanne's direction. "If what you're saying is true, that gender in the end doesn't matter and all sexual orientation is relative, then doesn't that, and I'm shooting from the hip here, I know, but following Valerie's line of thinking...doesn't that devalue your argument? How can you construct an argument without a foundation? What's your lynchpin or cornerstone? What are your theorems or postulates? I say that as someone with a technical background, but I don't see how your logic works...even if sexual identity really is nothing more than rhetoric. And if it's something imposed on someone in a socially constructed way, then can't it also be taken away just as easily?" His last comment made him suddenly shudder.

Lisa's eyes glared at Carl's, her face conveying arrogance and condescension. She kept her eyes transfixed on Carl, as saying, "Out of my house, now," but said nothing. Jill whistled over his moxie.

Knowing he was getting under Suzanne's skin, Carl raised his voice slightly. "There's no gender at all in some organisms. But on the subject of sexual orientation, if you say male-female relations are not inherently natural, and we don't define this relationship as the anchor categorization, if you will, despite its biological relevance and prevalence in human populations, then aren't you also saying, by extension, that homosexual, bisexual, and asexual categories are also unnatural? And wouldn't this invalidate gay rights, for instance, by undermining the basic substance of and rational for this form of justice?" When he finished, Carl was amazed this had come from his own mouth.

"That's ridiculous," Lisa quickly and defiantly broke in. "There are two kinds of men. Those who make babies, and those who take care of them! The first kind is something you are *not*, Carl Moretti. *Real men* don't get thrown out of their apartments by their girlfriends!" she dug, her tone more biting and nastier than before.

Even Suzanne and Jill, not expecting such intensity, became speechless. Suzanne looked at Lisa as if to say "Calm down. Not so strident." At first, Lisa backed off, but after a long and awkward pause, she added, "And that's why he's homeless now."

Carl felt deeply humiliated. He stood up, pointed at her and declared, "You'll say anything to get revenge for my not caring we broke up!"

"Didn't care? Who said we should work things out?"

Tabitha motioned toward Carl, then grabbing his attention, offered a kind and helpless shrug. Carl's face suggested it was not her fault and she smiled faintly.

Suzanne attempted to clear the atmosphere with levity.

"Let's throw Ben and Carl together and find out if they're real men!" she said, battling over her dual attempts to support and humiliate a male opponent…and perhaps rally her female alliance, which appeared to be crumbling.

Jill clapped her hands. "Oh my God, did you see the episode of *Sex in the City* where she dumps that poet guy? Hysterical! What a *loser* he was," she cackled, forming the "L-for-loser" sign, the perpendicular thumb and forefinger pressed against her forehead.

Suzanne clapped her hands, laughing riotously. "I saw it! I saw it! Oh my God! He was soooo shocked, but I mean, duhhhh…you tell her you love her so sappy like that and what do you expect? A dozen roses? Ew, what a creep!" She winced, shuddering. "Served him right to get waylaid like that! Pathetic. But great! A whole show about dumping dweebs! Ha, don't ya love it?" The pair proceeded to hack and cough, faces turning beet red as they recounted the episode, but the rest of the table remained stiff, disturbed, and silent.

Valerie shot Lisa and Jill the evil eye. "Hah! Don't delude yourselves, sweet cakes. You're hooked on the all-time, premiere saga of Landing Mr. Right. As a career woman myself I find the whole thing offensive. Why all this attention on meeting guys? Those Amazons keep searching...and searching...for what? Reminds me of some prissy, little...oh, it makes me cringe...antebellum-era debutantes sitting around...drinking tea...pining for love. Puh-lease. Or at least a quick shag until the ship comes in. Without all this going on under the surface, there'd be no story. Don't kid yourself, honey. Women with any kind of self-respect...have more to do with their time than let some dork...and that's how these men are portrayed...slobber all over them. It's like some woman's idea of what a man is, then she tries to be him. Pathetic."

"Ha!" Lisa snapped, joining the attack. "That's not the half of it, dearie! Maybe they like getting knocked up. Maybe I'm pregnant, too! Do you know? I know lots of *real* women who are having babies with whoever they feel like now. Movie stars are doing it, and look where they are!" She said this with a hint of self-doubt, then cut herself off by sipping her drink.

Bemused and overwhelmed, Carl began to creep toward the door. He needed fresh air.

At first, Valerie didn't notice Carl's edging away, and sensing she'd scored points with some of the other women and Carl, too, she continued, this time more confident and cool. "Suzanne, you mentioned a desire to land a rich gentleman. If you want to be liberated, fine, but then you still expect the man to be having more economic resources than you do? Now that we've ascended into positions of power and wealth, isn't there an ever-decreasing pool of available men up the economic ladder? How do you reconcile that? What if you're all alone at eighty and you should have married the plumber? He owns his own truck, you know. Not a bad catch. What you have to offer is so dehumanizing. You're a nihilist in the worst sense! Moreover," she said, losing control of her words, "you are base, vile, and cold as the winter's snow! You live for money, power, and your own, pathetic little satisfaction. In the meantime your heart is an empty trash can hoping to get filled!"

Carl surveyed the scene. *Have to get out of here. Maybe I'll run into Dasha back in the park.* He loved Valerie's appeal, though. He felt it in his bones; she'd touched his soul. *What's her last name?* he wondered. *Never got it. Oh, what's the use! They're all shouting. I've got to get out of here.*

Unable to bear the situation, let alone deal with someone so tangible when his life was so chaotic, he headed for the door where he paused, sighed, then exited. He clasped it shut as quietly as possible as he left.

Valerie noticed him leave, and crestfallen, she abandoned her argument. She loved his spunk and felt sorry for him. She felt he needed a friend. Her stomach fizzing, she hoped she might see him again.

CHAPTER NINETEEN

Carl walked back through Upper East Side streets, past the boutiques of Madison Avenue, now dimly lit and closed, past stately row houses with black iron gates and over the well-groomed environs of 5th Avenue. The air was warm and still, but his frayed nerves were incensed by his own outburst—losing control was something he loathed to do. He stepped briskly through the park entrance and onto the lawn, which, in the night's glow, shined both cool and soft.

He turned at the loop, walked into the center of the road, where he felt safer, and strode uptown toward the seventies, where he would change direction again, under lamplight's glow, and retire. With a day completed and a new one ahead, he tried to erase the altercation from his mind and gradually, without trying, the scene of the party passed into memory, but new memories lay all around and ahead. Once he reached the bushes, which basked under the moonlight shade of an oak tree, he shuffled his things in haphazard fashion, snuggled under his sheets, and gradually fell into a dream.

The young man found himself driving a carriage, alone and dressed in a camel hair overcoat, an amber sash and soldier's boots while working the reins of horses, whose hooves clip-clopped and echoed down a gaslit and cobblestoned street. On both sides of him, gargantuan houses towered overhead. The windows were elegant and large: some glowed softly, while others were dark. Little flames danced and flickered along the roadside, guiding him onward in the thrush of autumn. Except for his brisk-moving vehicle, the street was deserted.

When he arrived at the mansion, he stopped by yanking the horses' heads backwards and up; they responded by clomping their hooves on the ground. He tied them to a post, brushed the dust from his clothes, as he had been riding since late afternoon, and with a tilt of his hat and clearing his throat, he proceeded to the door, on which he knocked three times. A single candle burned in her living room window, but he could see her bedchamber above was unlit.

Moments later, footsteps approached the door, and at the strike of eleven, as a church's clock chimed in the distance, the passage swung open and he found himself facing the porter, who recognized his visitor at once.

"Marik Andropov, I presume," the man asked in perfunctory and formal fashion.

The nervous petitioner nodded, took off his hat, and bowed slightly.

The porter acknowledged the gesture, but his face remained crinkled with skepticism, even disapproval. "The lady will not see anyone at this hour. Her father has informed her to retire. She's under close watch, given the recent, anonymous letters we intercepted," he added, peering over his nose at Marik, who stood beneath the man on the home's granite step. "And I presume you're not aware of the authorship of these correspondences—"

Marik's face blanched. "That's correct. I'm not aware of who would disdain a lady of her caliber by attempting to contact her without revealing his name and outside the normal...and proper...channels. It would do her reputation a disservice, and anyone who respected her would not make such awkward attempts to win her favor."

Candlelight faintly reflecting in his eyes, the porter smiled approvingly, then responded in a more inviting tone, "Indeed. And you are a friend, I presume?" he asked, leading the young man inside with a slight bow and wave of the hand.

"Yes, yes, of course. We met at the ball. Last year, actually, when her younger sister was introduced into society—"

"Yes, of course. Young Katia. She's quite the rage now. Very well," the man said, waving him through. "There's no need for further explanation. As it turns out, her father's away on business and her mother's resting from a recent fall. It's not serious. The lady informed me of your visit in advance, and told me quite insistently I must let you in and inform her of your arrival at once. Very well...I won't be one to argue with a lady, but I must request you leave within one hour's time," he said, pointing to a gold pocket watch. "And I keep a strict schedule at the Konstantinov residence, naturally," he admonished.

Marik pressed his hat against his sternum. "Yes, yes, indeed. We can meet this criterion. I'll be gone by midnight," he said, stepping forward.

The porter halted the young man, reminding him who was boss in this house, then with a stiff upper lip, turned on his shoes and announced, "Follow me," then waltzed briskly down the corridor into the anteroom where the puzzled and nervous officer, having failed to anticipate this screening and tussle, found a seat and waited.

The man disappeared behind a door.

Several minutes passed as a grandfather clock tick-tocked along the wall; two lamps shined brightly in the room, casting ghostly light on the walls, doors, and ceiling. Fumbling his hat in his hands, Dasha's suitor listened to every creak and groan of this dignified home, which remained grey and subdued. He tried his best to practice what he might say, but by the time her soft footsteps brushed down the stairs, the knob of the door opened, and he caught his first glimpse of her gown, which swished past the crack in the opening, he could barely utter a word.

"Dasha—" he managed to utter, standing at attention and bowing fully.

Her eyes were warm and bright. "Yes, my errant little fox. You are a sly one, aren't you? Where have you been this past season? I've received the letters, as written in your hand, but your hand itself has gone missing."

"The lady is correct," he said, humble and submissive, yet holding his chin in the air. "I am in error for not visiting," he said, feigning diplomacy, "but the missus is aware I've been fighting Cossacks in the east. The uprising has been quite savage and, of course, this is no condition in which to consider the presence of a lady."

Her eyes flashed. "I see. And who would have considered requesting my presence in this wild frontier?" she coyly inferred. "Dare I think you, my dear captain?"

Nabbed, he bit his lip and gulped, seeking an artful way out. "I cannot divulge the shadows of my heart under such circumstances, although I request the permission to speak to the lady with candor."

She raised an eyebrow, eyes gleaming and nose crinkling in gleeful jest, then she alighted onto a chair, folded her legs one atop the other, and rested her hands on the armrest. Then she leaned toward him, intensely interested. "Go on, go on! You ask for permission as if I'm a general? Please, please...my father was a general once, as you know, but I'm not so simply defined. Please, I beg you...tell me," she played, voice smoky and vague.

"My dearest Dasha," he said, seating himself several paces from her. "In this late hour of night, I know fear unlike nothing in my garrison. At least when it comes to pistols and powder, which I know exceedingly well, I can define my quarry. But in the realm of ladies, I must confess to you, I'm quite the undefended fort."

She clapped softly, leaning further over her toes in his direction. "Excellent! Well said. You are, indeed, the author of your epistles. These were not copied from books. Please continue, and why...my dear, I must say...you are a most handsome...if not a wholly qualified...suitor," she said, grimacing through twin barrels of kindness and heartache.

He bowed his head. "I'm aware of our father's quarrels and my relative lack of fortune. Has the lady asked her father, in passing, what he might think of this match?"

Dasha reared up and winced. "He'll have none of it. Once I dropped a hint, when he found your third letter, which I'd foolishly left opened on my dresser. I asked him what if it were you. He stormed out of the room, his sword chipping the frame of my door with its metal edge! As I heard his boots stomping down the hallway, I heard something that sounded more like a shriek than a man's voice, and he called after me with, 'Never, as long as I'm a Konstantinov!'"

Heaving a big sigh, Marik looked up at her disappointed eyes, feeling beaten. "It is thus, as it were."

"He'll not change his mind. To him, our family's honor is everything. Of course, my mother has powers of persuasion," she added, luring him on. "And she has a different opinion of these family quarrels. She says, and I agree, of course, we're in modern St. Petersburg now. Let's not let the samovar boil all day and night over such trifles, she says. Her overruling him, in the way she has with him to this day, is always possible, but she, too, has her objections."

Anguished by the news, his eyes watered.

"And it's related, as you might have guessed, to her... assessment...of your opportunities. I, of course, think she's a prattling old fool at times, but I'm bound to respect her all the same. But tell me, my dear Marik, do you consider yourself worthy?"

Again, he gulped, then looked surely into her eyes. "I do."

She paused and smiled demurely, enjoying his supplication and effort. "I see. Well then, we do have a challenge, do we not? I've found your letters most tenderhearted and fair. And your efforts on the front most dashing and thrilling. It's all a poor city lass can do, when receiving such epistles, not to throw herself onto a carriage and race toward her heart's desire, when words stir the soul as yours do," she said, her eyes soft and wet. "When we danced at the ball, my heart moved with my slippers...every beat, every word. Do you understand the cage within which I've placed our love?" she pined, wistfully.

Both moved and relieved, he stumbled and stammered. "I...I'm deeply honored...by your reception to my churlish advances. Shall I make arrangements to—"

"Let's not cavil over trifles today," she said, her face relaxing. "I'm not ready with my decision which, furthermore, I cannot make without a formal proposal. But if, hypothetically, you were to suggest we—"

"I know a church near Omsk," he interjected, breathless and intense. "It's a day's ride from here. We could—"

"Enough, my love," she said, peering toward the clock. "Time flitters on, and I need to retire. Write me again soon. I'll await your warm words, which fill my heart with joy. Here, kiss me on the cheek and say your goodbyes."

(19)

He kissed her cheek and hand, which she extended with grace and passion. But checking his emotions, as much to impress her as for propriety, he turned on his heels and left the room, donned his hat, and proceeded onto the bleary street.

CHAPTER TWENTY

(1)

Cool air settled over the park as Carl, not wanting to leave his previous night's dream world, pulled the bed sheet tightly over his chin; when that was not enough, he grabbed a stray sweatshirt, pulled it over his mouth, and breathed slowly through snorkel-like nostrils. He shivered once, but as his body heat filled the makeshift cocoon, the chill subsided. He stared into the leaves and orange skies above: a robin shook its wings overhead, and higher above, gentle branches swayed like flamingo dancers on a Tuesday night stage.

Having pushed himself hard enough over the past few weeks, he drew a long breath, exhaled, and closed his eyes. *Sleep, time to sleep*, he thought. Due to the cold front now creeping inland from Long Island Sound, the ordinary din was subdued, the loop empty, and Carl's mind drifted toward maidens, brooks, and country thickets. But Dasha failed to arrive, despite these thoughts that somehow, as he thought them, hinted she might appear.

It rained until evening, and throughout the day, Carl remained under a parka, unwilling to budge. Misting rain, blanketing the streets, grasses, and leaves with an iridescent gleam, deposited itself in sheets, then trickled its way through soil and gutters.

The next shift at the bar would be Thursday night, still two days away, and pressing matters of credit card payments could wait another few days, so lacking a particular structure for the day and needing a break, he chose this languid option.

Dasha, in kind, let him rest, only appearing at dusk.

"Get up, get up, lazy bones," she said, tugging on his shoulder. He turned over to see her smiling warmly, her expression similar to that of the dream: excited, yet muted and cautious. Her presence brought a salutary effect on his soul, such that even in the midst of the foggy, rainy clouds overhead, her face seemed angelic. He rolled over several inches, resting his cheek on his hand.

"I dreamed of you last night," he muttered, searching her face.

"And I of you, of course. But whether it was a good dream or a bad one, I cannot say. It would reveal my hand in a way I'm not prepared, and besides it's against the rules," she confessed, frowning.

"Whose rules? What—"

"*C'est pas grave*," she replied, her face soft through lack of concern.

"I once loved you."And I you," she replied.

He wet his lips pensively, then searched for a way to continue this subject without sounding too foolish or worse, scaring her off. But the radiant shine of her eyes, and the way her brown hair dangled over her lips, encouraged him, and he stepped closer to the ledge. "I've been thinking today. We don't love like that anymore."

"We?" she gasped, gathering her breath. "I think *we* don't love at all."

"I mean, the collective we," he said, tenderly. "Of course it's not you and me, at least not today. But yesterday...tomorrow. How long can we love?" he asked, testing her with challenging eyes.

She heaved a sigh. "It's not a question of how long. It's a question of how much. Don't you agree? When two people in torrid, wicked love catch the fatal sting of Cupid's bow, it might as well be a poison dart through their hearts. The curse of it all! The heart, struggling to breathe, cries out for air as it beats at this furious pace, but if the love is snatched away suddenly for some reason or none at all, the beating cannot stop although the object of that beating is gone. Then one, to end this love, must pull this arrow from the body—thorns, barbs, and all—if we want any respite. But is that possible? I've known Cupid quite well; I've called for him amidst these trees more than once, and here he's not appeared. He's gone to some other time and place, and for us he's not stirred. This is my lot, and I expect nothing more, you must know," she added, frowning.

Carl looked at her inquisitively, feeling a sense of déjà vu in her melancholy. "Long ago—before we had cars, phones, and Internet—when people wrote passionate letters by hand and sealed them in wax. Was there more satisfaction?"

"Perhaps," she said, tilting her eyes away and beyond. "They say we had strictures and mores, and that is quite true. But you have your own today, and often based on the same, vile reasons. Yet understandable, in their own ways. Love itself has not changed," she sighed, "but people get in its way."

"So there's hope for us now?"

"Who? My dear Marik, I'm at wit's end and I must find resolution to this...this string on which we dangle. Yes, indeed. I'll work on it. But here...I can...here, I have a piece of paper for you," she said, suddenly shifting tone. "Have you called my contact yet?"

"No, I've—"

She tapped him on the wrist with her wand. "Shame on you! But that's okay, you have time. You see, I have great designs for you. I know you're struggling and need my assistance, and for that I'm quite honored, of course. I can fix you, don't worry. But you need to release these thoughts you have, such as I cannot find a woman because I'm not rich. This is nonsense. Once, when I knew you, as you're starting to see, I suspect, you were much more bold although, perhaps, equally as harsh with yourself. You see, you didn't like the war, the fighting; you were never the natural officer, like my father, and that's why I loved you. Yes, it's true, we were in love. Then you abandoned me."

"What? I abandoned you? What are you talking about?" he guffawed.

She was supple and lithe as she spoke. Her eyes remained soft. "It was a cold day in spring, some six months after you came calling in my anteroom. I had responded to your letters at last with an agreement to marry you in the church, as you requested. Then...I'm sorry," she said, eyes welling with tears. "I cannot finish this story now. It's too painful for me, and it may affect you in some way I don't intend. I've been given limited freedom by the powers that be, if you will; they were kind enough to let me visit you, having heard my pleas for your happiness, but this is all I can say."

He looked at her askance, wondering how much to believe, but feeling a strong sense of familiarity in her intimate tone of voice. "If it's any consolation, you abandon me, too. Is this revenge?"

"No! Heaven's no! But I'll work on it. I promise. What's meant to be will be. That I can assure you. What's not meant to be can still be worthwhile. It's that complex." Dasha gathered herself and continued more strongly. "May I suggest, at least, you call the woman whose name is on this note? I found her through some investigation, if you will...it was some horoscope posting and she could care less about your station and status... and although I don't know her, perhaps it will be the start of something."

He shrugged. "I'll think about it."

Satisfied, she stood up, then tossed her wand over her shoulder. "Do you like this pose?" she teased. "If I'm to be this love faerie, then I must relish the part." Then criss-crossing both arms across her chest, she turned up her chin, crinkled her nose, and exclaimed, "Hm, I think I'm quite beautiful!"

Bing!

(2)

Later that evening, he stood before a tiny shop.

Situated on a side street of Clinton, the place appeared closed. The curtains, dyed sandstone and purple, were drawn shut, the door was closed. An electric candle was the only light emanating from the window, in which a sign stated: "Fortunes Read. $5." Beside the sign were plastic beads, a silver necklace, and a sign that read: "Closed." Several people strolled by, and for a moment Carl felt too self-conscious to knock; for all he knew, it was a front for a massage parlor—or worse. *Surely, she doesn't mean*, he thought. *No, that wasn't the look she gave me.*

Curious, and lacking alternative entertainment for this desolate night, he straightened his collar, combed his hair, cleared his throat, then knocked three times. He stood still, waiting patiently.

Some thirty seconds passed before he heard a keychain jangle, a latch open, and the weary creak of the old door. A nose and two eyes appeared in the crack, and Carl mustered his least-intimidating hello. The door swung wider, and a crackling voice rang out in the night. "Closed tonight. How may I help you, young man?" she asked. The woman, who now stood in the light, was in her sixties. Her grey hair, intermixed with brown, was bundled into a knot on the back of her head, and her dress, embroidered with crimson flowers and violet pastels, was thin enough to flutter in the vortex of air around the passageway. Her face, deeply lined and wide, yet pleasant and taut, bespoke a woman who, upon glancing at a stranger, could size him up well. She smiled faintly. "But come in... come in. I see you're here for a reason."

So he stepped inside, where the room was musty and dank. A crystal ball, polished and glimmering, stood alone on a table, which stood between a love seat and a velvet-lined chair that in another setting might pass for a throne. Noting his wandering eyes, she smiled again, then suggested he make himself at home while she fetched a pot of tea.

She shut the door behind him, locked it, and proceeded to a back room.

For the next several minutes, which seemed like an hour, he watched the passing scene along the street, although the occasional taxicab, pedestrian, and squad car remained obscured by the smoky glass and the overall somnolent effect of the shop. He sank deeper into his seat, trying to remember which questions to ask, and even more to the point, why he had walked some twenty-five blocks to get here. But the longer he sat, the more subdued he became, and by the time she returned with his steaming cup of jasmine, he might have preferred a nap to her inquiries.

"What brings you to me today, young man?" she asked, facing him from her cushiony seat, placing both hands beside the globe. "I'll pay you a nickel for your thoughts," she quipped.

He smiled politely, recognizing her goodwill gesture. "I was hoping you could answer that one."

Clasping her fingers, she tensed her forehead, then peered long into his soul. "Your eyes are troubled," she observed. "And I suspect," she said, studying him closer, then turning toward her crystal ball, "it's due to someone, very close, in your life."

He agreed, hesitantly.

"A young lady!" she announced, casting a knowing glance in his direction. "But someone who, I can see, holds some mystery in your heart. You don't know whether she loves you. And you, I sense, aren't sure whether you love her, either. There's been a misunderstanding. Some conflict...disruption. You think about her night and day, you recall her smile with warmth and love, but there's something holding you back. Something you, and perhaps she, cannot resolve. Am I getting close?" she asked with a rhetorical tilt of her head.

He nodded, sheepishly.

Thinking carefully, she rubbed her chin and hummed. "And this young lady, her name begins with a B, a D—"

"D," he said, spirits soaring. "That's right. How did you know?"

"I didn't," she answered, wisely. "What does an old gypsy woman know that her visions don't tell her? I could go on and on about that. Let's not go there," she said, waving a hand and chuckling to herself. She locked her eyes on his, sounding intimate and cordial. "Listen, at this point I usually hit them up for $5, but since you seem like a fine fellow, and all...and I'm officially closed for the night...I'll make it a freebie...on condition, of course, you don't tell my union." She smirked, ironically. "Some of my best readings have been freebies, I must tell you, so better buckle your seat belt in that couch, young man."

Feeling the intensity of her stare, he shifted uncomfortably, but tried to smile.

"Very well," she said, returning to her crystal ball. Then she rubbed the globe with thick, ring-adorned fingers and chanted,

"Rainbows, clovers and handsome, rich earl,
Show me his flame, show me the girl."

She looked up, her face brightening. "Oh, oh, I have an image! I see she's wearing a dress. Is that right? Yes, you're nodding your head. Good, you're with me. And yes, faintly through the glass I can see one, two...you're at a ball. A fete of some kind, yes?"

He began to feel strange, but nodded softly.

"There's some history between you two, I see. Is that correct? Some long history. You've known her since childhood?" she inquired, sniffing her nose.

"At least," he said, leaning closer. "Actually, I don't know. But I've been...I guess the reason I called on you. She gave me your address, actually. I don't know, but I...I—" he stammered, eyes darting around the room while she watched him closely. "I...I wanted to ask you whether...and I know this sounds crazy. Maybe not to you, I hope. I want to ask whether—"

"Stop!" she ordered, holding a palm to his face. "I see where you're heading. You're asking me, are you not, whether there is, in fact, such a thing as a past life? Is that correct?"

"I might be. And what of it?" he blurted, feeling stupid.

She laughed. "Aha, the man who doesn't believe is the proudest of all! On what are you standing, young man?

I see you're intrepid, but come on, are you concerned about conventions…here with me? Nonsense! The other day, a young woman came here…she was pregnant with a near-stranger's child. Said it was a wild affair, and before she knew it, wham! She was pregnant, and now suddenly she feels this is punishment for sins of her past life. How karmic, imagine that! The things people say these days. Oh, I could write a book. Tsk, tsk," she continued, shaking her head. "Now, I don't mean to belittle your visions, which are no doubt sincere. But as much as I'd like to help, and I can certainly give you your fortune with this lady, if you like, although I think it's a murky case at best…there are heavy forces at work here, you see?" she confided. "Perhaps you should speak with a friend of mine… she's from Calcutta. No, never mind, hmph, she'll tell you the same thing. You can try meditation. That may do the trick, but the best way to explore what you had with this woman in the past is to spend time with her in the present. This is the only way to assess whether you're on the same path. Give her a try! I'm sure she's struggling with the same things. See where it goes! I mean, if you have that much baggage with her, one night you'll both wake from your dreams laughing, or crying, or doing something, because you'll both know. And then you won't need to ask me," she said with finality.

"That's my fortune?"

"I'm sorry, I'm having an off night. Really, I'm as sorry as an old gypsy can be under the circumstances. Maybe I should have demanded payment. I'll have to remember that in the future. But be that as it may, I am certain you two can work this out between yourselves. I saw great admiration and respect in my ball tonight, and I can see this is your natural disposition…so I'm not worried. Will you betroth yourselves in everlasting love, or part your ways as your paths diverge, far over the bend,

I have no idea. I admit it! What am I, a prophet? I earn the other kind of profit, naturally, but all I can see tonight, if I may be so bold, is a path of mystery and wonder, and where your lifelines will take you...God knows where. Let me see your palms, yes? I can see clearly, and farther than the eye can see. Beyond life, beyond death, and into the stars," she finished, wondrous and light. "That's your fortune."

He thanked her and left, wondering how matters would be resolved with Dasha.

CHAPTER TWENTY ONE

(1)

Needing to release pent-up frustration and confusion, Carl went to work the following evening on a tear. After immersing himself in the art of making drinks and jokes at the same time, and scurrying from customer to customer, wiping counters, and hauling ice from the kitchen for eight hours, he finally recharged with a five-minute break.

As he stood, pensive and alone, he decided he had developed a devil-may-care attitude. The money was good, the pressure to perform was minimal, the atmosphere was festive, and his behind-the-bar colleague, Isabelle, maintained a down-to-earth, nonjudgmental attitude that soothed Carl's ego, although he continually suffered lingering feelings of humiliation for falling from high-tech brilliance to tending a bar.

Eyeing her, he sighed.

But working around an attractive female, no matter how untouchable she might be, had its own rewards. Beside filling his long nights with feelings of hope and validation, he found she had a subtle influence on him. He began to work harder, began to think more about the future, and began to consider ways he might escape this cycle of poverty and instability in which he found himself. With this in mind, he resolved to jettison the digs in Central Park and find a real apartment.

So after waking the next day, he trotted to the nearest newsstand, picked up several city papers—one caught his eye

due to a big scandal that was uncovered in the police force—
and proceeded to thumb through the apartment listings. After
sifting out the ones with strict covenants, he found several
on the Upper West Side, where he wanted to stay, that were
within his budget. They all required room mating with a total
stranger, but in his current circumstances, he knew he rolled
the dice every time gentle sleep closed his eyes in the middle
of a public park.

Soon he found an apartment: the roommate, a twenty-
something architect who appeared almost as poor as he, would
be in San Francisco on business for six months, but wanted to
keep his apartment in Manhattan. They shook hands, signed
an agreement, and Carl moved in the same day. The move took
one trip: with three bags to carry, it was the easiest move of his
relatively short life.

Then the following afternoon, feeling optimistic, he
decided to call the woman whose name Dasha had given
him. As if daring himself, he made the call, set up the date,
and discovered the stranger would receive him warmly, even
passionately, because they shared the same zodiac sign.

The next evening, he met her at her apartment, five blocks
south of Columbia University.

She called herself Candy, apparently a pet name, he
thought.

She arrived at the door wearing a silk slip dress, bare
feet, and a leather ankle bracelet. In the background, dozens
of candles shimmered around the room—on tables, window
sills, and all atop the counters—and soft music wafted from
stereo speakers that remained hidden from view. She was about
five-foot-five, with reddish-blonde hair down to her shoulders,
dazzling green eyes, and a slender, firm frame that curved

down her waist and beyond. In terms of how she looked, he knew, Candy was a work of art.

"Hi, baby," she said, her voice tender and smoky.

He stepped inside, handing her a bottle of wine. "You exceed your description," he said.

"Yes, I like to exceed expectations," she replied, leading him into the room. "Tell me again, you say you're a Taurus?"

"I am."

"Ooh, yummy," she cooed. "But let me see your ID."

Not sure whether she was joking, he pulled out his wallet and showed her his driver's license.

She leaned her shoulder against him and she read it, running a finger along the card. "Oooo, you are! And May 16th, that's one day sooner than mine! An older man...fuuunzieees." Then she cast him a pouting glance, running a hand along his arm and sauntering toward the couch, where two glasses of wine awaited them. "But do you think two Tauruses will clash?"

He breathed out, eyeing her firmly. "Most likely."

She smiled demurely, then sat on the couch, where he joined her.

"So your horoscope said look for a Taurus?" he asked.

"Oh," she said, taking a sip of her drink, "Venus is rising but the whole world's turned upside down, and it's going to get wild," she purred. "But my horoscope said grab hold of your nearest Taurus and *enjoy the ride*," she said, eyes burning into his.

Aggressive, he thought. "But what's in it for you?"

"I need some love potion," she said, stinking her double-entendre into his heart. "And then I'll feel better. But only then. And you, baby-waybee, are going to be my bull."

"You always primed up like this?"

"Mmm-hmmm," she said, nuzzling her nose against his and pressing her lips into his. Her lips were warm and moist, and their mouths stuck together as they kissed once, passionately, her neck arcing back, both exposed and delicate.

With things going so well, he sank her back into the couch, holding her closely, rubbing his fingers along the smoothness of her back. He took her glass from her, and she moaned softly, loving his control. But as they continued, and without his full awareness, she began to break free, having wishes of her own, and while locked in their embrace, she slipped her hand over the couch, fumbled around the shelf behind it, and seized a candle, raised it over his neck, then poured an allotment of singeing wax down his neck.

"Ow! Damn, what was that? That hurt!" he said.

She smiled an evil grin.

He pulled back, incredulous, staring at her with wide-open eyes. "You bitch! You just poured hot wax on me!" he exclaimed, seeing the weapon in her hand from the corner of his eye. "What the hell?"

"Don't you like my aggression, my everlasting *Taurus*?" she insisted, nudging closer.

"That was so unexpected. You didn't even warn me," he said, shocked and amazed.

She frowned, putting on a false air of hurt.

"What kind of person would do that?"

"Maybe...I don't know...the same kind who'd kiss a total stranger like that?" she replied, somewhat humbled. "Don't mind me. That's part of the package. Call me a caster of spells," she said, moving closer again.

He shifted away. "Listen, before we continue. If we continue. I mean, you pulled that stunt at exactly the wrong time—"

"Exactly the right time," she said, inching closer. "You're feeling frustrated? Here, let me see if I can help."

Concerned over what she might do if he gave her *that*, he held up his hand. At this point, the spell was broken, anyway, and he began scrambling to think, having conceded his reason only moments before.

"I'm going to win you over," she said, getting upset. "Don't you realize? Our birthdays are one day apart, and on exactly the day they predicted…when they said my one, true love would walk into my life…here you are. And I can feel the chemistry…it's so obvious. Let me take things from here. I know you're feeling shy. Maybe you're not ready for me…and my rivers of tears…my darkest emotions…yet. I can be flexible. But you're mine now. Alllll mine."

She's insane, he thought, hair rising on the back of his neck.

Unconvinced by his reluctance, she slid closer on the couch. "I will drag my body through mud for you, I will slide down mountains of ice for your love. I will die for you. Breathe for you. Live out my deepest passions, fantasize about you morning and night, I will—"

"Stop!" he said, not able to control himself and flabbergasted to learn he'd arrest a woman so in the throes of passion, especially when he'd lived long in deficit. His level of fear rising, he stood up, preparing to excuse himself.

"Don't go!" she screamed, pointing a finger at his chest. "You will not leave until I say you can leave!"

Carl gulped. His only consolations were his ability to walk out the same door through which he came and the likelihood she'd alarm the neighbors if matters too a turn for the worst.

She leaped up; his heart leaped, in kind.

Enraged and trembling, she raced for the kitchen, where she grabbed a meat cleaver. "Let me help you!" she cried, moving towards him. "I can show you we're meant to be."

"If we're meant to be," he said, holding his ground but preparing to run, "then take me to another planet!"

"I can arrange that!" she cried, wild-eyed and mad.

"And I'm outta here!" he said to no one in particular. Then he broke off into a run toward the door. She tried to intercept him, but he ducked, she swung, but he threw out a leg, knocking her off balance, and proceeded to undo the latch and slide around the door before she could hit him, while his heart pounded at a furious pace. He slipped onto the staircase and leaped, with all his might, onto the first landing, then careened around the banister and headed down the next flight.

"I own you forever! I'm your destiny, baby!" she roared.

But by this time, he was already at the front door and not listening.

The terrified man, too shaken to think, wheeled himself onto the street, turned south, then raced down the sidewalk as fast as he could go.

(2)

Sitting astride a cloud, thousands of feet above the unraveling scene, with feet dangling over the puffy edge, Dasha popped open her fright-filled eyes. "There! At last...I hear him leaving now. Oh, I can't bear watching this! I should have flown to the wrong side of the moon! Ew....oh! What have I done? My poor, mortal flame: my dear Marik burns in me so, yet I'm the fool, sending a man I love into the arms of another woman only to watch him suffer so! This was not my intention, of course. Hm. Or was it? Perhaps I needed to make matters even. To take his kiss with me and go, forever consummated. Is that possible? Poof...poof. Such silliness. Of course not. What am I thinking? I saw this man in distress and here I am to rescue him. But this awful woman! A thousand boils on her face! I'm in the world now, ha! I can sense these thoughts again. Heaven, this is not. Do I not feel myself slipping? Don't I deserve to be punished for this? Never mind now. I must fly down to him at once and see if I can mend this terrible mess I've made! Down I must fly! Into the flesh once again! Such pain awaits me! May God forgive me!"

Down she flew; into her body she went.

Upon returning to his apartment, Carl found Dasha waiting for him on the sofa. Legs daintily crossed, hands folded on her lap, and face sheepish but beaming, she seemed glad to see him. She bounced a leg over her other knee, expectant and lively, and the color in her cheeks, last time so drawn, had returned to their primrose glory. Indeed, she looked smashing, but in his frenzied state of mind, he overlooked her beauty, seeing only disgust over her little prank.

"You almost got me killed!" he said, drawing to a halt upon seeing her, gasping for air from the long sprint home. "That woman was a psycho!"

Although she maintained composure, her contorted cheeks conveyed a need to defend herself. "And you speak this way with a lady?" she said, slyly curling her nose upward. "I'm afraid I'm not aware of such people called psychos. But it didn't go well, that I can see. She threw herself at your feet?"

"Yes, and then some!" he complained.

"Was she pretty?"

Panting and leaning forward, as if to point at her, he nodded. "Pretty crazy. But yea, she was striking. And quite the hot pants, too. For a moment there I thought you were onto something."

She smiled subtly, relishing his mood, which stirred her soul with remembrance. "You have a lady who is beautiful and wants you as her own, and you did what?" she inquired.

"Ran like hell!"

She blushed. "I see. So much for finding The One this way. But you got a date. See? It's out there. And she didn't hurt you physically?"

He collapsed his arms by his side, eyes agape, continuing to glare. "No. No, she didn't. So I suppose I'm supposed to be glad she didn't carve me like a turkey and eat me for brunch?"

Dasha shook her head, sympathetically. "A tempest in a teapot you are. No wonder she liked you so much. But listen, I am truly sorry she turned into such a rotten apple. I had no idea. There was no way of knowing. But I'm thinking about this...hmmm...and there's much to be thankful for. You're not stuck with this wench, that's number one. But number two, you dumped her. Aha! Is this not excellent?"

"Faintly," he winced.

"Let me ask you, my dear Marik. If you're seeking Ms. Right as, after all, most men will do on occasion...and perhaps all the time in some inner way...and someone arrives who has been selected for you by Venus herself, or Aphrodite, if you will...this is your ideal match of body and soul, I might add...as aligned by moon and stars and all that is beyond until the end of time...and you *reject* her. What if you give her no explanation and do this in a cruel, even vicious, way? Won't that tear the fabric of the universe?"

"I don't follow you. Enough of this nonsense!" he exclaimed, nearly breathless. "Just tell me. Are you some kind of phantom from my past? Did I live a past life? I'm really wondering now.

The dreams, my feelings of déjà vu, your consistent appearances out of thin air: either I'm losing my marbles, and that's certainly possible, or else something magic is upon me. And I want to know more. Much more," he said, finding a chair and studying her beaming face closely. "For someone who almost set me up for murder, you sure don't look very contrite."

She waved a hand dismissively. "Oh, I am, I am. But you were not going to die. I peeked at your num...never mind. I don't tell such hallowed secrets. Can't, you know. By heavens, it's the rule. It was hard enough getting permission to come here and rescue my poor puppy."

He grunted in agony. "So what are you, visiting from the other side? If so, for what? To torment me with your barbs... your games...your tricks? Are you demon or angel?"

"The latter. That's my intention, at least. Cupid, oh, if only you would rescue me," she lamented, "and strike your poison dart in his heart! And if you miss his heart, then shall you, as God is my witness, shoot mine, instead, for my misery."

He looked her up and down.

"Forgive me, here I am in your modern world and, oh, where's forest sprite when I need it? Hm. I don't know. There's nothing magic here at all except me, and my wand, and— nothing."

"So you don't exist, you're telling me? You're only a figment of my imagination?"

"*Lese majeste*! A fiery man!" she exclaimed, eyes aglow. "Have you considered opening your heart to my possibility, at least? Of course, I cannot divulge myself to this world, or suddenly the whole world might lose faith. You know how that works, right? If the sun shines all day and night, then you know there is sun. But if it disappears every night, then only the faithful will prepare for the next day. And it's true; your life is like nighttime right now. Your pride, your honor, the very fiber of your identity, have been snatched by thieves in the night. It's an injustice, and you must fight! Are you not enraged to the point of cannon fire? Do you feel powerless? Is that it? Do you feel oppressed? I'm here to release you! That, my dearest Marik, I say with all my heart," she added, her voice turning more sincere, less prim, once again. "Yet retrieve you at the same time. Is it worth fighting for something so intangible? Something you cannot hold in your arms? Hm. I wonder this myself."

He leaned forward, resting his arms on his knees and watching her closely. "Not in my future, but you know my past. Tell me more. I need to know."

"It's impossible for me to say. That would be against all the regulations of my furlough, if you will." She looked hopelessly vulnerable now.

Anxious, he moved closer, wanting to kiss her.

She shuddered and winced, but her face sparkled, too, revealing her feelings. She held up a hand. "Marik...I cannot. As much as I might wish, these feelings...I'd forgotten. I did not anticipate this. But darling, I must give you freedom...to seek all the love you may have in this life. My world and yours, they're so different."

Tears welled up in his eyes. "Come on. I can see it. You've fallen for me," he said, teasing her. "I love you. You love me. Why can't we consummate our love? I feel this...infinite urgency...to do so, before you're gone for good! When will I see you again?" He began to feel mad with passion.

She smiled faintly, attempting to calm his spirits. "Soon enough. Now I have one more power to share with you. All I can say is this: in three days hence, my dear, enter your dreams. I'll give you this potion to sprinkle on your head," she said, handing him a vial. "Have it before bed. It's nothing to harm you, but it will fire your imagination. This you will see…then you will understand my position…even thank me for coming!" She stood, pointing herself on her toes, and with a wave of her wand, she opened her arms with sumptuous eyes. "I'm here for you. Come and take me, my dearest," she added, heaving a sigh.

He moved closer, but again she brushed him off.

Beginning to wave her wand, she whispered to herself, "But first, I'll need to find where his heart resides. Am I projecting a former man on this man's soul? I have no idea! What does this man truly desire? *Tant pis! Tant pis!* Hm. A disguise. Yes, I need a disguise!" At this juncture, having said all she needed to say and having crafted a plan, she rapped her wand once more in his direction, as if to bless and to freeze, and with a magnificent twirl, she swirled the little star in the air, brought it gently to her left shoulder, then tapped. And as quickly as she had, she winced, then crinkled her nose, and,
Bing!

CHAPTER TWENTY TWO

Carl worked his job at half speed, having remained at his post for three-and-a-half straight hours and knowing his mind belonged elsewhere. During the previous rush, he completely forgot to take a break. He looked around him, wiped the counter, and tried not to think much.

With memories of Dasha vivid, the young man went about his chores with a rising sense of strength, determination and freedom in his soul. *Wish I could have her all the time,* he thought. *Why does she keep coming back, even under my circumstances? She doesn't care I'm a washed up programmer at all. I know I've fallen in love with her. I'll allow myself that thought, however impossible it seems. No one can take a thought away or censure it. And I wonder... wouldn't it be special to consummate our deal? If we had one moment, one moment of truth, we'd know it, and we'd have it forever. But forever, what's that? Ridiculous. My mind plays tricks on me with Dasha. If I told anyone else, they're think I've flown the coop for sure. But something else is happening. It's not that I believe so much, or lost my ability to question. No...I think if anything I question still more.*

The outside door swung open.

Then a figure entered the room, spoke to the bouncer, and proceeded to approach the bar. Carl noticed, casually, but thought nothing of it until this person, quiet and modest in demeanor, stepped into the light.

Carl stopped cleaning. *A friar?*

There in a frock, golden cross dangling from his neck and his face shrouded in darkness stood a monk who, as far as Carl could tell, seemed parched enough. *Maybe he wants a drink*, Carl wondered, and sure enough, within seconds the mysterious visitor saw him, drew in a long, deep breath, and sauntered to the counter. He shuffled to the end of the bar, on the side closest to the corridor leading to the kitchen and bathrooms, chose a seat, and leaned his shoulders over the oakwood shine.

"Vodka, straight up," he said, speaking in as deep a voice as possible.

Startled, Carl looked at the dark figure, the shadow veiling his face from sight, and asked himself why an obvious man-of-the-church would be here, in this bar, on a Friday night. But as a Catholic, he reminded himself there were no prohibitions against drinking in the monastery, per se, and moreover there were no explicit rules concerning the orientation of the denizens of said institutions, so he addressed him in as nonchalant a manner as possible.

"What brand?"

"Stolichnaya," the stranger replied.

Carl shook six ounces of Stoli in a tumbler with crushed ice, filtered the elixir into a glass, and popped the drink onto the bar top. "Six dollars."

"You would charge a man of the cloth for a drink?"

"I'd charge St. Bartholomew himself," Carl responded, tapping the bottle with his index finger.

"He would give you drink if you were thirsty." Acting annoyed, the friar reached underneath the sack-like garment, grabbed a wool sack from his pocket, and pulled out six one-dollar coins. He stacked them on the counter with a click. "Donations," he said.

Raising an eyebrow, Carl swept the coins into his free hand. "Haven't seen these in a while," he observed. "So tell me, I'm curious. What brings a monk to these parts on a Friday night? Joining the fray...saving souls?"

"In order to save souls, one needs to be where they need saving," he said, bowing his head and sipping. "Do you speak this way because you need to be saved?"

Carl shrugged, then curious where this would lead, he began wiping the counter again, trying to place the voice, which sounded vaguely familiar. "Not really. It's not my soul that needs saving. My life here on Earth that's a mess, but I could write a whole book about that. Anything you can do to help? Huh? Any connections up there? Have a direct line?" he teased, hoping to elicit some wit from within the mien.

The friar continued staring down. "We all have a direct line, of course, but as for matters of this world, you may be on your own. I can't second-guess the one upstairs. Tried to do it once, twice...but ended up in a tizzy. Life's too stressful already."

"Even in a monastery?"

"You ever live in self-denial? What do you think I am, a martyr?"

At this point, several men burst out laughing over a bawdy joke, and the noise picked up as the band returned for its next set. Carl leaned on the bar, his head inches away from the friar, and proceeded to speak loudly through the noise, straining his ears as best he could.

The man seemed unperturbed by the pyrotechnics around him.

"Need any advice? Love interests?" the monk asked. "Fifty cents a pop. You might do better with me than, you know...a horoscope."

Carl shivered uncontrollably. "You're not kidding," he replied, his voice turning more sincere. "You have no idea how much trouble that's gotten me into recently."

"Really?"

"Really."

Hidden underneath the hood, the monk said nothing, but Carl could tell his mind was engaged. "Let me ask you something," Carl continued, suspicious and wanting to dig deeper. "How do you stay...you know, celibate? Or do you? Do you get none...never mind, reminds me of an old joke."

"I'm fortunate because I love God," the friar said, taking a swig.

"No one else?"

This made the friar look uncomfortable, although with the face hidden under the shroud, it was hard for Carl tell. "Maybe one."

"Who?"

"A being of exceptional elusiveness, yet with a warm heart, and strong."

"Who is she? Or...um," Carl continued, remembering the nature of the bar, "you know...he?"

"It is a he, if you must know. But it's not as it seems."

"Wait. How so? What, you mean the love's platonic? Or you're a woman dressed up as a guy, or what?"

The friar took a long pause, contemplating an answer.

"Brother. These are temporal things you describe...it's all for mortals. Mine is neither platonic nor of the flesh. It's infinite. Although...I must say, it is replenished by the infinite as well. To say otherwise would be blasphemy to me. This love interest of mine is temporary. I must leave soon. You understand...sometimes you meet someone, then the storm passes."

Intrigued, Carl leaned closer, pressing his hands against the counter. "That reminds me of my own love interest. Remarkable."

The friar shook, as if excited, then sipped his vodka. "Love interest? Then I suspect God brought us to this time and place for a reason. What about this love? How do you feel?"

"Drives me crazy. She comes and goes like the wind."

"Oh, gracious! That's...what a pity. But remember, love and madness are nearly the same thing. Your dilemma is not surprising. Please...have sympathy and understanding for her. Have her comings and goings made you feel shy or cynical about love, or do you still cling to hope?"

Carl scratched his head. After looking around to make certain no one needed him urgently or might be eavesdropping on their conversation, he continued, his voice more insistent. "I'm still hopeful. Now tell me...I'm sorry, I don't have your name."

The friar sighed. "Francisca."

"Francisca. I see. Your voice sounds funny. Not that it's a bad thing. But anyway, my name's Carl."

The man stopped drinking. "Tell me more about this love interest. What is your impression of her? Is she fair? Charming? Graceful?"

"Yea, you could say that. But she's also someone I hardly know."

Francisca slumped his shoulders. "Oh."

"Anyway, tell me, and I know this sounds crazy...do you believe in ghosts...déjà vu...past lives? Is this consistent with your beliefs?"

"Spirits? Yes! Yes! Do they visit? I don't know. I've never been visited. Have you?" he inquired, leaning closer. "I'm following someone's trail."

Carl leaned closer, resting his elbows on the bar. "Who? A girl? Maybe I've seen one…but recently it's more like haunted than visited."

The friar gasped. "Yes, continue…what do you think of her? This soul?"

"Attractive, but like everything else I want in my life, I can't have her. She's always running off."

"But my brother, we are all running off! This is the way it is…Yesterday I counseled a woman who's husband of 50 years died of cancer. So sad."

The band struck up a tune, and the place began to rock again. Having trouble hearing now, Carl leaned closer, holding his mouth against the man's hood.

Francisca continued in muted, noncommittal tone. "As a monk, my perspective is to pray. As a human, my perspective is to wonder. But tell me, why do you look for constancy? What are you seeking? Are you looking for everlasting and unconditional love? Oh, the burdens! What if she disappears, and you're calling out to her…say she's sick, or falling from your grasp into the love-stricken ocean? Will you get on with your life or will you cling to her image instead of God's?"

"Call me romantic," Carl admitted.

"One of those. I see. You torture yourself."

Carl shook his head. "You make it sound hopeless."

"Not at all," Francisca replied, warm to the topic. "It's joyous! That is, when we accept we're dealing with mortals. You are mortal, yes? God made you this way?"

"Have you ever met an immortal?"

"Maybe," the man said, rising from his seat. "I've met you."

"Hm. But I hardly think you know me."

Francisca laughed. "Oh, but I do, I do! That's your mistake. The problem, dear sir, is you may not know yourself. And if you don't, you can grasp at any tin bit of advice that comes your way." The hood moved closer. "Don't get me wrong, though. I admire your pluck. I've seen your work from afar, and it's charming. Really. Keep the faith! And don't take any wooden nickels," he said, tossing a tip on the counter.

Carl eyed him carefully. *Who in the world is this?*

"In the world?

"I'm here not through trick...of mind, world or nation;
Whether real or imagined...here...see God's creation."

Startled, Carl's eyes misted. "Um...you read my mind." His voice sounded scared.

"Call it a gift...for you. Now I must leave your world." The mysterious customer thanked him for the drink and left the bar. Bemused, Carl watched this peculiar character pass through the door and into the dim light of the street.

Carl left the place two hours later. And as he locked up the door with Isabelle, his fellow bartender remarked, "Don't go chasing your dreams too far, now. We need you back next Friday...because I have someone I want you to meet."

"Oh," Carl said, noting her urgency but feeling too exhausted to care. "I meet a lot of people lately."

He walked home.

In the wee hours of morning, as a pink moon shined through his bedroom window—at once intimate and warm— Carl tucked himself into bed. Compared with the recent, hard accommodations, this place felt infinitely more restful, and he fell into a deep sleep, whereupon he slipped to enchantment. Eyes flickering and body atremble, he fell into a world of subconscious, where reality and the ever-stretching truth mixed and matched.

He found himself riding a steed through fields of mud.

The horse's hooves kicked damp earth in all directions as it galloped.

"C'mon, Thunder!" he cried, addressing his mount by name.

The animal continued to charge across wide-open plain, then past groves of sycamore trees, the last checkpoint at the river's edge. He saw a ferry ahead and the captain, a kindly old fellow whom locals called by his last name, Hastings. The gentleman, whose hearing was faint, didn't hear the ruckus charging in his direction, and heading for his controls, slipped the watercraft into gear. The engine began to chug.

At this point, Carl pulled up to the water's edge and waved furiously. "Hastings! Don't leave me on my parents' farm!"

Seeing him at last, the old man waved his hat, as if to say don't worry, I see you, and proceeded to lower the gangway. With this, Carl walked the horse onto the boat, found a spot in the corner, leaned over to shake his friend's hand, and proceeded to ride over the choppy, slow-moving waters.

Several hours later, which passed like a minute, Carl and his ride left the craft, and with wonderment and awe in his soul, the dream shifted to new and unexpected venues.

CHAPTER TWENTY THREE

Russia 1830

(1)

After dismounting, they tied their mounts to a picket fence that stretched from the hill to their north to an alpine brook, some 100 arshin to their south.[xiv] "Remember...pull down your flintlock and fire when ready," said Captain Federov, his wide mustache fluttering in the wind, which swept over the steppes and onto their grassy plain like ghosts fleeing from their graves. Three other men watched the recruit, who would fire his first shot at this moment. For their amusement, the men had set up an Ace of Hearts as the makeshift target; they lacked the resources of a full garrison. Their fort, hidden beyond hills and evergreens that dotted the lands around them, lay three versta to the east.[xv]

Marik Andropov, wearing his dashing uniform, a sword, and leather boots, raised his pistol, clasped the latch downward, aimed, and closed one eye. As he'd been taught, he took a quick breath and held it. Wincing, he grimaced, zeroed his focus on the target, shifted the barrel a centimeter up and to the left, then squeezed the trigger. The gun recoiled into the air, spewing his hand with stinging powder and smoke.

The musket ball sailed past the card. He'd missed.

The men laughed.

"You mimic your aim in love," scolded Gregorio Volkovensky. In his late twenties with pepper-black hair and a scruffy shock that he swept to the side, and with deep-set, blue eyes that were at once intelligent and taunting, he chided Marik with a grin. Then he pulled a tarot card from his trouser pocket. "Perhaps your marksmanship would improve if we placed misfortune in its place?" he said, holding the card toward the bull's-eye. A cavalry poruchik one level above Marik's rank of wachtmeister, the officer gave his comrade a collegial, but condescending, slap on the back.[xvi]

"If my aim's true in battle," Marik replied with a mischievous pinch in his cheeks, "you'll wish me luck for your salvation."

Gregorio turned crimson while the other men guffawed.

"My lady," said Marik, ramming another ball down the muzzle, "will be lucky if she draws me instead of the fops her mother parades through their parlor."

"Your lady," replied Gregorio with a tone of censure, "would be more your lady if she replied to your letters. At the moment, I'd say, if I may be so intrusive, she's more a figment of your imagination."

Marik raised his pistol and took aim. "This may be true," he said, "but I'd rather dream of fairies than marry this army."

"Don't be certain they're separate," said the captain, chuckling at the love-struck young man and admiring his willingness to spar. "Fire when ready," he commanded.

Marik squeezed the trigger, releasing the flintlock, and a furious musket ball sailed at the target. This time it grazed the upper-right edge of the card, chipping the corner.

The men applauded politely, slowly, and with measured surprise.

"You see," said Marik, grinning broadly, breathing deeply, then speaking on a fresh rush of air. "After two times' persistence, I've landed my target." To the other men, he was beginning to sound cocky.

Gregorio, not to cede the last word to a subordinate, rested his arm over his colleague's shoulder. "No, my dear wachtmeister, you've made an impression, but you missed your true target. You failed to pierce the heart, and when it comes to women and battle, a mere graze won't suffice."

The men chuckled at Marik, who placed the pistol back in its sheath and clapped the dust off his hands. "Also true, but often in this realm, as you might know, the most creeping of wounds is also the most artful."

With this, the men roared with laughter, and Gregorio, whose face blushed again, managed a wry smile. "Congratulations, then, my friend. If your wit has wings, now we can await her letter."

Despite Marik's confidence, resiliency and ever-upbeat nature, however, two seasons passed and no letter arrived. In fact, it became a running joke in the barracks. When mail arrived, a junior officer would summon the troops in the square, shout out a quick drill, then announce they had correspondence in the bag.

"Except for our comrade, Marik," he would announce at the very end, after rummaging through the bag, even shaking it upside down for extra effect. "Whose aim will be true when his expectations become truthful," and so on.

Ever intrepid and defiant, to the point of encouraging more ribbing, Marik continued to have faith in his distant paramour who, he reasoned, could easily settle into the fort, and later some quaint dacha, as his life circumstances changed.

(2)

Marik maintained a melancholy relationship with his heart. When added to persistent doubts regarding the worthiness of his cause in this remote outpost, he blasted rebels and outlaws to Kingdom Come with reluctance: all to maintain order on the frontier for distant authorities who, although they'd never visit these lands, considered the territory strategic property.

Complicating matters was a peasant girl named Olga who frequented the fort's town and barracks. Although they gained an instant affection for each other, she told Marik the men on the base were ill-mannered and rude. With pale-blonde tresses, eyes of cobalt, and a quiet yet complex personality, she seemed aware of his interest despite the lady he maintained in St. Petersburg. So despite his decent pay, relative social status, and striking appearance, she veiled her reciprocal feelings. Her mother had warned her explicitly: "Take care of your heart with these visiting soldiers, because when the insensitive debauch takes it, what will you give to the man who truly loves you?"

Olga's mother insisted she had seen this before.

They began to walk through gardens and fields when she visited. The older men noticed at once, but blinded by his passion for Dasha, and not wanting to accept anything less than his full heart's desire, Marik maintained a warm distance of friendship, making Olga admire his restraint even more.

In their jaunts through the countryside, Olga surprised Marik with her outbursts of joy and good humor, her incessant charm, and the friendly way in which she greeted his colleagues, all of whom admired the young lady. Behind Marik's back, the men whispered that, although he had her by station, she was the better catch for this hopeless dreamer, and she'd be wise to choose another suitor. Their envy and scorn, matched by their admiration for this warmhearted soul, soon led them to loathe the young officer Marik. They considered him repulsive, and this disgust showed itself on their faces as they addressed him, which she naturally noticed, but dismissed. She had already made up her mind. While his comrades were more dangerous, more duplicitous, and more sly, Marik maintained an endearing and straightforward innocence. She felt if his passions ever turned to her, they would last a lifetime.

Scarcely the fool, Marik was aware of the men's whispers and slights, but as a soldier of His Majesty's army first, and as a sensible man to boot, he was loathe to respond to innuendo that would, invariably, culminate in a duel. His rank might not survive such a mark on his record, and moreover, he realized, grim death would guarantee he'd never see his St. Petersburg damsel again.

So he bit his tongue and trudged on.

Olga loved his reticence, as she could fill in his thoughts as she wished, and instead she infused their walks with songs, laughter, and stories of youth. Once she climbed an apple tree, ambushing her friends with the fruit of knowledge she said. "Perhaps you should let me aim your batteries," she said, giggling. She told him stories of spying on travelers who stopped in their cottage for a night's rest, and recounted tales of myth related to the surrounding timberlines. With an imagination so vivid and a soul so merry and bright, Marik struggled to hold Olga at bay against his need for resolution from Dasha.

In his quiet moments alone, he gazed at the fields where they traipsed, his heart solemn and dark, not wanting to let Dasha, his angel, go. In his mind's eye, he revisited the parlor where he last met Dasha, over and over, trying to gain some sense, some glimpse, of her intentions, and churning through phrase after phrase, he searched furiously and in vain for a convincing hint or suggestion.

But rumors of a new uprising arrived, and they began drilling intensively.

Up before dawn—marching, shooting, riding, and fencing—they practiced their full range of tactics, and with the help of books on battlefield tactics, but most of all with the experience of their officers, they analyzed every move they could conceive the rebels might make. Along the way, Marik felt a stir in his soul. How could he be so adept in war—outflanking, out-training, and outfighting a worthy opponent—when he felt so helpless with Dasha? Why was there not a book on how to convince a woman to love you when she might or marry you when she won't? He found himself perplexed by these questions, yet it was not a matter of gaining answers to the questions themselves, all of which he found trivial; instead, these ruminations pertained solely and specifically to Dasha's much-overdue letter.

In there would be his answer.

What would she say? How would she respond?

Marik had written her eleven times since their last meeting, and his weary heart merely needed an answer—any answer—so he could move on with his life. He scrolled back in his mind: the last time he saw her face, he remembered, she welcomed him into her home. Her face shined brighter than Venus; she must have been flattered by his attention. She spoke in a whisper, as lovers and confidants do. Surely, he thought, a woman of her honor would not signal such feelings without interest. If she did, she would make herself a scoundrel, and who of such lofty station would lower herself to that wretched level? *There must be something between us*, he thought, *otherwise, she would not have received me.*

As the months wore on, he maintained hope for a letter. Occasionally, he saw signs, too: a shooting star, a break in the rain, a shot landing true. Such occurrences portended a happy outcome for his plight during the long, winter months, as snow blanketed the hinterland in its milky-white glaze, then in spring when ducks flew overhead, returning to home and hearth. But although day fell to night and moisture turned like clockwork from snow to rain to sleet and back to snow again, her post never arrived.

"Perhaps her father has intercepted your letters," suggested Gregorio one summer night as Marik, lost in thought, sat by the windowsill of his cabin, teacup in hand. "How long will you wait? It's been almost two years. Does she not abandon you in these frigid wastelands, where your only warmth is the drink in your hand, the roar of the fire, and the animal pelt on which you rest?"

He sighed, remembering the sparkling life behind Dasha's eyes. "You're right, Gregorio, but as long as I hear winds on this sullen frontier, I'll listen for her voice. It's odd," he added, looking outside, "but last night I dreamed I was an American. Someday I'll take her there."

CHAPTER TWENTY FOUR

(1)

By early May, although the snow and ice had faded to withering grass, the battalion had settled into a routine of eating, hunting, sleeping, cleaning their guns, and not much else. The boredom was excruciating and numbing, but occasional skirmishes with a band of renegades that haunted the area kept them, at least, on the lookout. A wider conflagration had developed in the hinterlands to the east, where imperial troops had begun an offensive, and rumors persisted they would soon need to decamp and join the fray.

One silvery night while drinking by firelight, a rider approached the commander's house, the place where they most often gathered, hopped off his horse, and clambered to the main door, on which he knocked insistently. Once inside, he collapsed in a chair, asked for a glass of water, and read them a letter:

> Major General Ivan Nikonov of the 72nd
> Regiment insists on your immediate
> presence to support anti-insurgent offensives
> in the east. Leave a small security
> detail at your fort and proceed at once.
> We await your arrival. Respectfully yours,
> A. Ivanov.

"Marik will get his first taste of war," jibed Gregorio, his voice supercilious and cold. "Perhaps his wait for the letter will be resolved in blood." A more spurious man might have demanded seconds and an appointment at dawn, but Marik wrote the barb off as so much blather, understanding the consequence of fighting among troops.

The pressing issue became how to say goodbye to Olga.

She arrived in the afternoon, as she usually did, and as soon as she saw Marik's face, she knew he was shipping out. Her contagious smile, so often comforting, suddenly turned awkward and stiff. Noting this deterioration in his damsel, he couldn't help feeling like a wretch. He took her hand, rubbing her palm gently against his, and told her in no uncertain terms he would miss their walks and conversations, but this only made her feel worse; tears welled in her eyes and his heart rended with pain and self-loathing. They talked for hours on end until the sun began setting in the distance. Then knowing she needed to go home, they parted with a kiss—one of love tasted but never consummated.

The soldiers rode off to the front the following morning, two batteries trailing behind their sturdiest horses. Along the way Marik, otherwise anxious to test his mettle in combat, lamented his parting with Olga, but soon found himself stewing over Dasha's failure to write. He wondered whether he'd see her again.

Has she found someone else now? he asked himself.

Even more tragic, he realized, was the possibility he might lose his life at the precise time she decided she loved him. What a tragic end it would be, leaving her in his wake to pine over his letters all her living days, longing for him within her quaking, trembling soul!

And the rationale for Marik's life of war, overall, remained opaque. Although he felt compelled to fight for Dasha's safety and honor, and certainly for his beloved country, without her by his side, it seemed as if it were all for naught, and for this reason, he feared Russia itself had abandoned him, leaving him to fight for a scrap of pay, a warm meal, and little else.

Marik's garrison reconnoitered with the other imperial troops as scheduled, and with sullen thoughts in mind, Marik rode his horse around ashen-green forests, preparing his mind for battle. Later, amidst the pother of troops who worked at a furious pace to entrench themselves within eyesight of the rebel fort, he continued to fret. In his new circumstance, it was no longer the separation or the uncertainty of his relations with Dasha that bothered him. Rather, it was the point of his lamentations. *Even if she loves me now,* he thought, *what's the use?* Now hundreds of miles from St. Petersburg, and an honorable discharge many battles away, even an open declaration from her, combined with an agreement to consummate their relationship at the designated church, would pale against his obligation to serve. He'd need to put her off, even promise her nothing. Such was his predicament in time of war.

Still, on many occasions he stayed awake long after the last bugle call, hoping for a heavenly sign or better yet, a smiling soldier announcing he had mail. Even a no, at this point, would satisfy his craving for answers: maybe he needed her out of his life. Maybe he should ride back to Olga, sweep her off her feet and make her an officer's wife. What good was coming out of this endless waiting? And why did he, a young man trapped in the service, burden her with his wish for a life-long commitment? Why not dance the night away, consider her won, and leave her pining for more, taking the affections she bade him as encouragement for his next exploit?

All these day, the letter failed to arrive.

Or so he thought.

One afternoon, eight days into the siege and hours after his garrison arrived, Marik had received her first letter, but the commanding officer, not wanting to agonize or otherwise distract this important young officer, ordered the letter hidden. Only the officers knew of the note, and fearing reprisals, they declined to distribute it. So as dust settled over the garrison and the enemy, who looked increasingly pathetic as the blockade strangled them, Marik despaired.

Matters became even more complex as the iniquitous battle approached when pangs of sympathy for the enemy, whose position appeared hopeless, began to creep into Marik's conscience, not least because he could see in himself, in some ethereal way, mired within the same fate of doom. His life unraveled, like them he could do nothing except fulfill a role: remain in position, take whatever precautions he might, and wait for a response. Furthermore, as the days dragged on Marik increasingly felt her response would be no. This thought, which began to seem an inevitability, clouded his mind with a jaded sense of indignation. But this is the way of the world, and he'd better learn to accept it, he reasoned. Love's a trifling conceit, and everlasting love, the kind where two people stood fated from birth to bond between two souls, seemed nothing more than a tawdry pronouncement of bards and degenerates.

When a battery officer became ill, Marik paced back and forth between their two guns while the attendant feldwebel fretted over issues of placement and aim.[xvii] As a cavalry officer, Marik typically drowned out the cannon fire and charged, but now he had this responsibility on top of everything else and knew that soon the cannons would rage both hot and fearsome

loud. This kept him on edge. Another officer reminded the
greenhorn crew to stand back when firing, as the barrels could
explode, but stood too close himself.

The pounding would take its toll on their ears.

Feeling himself starting to crack, Marik engaged his mind
in more everyday matters as much as he could bear. He cleaned
his gun, fetched buckets of water, boiled water for tea, and
generally did chores he was not required to do simply because
he needed a reprise. Now standing on a rampart, gazing with
binoculars at the sentries at the fort, all of whom had guns
slung over their shoulders, he imagined he would soon need
to either shoot them or be shot. Agonized, he rammed his
sword into the dirt. "The woman of my dreams anguishes
me! Perhaps I'll be better off seeking Olga's hand, if she'll still
take me. Lord knows she has a kind heart. Instead, I live this
life of desperation, hoping one love will scorn her parents...
while I hold the love I can have at arm's length. This vexing
uncertainty...devil take it!"

Several days passed, and in the midst of his deteriorating
state, he still had no letter. Needing an escape from his incessant
stress, he turned his focus onto the rebels. They needed no
sympathy, the troops were reminded, as the Cossacks had
butchered and shot and otherwise menaced the countryside
for almost a year before the crackdown began. Many of his
countrymen perished in the carnage, such that Marik and
his men had orders to identify, arrest, and execute the main
perpetrators. Already, several likely candidates had been
identified; they would be targeted during the raid. Despite the
butchery on the other side, however, Marik remained contrite
over the cruelty of their siege, which affected men, women, and
children alike. The outlaws, faces soiled and thin, seemed eager
to live; they were human, after all. Certainly they huddled

within the safety of their fort, straying only for necessities, and then only in the stillness of night, remaining crouched behind barriers otherwise. At times, they built bonfires and rang out in song, filling the air with lyrical highs; occasionally, their grey patina of work subsided, revealing an easygoing side to their choleric reputation. Some laughed heartily and quite sincerely in the campfire glow, feasting on whatever scraps they had on hand.

This state of affairs persisted for several weeks.

But the eve of battle arrived.

For many imperial soldiers, this represented the first taste of war, and with hundreds of rebels aligned along the battlements of their fort, matters were tense. Marik's horse, sensing the danger, persistently stomped the ground with impatience.

The tactics, as explained in the officers' tent, would be to bombard the fort with cannon fire all night, then launch the cavalry assault at dawn. The sun arced downward in the west, spilling tangerine paint across the sky, and with the Cossack forces under siege and their supplies dwindling—the imperial scouts had noted their enemies' gauntness in periodic reports—the Major General assured his ranks of a swift and total victory.

A rebel flag waved defiantly over the fort, rippling delicately in the breeze.

Once the batteries were aimed and in place, Marik mounted his horse and surveyed the guns scattered along their lines, determining there were a few problems with placement here and there, then reported their readiness to his fellow under-officer, who thanked him for the effort.

The evening was tepid, and the few clouds scattered across the horizon—non-menacing, peaceful, and soft—cast a fragile net of security over the landscape. The night settled into darkness, and at 1:00 AM, they gave the order to fire. Guns raged and blazed across the line as cannon shot flew, smashing into logs, stones, and sand, and exploding in rings of fire. Out of rifle range, the fort's defenders hunkered down, scurrying back and forth while tending to the wounded or running a message, but otherwise they remained calm and eerily silent. The imperial guns hammered the fortress; the bombardment continued all night.

But as the explosions rocked the fortress, and as the agonized screams of men, women, and children wafted into his zone, Marik Andropov's thoughts continued re-centering on Dasha. He tried to block out her image, even the mere suggestion or association of it, but as the guns wrangled on and fires broke out, sending out waves of flesh-scalding heat, and the sounds of cannon fire rocked his soul, he wanted to escape.

He needed to escape.

"Stop...stop these torments," he whispered to himself. "Someone make them go away!"

Thunderous blasts rocked the air, spewing splinters and arms into the sky, all of which landed in heaps of rubble and dust. Hearing the cries of agonized men and listening to the sounds of humanity crying for help, his first instinct was to cover his ears, already stuffed with cotton balls, with his hands. He squeezed his palms against his skull, drowning out more, but it was not enough.

Trembling now, although no one noticed his worsening state, he watched flashes of light, as if in a dream, and barked out orders he could not hear, always ordering his men to stay ready.

Suddenly, a heartrending voice pierced the night.

He became wild with fatigue and anguish.

He glanced up, and there on the plain between the fort and the guns, to his bewilderment and shock, stood Dasha. He blinked, realizing he'd gone mad, but she wouldn't leave. He cried out to her, "Come here, my love! Out of the field! It's dangerous! You'll be safe under my wing!" Fingers outstretched, she ran toward him, guns raging around, explosions rocking the earth around her, braving an ever-present risk of a marksman's shot imperiling her flight.

"We wasted time!" Marik cried.

She tripped, then slumped the ground. He dropped his weapon and ran toward her, but as he approached, bullets whistling overhead, her still form on the ground faded, glowed with a heavenly light, then disappeared.

"Is this my last chance to see her?" he exclaimed, distraught and confused.

Gasping for breath, he ran to the spot where only moments before she'd lain on the earth, threw himself down, and hearing the screams and thunders and horrors of the battlefield, he pulled the cotton from his ears, bringing all the noise and agony to full strength.

He wheeled around and sprinted back to his cannon where, by morning fall, he became deaf.

(2)

Gazing over the ramparts, the men could see the extent of the damage they had caused the previous night. Wooden structures lay in ruins: black smoke rose from ashen ruins into the clear, morning air. Rebels, both adults and children, raced about the battle zone, transporting water to the wounded, tending to makeshift defenses, and arranging themselves into new formations along the front wall, which remained in place here and there. A large hole had been blasted to the right of the gate; where once there had been wooden logs, now there was nothing but smoldering debris and jagged-edged spears.

With the job of softening their opponent complete, Major General Nikonov ordered three, smaller contingents to the side and rear walls, over which the rebels might attempt an escape. In the haze, nervousness and confusion, those who remained facing the main gate shifted in their places, partook in a last smoke, or stared numbly, eyes transfixed and perturbed, at the unfolding horror.

Marik waited among them, hand resting on the saddle, picking out the best path over the top; they would charge in a moment the commander said, and the young man noted how many paces it would take to storm the breach. He would save his musket ball for the last possible moment, he thought, to ensure a clean hit. Ahead and to his left, he spotted two rebels, who were apparently watching him; one pointed while the other nodded. Marik called over two hussars, announcing he would lead them in charge across the leftmost plain. However, unable to hear his own voice, this order seemed strange and unreal to him.

The Cossacks, noting his hand motions, disappeared behind the wall, apparently searching for reinforcements.

The imperial troops would secure the inner buildings and magazine, then round up the rebel leaders for summary execution. The rest would be imprisoned in the fort by a special contingent that would be left behind while the main force continued east, where fighting remained. Sizing up the task, Marik considered the risks manageable, if not wholly certain, and with intrepid spirit, he itched for the fight to begin. Now on the cusp of battle, thoughts of Dasha faded from his mind; his single-minded focus became the importance of seeing this conflict to a conclusion.

At 8:00, the general gave the order to charge. Charging over the ramparts, he broke his horse into a trot, then a run, as his chosen men raced close behind and on either flank. The day was glorious, with silent fields awakening under velvet-pink skies—and on another morning Marik would have noticed. Today, he stared in muted silence as the imperial forces, two thousand strong, closed the vice on the doomed rebels. The ground beneath them shook from the energy of hooves and fear and guns that began popping in staccato fashion as they moved toward the fort. Bodies waddling under the weight of light packs and guns, the Russian cavalry streamed over thick grasses and dusty earth.

The enemy loomed closer, but Marik's soul stood still.

The enemy loomed in the foreground and Marik raised his pistol, eyeing a leader.

Determined to make his one musket ball count, he took careful aim and squeezed out a shot, which hit the leftmost guard instead, toppling him backwards. Two of Marik's men raced several arshin ahead, came to a halt, and holding their horses steady, sent two rounds into the remaining sentry and officer, both of whom slumped over the fort, trickling blood. Marik and his cavalrymen jumped the rubble that was once the wall, then raced toward the town center where several men were surrendering. Other soldiers flooded the gates, firing pistols and brandishing swords as they flew. Within less than a minute of scaling the wall, Marik could see the fight was over. Triumphant and panting for breath, he approached his general, saluted, and announced his corridor was secure.

After rounding up six leaders, the regiment yanked sacks over their heads, marched them to the makeshift gallows, and proceeded to hang them as common criminals. The pall of death hung over the air as the bodies hung from the sky, lifeless and inert. Family members—those who weren't huddled inside—stood outside in shock, some sobbing softly while others were mute.

A grey cloud of smoke filled the atmosphere above as ashes burned.

Marik removed his hat, patted his horse on the neck, and taking in the carnage and wreckage, found a seat on the ground.

And it was not until the following day that he learned the news.

CHAPTER TWENTY FIVE

"Andropov!" announced Major General Nikonov, whose voice echoed about the fort. "Front and center!" Since Marik, ears ringing and damaged, failed to hear him, his comrades on the right and left nudged him. "Go, go! Front and center!" he saw one lip to him. The surprised young man scampered down the line, turned squarely, then proceeded to face his general, whose eyes shined with glory and good humor, and whose face belied affection and sympathy for the young hero, whose face indicated long suffering despite his age.

"Wachmeister Andropov, by authority of His Honorable Emperor himself, and in light of your leadership along the batteries, which softened our enemy irreparably on the eve of battle, I hereby hand you this medal. Congratulations," he said, shaking the man's hand warmly and placing the medal on him.

Receiving this honor, Marik felt his spirit lifting—the world seeming brighter—and with their flag waving over the fort and free-spirited birds gliding further above, he felt, for an instant, he would like to capture a moment of glory. His cheeks flooded with color and his heart, still heavy and anguished, began to beat softly, calming his shattered nerves. He clicked his heels together, saluted, and headed back toward his place among the men.

"Andropov!" announced the general, grinning with glee over the young man's charming ignorance, "come back. We aren't through with you!" Confused laughter spread through the lines.

But not hearing his commander, Marik continued to walk. As he rounded the bend, one of the men stuck out his arm, grabbed the stunned soldier by the shoulder, and pointed toward the general. "That way, fool!" He laughed. Marik's hopes soared. *Could this be the letter?* And turning to face his commander, he saw that indeed something lighter and more soul-stirring was amiss.

General Nikonov, with an ebullient expression of mirth, reached into a pocket, pulled out a tattered letter, and held it, searchingly, toward Marik.

Marik's heart pounded. *Is this from her?* As he stepped quickly and lightly toward the grandfatherly man, he was in his commander's eyes that yes, it was the long-sought letter from Dasha herself. Quickly, he assessed the situation. *It's been opened, and the general's smiling, too!* Marik ran a gritty hand over his chin, jaw dropped. His lips began to tingle. He ripped open the envelope, forgetting it had already been opened, and with trembling hands, his face in a daze and his mouth as dry as wool, he read the following letter:

My Dearest Marik,

Today it rains, and sitting beside the window, moisture streaming down feeble cheeks, I ask myself why, why have we been fated thus? How could a man, whose aura so stirs my beating heart, be distanced by family trifles, circumstances, and war? As God is my witness, I've asked for some break, some sign from heaven, but still nothing arrives. Forlorn and all too lost, I've struggled alone in my stringent palace where guests and diplomats come and go, seeking my hand, and I cannot accept them, if not for your love, then for want of my heart, which I save always for you.

My sister gives her kindest regards, and my tormented mother continues in her vexed state, hoping I'll agree to one of her matches. The heartbreak is getting to her, and I fear for her health, but my father leaves these decisions to her, as he's too busy with his affairs of state. Here I coo like a nightingale for love that is as real as it feels in my soul, yet only a mirage. Perhaps you feel this way, too.

I must go now, for at any time they may burst through my door and discover my letter, and thus my intentions. They're suspicious now, you might know, and they fear this very thing. I will miss home so, despite the desolation I feel here, but yes, yes my love. I will meet you at the church as planned and wed you upon earliest convenience. Make haste, my love! Let's delay no longer. I will await you at the church. I've already arranged matters with the father, with whom I'm scheduled to stay. Take care, I pray for your safety, and God bless. I will be with you always.

Yours forever,
Dasha

Overjoyed and amazed, Marik raised the letter in his hand, cheering the news. The general smiled kindly and knowingly, and once again shook Marik's hand. Eyes bright and deeply aware, the general gave his hero a solemn nod, then spoke in a husky voice. "Go. You're on leave. Marry your woman and bring her to Fort Ivangorod. Here are your new orders," he said, handing Marik a note. "We've brought them to a ceasefire on the frontier. Blessed peace has arrived."

"I can't hear. The guns last night—"

The Major General nodded, then pointed to the orders, and upon reading it, the young man felt overjoyed. "Peace and I get my beloved Dasha. I must be in heaven!" he cried to himself, tears welling in his eyes.

Quickly growing impatient, having other matters at hand, the general shooed him away. "Go, go," he insisted, "there's no time for dalliance." With a salute, Marik raced back in place, finished the ceremony, and too anxious to wait for morning, mounted his horse in the calm of evening, said his goodbyes to his mates, and galloped under the starlight toward his awaiting nuptials.

Hard and fast he rode, only stopping when the horse could bear it no more. The countryside raced past him: dark forests, an occasional cottage, a wayward fox, or a peeking bear. The jubilant lover speeded ahead.

The first night he stayed at an inn, where he garnered a hot meal. The second he slept on bales of hay, leaving fifty kopecks for a grateful family of serfs, and on the third he slept under a pine tree, his horse tethered beside him, but as the fifth and final day arrived, he noticed clouds rolling in from the north. A late spring thunderstorm approached, and within several hours both horse and man were soaked with rain. The mud, now thick and impassable, proved more than his horse could bear, and needing to rest, Marik found a grove of trees, walked underneath it, and proceeded to wait. Lightning struck the horizon in the distance while the ground shook with thunder, and with a timorous heart, he lamented the delay. Would she wait for him? How long had she been there? When could he finally pass through?

Over the ensuing hours, he grew famished, too. His horse was exhausted. He waited this way for the night, which seemed an eternity. Only in the morning, as dark clouds receded again over the horizon, did he continue his journey through the wet and sullen landscapes, pursuing love as far as the journey might take him, but this time at a slower pace, lest he lose his mount beneath him.

He reached the church the following afternoon. Things were quiet. No horses stood outside, no people stirred on the grounds, and if it weren't for a single candle burning in the window, the place would have seemed deserted.

By now, some of his hearing had returned. He could hear close noises, when loud enough, but higher pitches, especially from a distance, eluded him, and an incessant ringing remained, a constant reminder of his impetuous decision.

Approaching the church on his mount, who strained slowly ahead, his heart sank at the thought, ever-present in his mind, that she might not be there—that someone would intercept her, or she might otherwise change her plans. Feeling cautious and alert, he rolled off his horse, hitched it to a post, stepped to the front door, and knocked.

The sound echoed inside, and at first, no one stirred.

But after a minute had passed, he heard footsteps approaching, boards on the floor creaking in kind, and with a rustling of bracelets and a pop of the latch, the door swung open, revealing an elderly woman. It must be the parishioner's wife, he reasoned, politely removing his hat and bowing. "My name is Mark Kuzmin Andropov," he said, crisp and respectful, "and I'm here to see Dasha. She *is* here?"

Grey-haired and weary, but with a gentle expression, she responded, "I'm afraid the lady has been moved to Vladavoosk, to the south. She waited two months, then when you hadn't arrived, she developed a fever. We were concerned, of course, and the doctor sent her to convalesce. We hear she's been faring well, but I can't guarantee how long they'll keep her. She's run astray from her family, as you know."

Marik squeezed his hat. "Forgive me, but how do I get there?" he asked, feeling despondent.

"You'll follow the road on which you came until the next town, then bear south on hundred-twenty versta. The road ends at one point, you should know, and your best bet will be to travel by sun or stars. The lands are monotonous, and I fear you might become lost."

Thanking her, he asked for one night's room and board, then resolved to leave in the morning. He stayed up half the night, his earlier feelings of despair creeping back in, testing his faith and sending him into fits of worry. The strain was nearly unbearable.

When daybreak struck, he left the woman two rubles, which she took with pleasure, packed his solitary bag, and rode his mount down the dusty, narrow road to the next town. His heart was consumed with guilt over not standing by her side during this time of illness. *Lord knows where this fever could take her*, he thought, grimacing. The trail into town was overgrown and windy; along the way stood scrub brushes and tall, flowing weeds.

Needing more than her letter now, he imagined her visage— her rosy cheeks, the pearly-bright light in her eyes, her crimson lips, her reserved laughter—it all came together into something both exquisite and rare. Dasha seemed like something from a faerie tale, and realizing how much he idealized her image, he managed to laugh aloud, scolding himself.

Marik stopped and asked for directions, just to make sure.

"Yes, you're moving in the right direction," said the peasant woman who stood by the road.

He thanked her and continued.

The country air felt brisk and clean, nothing like the rancid, dusty air of St. Petersburg in summertime, or the thick and choking air of war. It helped to escape the violence; despite his fatigue, uncertainty, and angst, he found he could breathe more naturally in this salutary climate.

He rode for several days, stopping as needed to rest and feed the horse, but virtually ignoring his own famished and tired self. Finally, he arrived at the convalescence home, which unlike the church, bustled with activity. Children played in the lawns surrounding the place and horses, buggies, doctors, and nurses bustled in and out the building's many entrances, their faces optimistic and cheerful. Indeed, the institution had a joyous atmosphere on the face of it, he felt, although keeping up one's spirits, he noted, would be part of the challenge in living here. On the right stood a well, where a woman drew up buckets of water. On the far side of the building, rows of bed sheets, all glistening and white, rustled along a clothesline. And the lush field around it, springing upward, complimented the home's ivory paint and even softened the glare.

Pulling up to the main entrance, where a cul-de-sac traced around a sprinkling fountain, he felt revived, refreshed, and cautiously hopeful. He dismounted, gave his steed to a man who identified himself as a livery man, tipped five kopecks, and proceeded through the tall entranceway and into the foyer.

Dasha

The floors of black-and-white tiles were waxed and polished, enhancing the image of freshness and light—sunbeams streamed through well-cleaned glass on all sides—and to the left stood a lively reading room, where people in wheelchairs and standing attendants casually passed the time. Some of the patients, he noted, were sickly and dazed, while others smiled and laughed easily, apparently near the end of their stays.

A nurse passed by, ignoring him, and he reached out his hand, touching her on the sleeve. "Excuse me," he said, as politely as possible, "I'm here to see Dasha Ivanova Konstantinov. My name's Marik; I'm on leave from the 3rd Regiment. Is she available?"

The woman, attractive and in her thirties, smiled warmly. "Dasha Konstantinov. I'm new here. Let me check." Then she disappeared.

With this uncertain answer, his anxiety grew again, and amidst the din of the home's interior he found himself unable to think clearly. As he had experienced on the front, a creeping feeling of isolation and doom crept in, bearing a negative pall to this man who was at this moment so surrounded by support and healing. He tried to feed off the energy of his surroundings, even attempted to smile at passing children, but it was to no avail. His heart rate increased, his palms became sweaty, and his forehead, already sticky with sweat, began feeling clammy again. He was suddenly thirsty.

Minutes passed, then a half hour, and still the nurse did not come.

Now overloaded with anxiousness, the young man stood up, straightened his coat, and with a determined sense of mission, headed straight for another nurse, who answered curtly, "No, she's away!" She continued to work.

Marik's heart sank.

Stricken by the news, he managed to swallow slowly, then feeling dizzy and weak, he stumbled to an open chair where he collapsed. *Where is she? How can I have made this long journey for nothing?*

He stewed and hurt in agony, but after several minutes passed, the first nurse approached him, kindness written all over her face. She leaned over him, smiling knowingly, and her voice was soothing. "Yes, I've heard she's gone missing," she said. "But it's been only one day so far. Sometimes young ladies…they stray into town as they're feeling better. Your best bet will be to stay here a few more days, then see whether she appears."

"But you don't understand," he pleaded. "My leave of absence was only for a limited time. And that time's fast approaching. I can stay here overnight, that's all, then I must join my new regiment. It's a great distance from here." His heart sank. "I'm sorry. I know this is not your concern. But we were to be married. I cannot live without her."

She placed her hand on his shoulder, searching his eyes. "If she returns and you're not here, I'll be sure to tell her you came to see her. You can write…see her on your next furlough. If it's meant to be, you will see her."

Marik found her words soothing, but in his delirious frame of mind, he nevertheless found himself dealing with failure and loss rather than hope. Smiling faintly, he responded, "She said she'll love me forever. Now forever's between us."

With this, she patted him on the cheek, smiled demurely, and left.

By the following morning, Dasha had not returned, and with his head hanging low, having already checked the town, Marik finally decided he must fetch his horse to leave.

He trotted out slowly, heading for a road through the forest.

As he left the compound, the usual bustle continued—laughing, playing, healing—but in the midst of these upbeat spirits, he felt doubly beaten and savagely alone.

Suddenly however, from the other side of town and as he headed past the first trees of the adjoining forest, Dasha rode into view on a peasant couple's carriage, her face radiant and bright. Her eyes peeled for just this moment, she recognized him immediately, and with glistening eyes she stood up, waving, and shouted, "Marik, my love! I'm right here! Right here!" She began laughing and crying.

Unable to hear her shrill voice, Marik kept riding.

"What, he can't hear me?"

He glanced over his left shoulder then, giving the area a final look, but he only saw the horses, the edge of her carriage and the peasant driver—not her. Crestfallen, he pressed on, and devastated, she ordered the driver to whip the horse. "Faster! Faster! We must catch him!" she cried. "Marik, stop! Stop my darling!"

Marik could sense her pleas. He could imagine her but not see her. It was all like a dream. He knew he was leaving her, but it was to no avail. He felt he could do nothing as the horse trotted ahead. Infuriated, he dug his heels into his horse's ribs and rode off at a gallop, determined to get as far away from her despondent image as possible, if only because it was so painful to him. He couldn't bear to listen. "It'll be years...an eternity... until I see her again," he lamented, riding far past the clearing as the peasants' horses continued to race.

Bursting with regret, he knew it must be a dream because he felt so powerless. Their fate had been revealed. All was lost! All lay beyond his control.

Carl woke with a start.

CHAPTER TWENTY SIX

Manhattan July 2007

Carl found himself sweating profusely.

Another sticky day, the air of the apartment smelled acrid and rank. The place lacked an air conditioner. Miserable and reeling from his nightmare, Carl propped himself onto his pillows, eyes squinting into the sharp morning glare.

Ordinarily, he scarcely remembered his dreams; he barely paid them any attention. But today, in the sun-drenched bed, hovering several stories above Manhattan's blistering sidewalks, the dream of faraway places left him astonished. *Was this true?* he wondered.

The dream seemed too real.

For a while, lacking anything better to do and having no one to rouse him, he sat upright against the bed-board, staring emptily into the mirror that faced him—not at his own image, per se, but at the looking glass itself.

Once an hour had passed, he lost interest in rest. He wanted to get up, move about, get out of his tattered sweatpants and into something he could wear outside. It was a bright, cheerful day, he decided, and there was no point in roasting inside a stuffy, old apartment when the city was abuzz with life.

Feeling expressive, he imagined he'd like to don a sword, then head into the bustle of New York with an extra attitude, but he knew this was silly, yet overall, despite the sad dream and his perpetually difficult lot, he found himself uplifted.

He spent the whole day enjoying the city.

Then as nighttime approached, he returned to the apartment, needing to change and hoping, as his heart had stirred all day, to find Dasha waiting for him. He entered the apartment, widely swinging the door, but for the moment it was empty. Disappointed, he checked the kitchen, bathroom, and extra bedroom, but there were no signs of her. Not yet, anyway, he reassured himself.

It took an hour to wash the soot from his body, have his coffee, and prepare for work, and at 6:02 PM, less than an hour before his shift began, he headed for work, leaving the door locked behind him.

Tonight would be different, he thought, leaving the apartment and taking the subway, which would carry him there in plenty of time. For the entire day, he had mulled over his circumstances and decided, in the end, he needed a change. It was not a matter of shame over status, or income, or address, or any other measures of his success or failure. Nor was it distress over the way his parents turned their backs on him, or Lisa's cold-hearted attitude, or even, still to his amazement, the combination of having two graduate degrees and living for weeks, by necessity, in a public park. The issue, in truth, was a sense of getting kicked around. Of becoming, somehow, the victim, whereas only recently in his life, he was out to conquer the world. He fondly remembered graduation day, the accolades from family and friends, the admiration he received and the endless stream of fortune that seemed headed his way. Then one man, an arrogant sap without the good sense to keep his best employees, had yanked the rug out from under his life, and falling into a tailspin, he had grasped and fired in every direction, heading down the long, wicked shoot, grasping his fingers in vain.

Time passed quickly at the bar, and by 2:00 AM the tally had been counted: they split $900 in tips, calling it a night. Carl and Isabelle, together the entire bartending team, celebrated by sharing a bottle of wine at the centermost table. The place was quiet, dark, and intimate.

They had chemistry, Carl felt, but they could only be friends.

He poured her a glass of cabernet, not wanting to broach the subject of his possibly leaving. "We're making good money here," he said, raising a toast with a nod. "But when I wake up the next day and see my pile of bills...the student loans I can't defer forever, the rent, the electric, my cell phone, and all those credit cards that keep coming back every month...I used them as a bridge loan to finish school and book my first apartment...it leaves me no room to breathe. Feel like I'm in a trash compactor with the four walls closing in fast."

She languished in a long sip. "Sounds familiar."

He leaned forward, folding his arms on the table. He felt a need to confess his previous night's dream. "Hm...maybe. I had a vivid dream last night, by the way."

Genuinely interested, she leaned toward him. "Really? What was that?"

"Dreamed I stormed an old fort, won a medal, only to lose my soul mate. I dreamed the whole thing in Russian. That's what happened when I learned the language. Sometimes I still dream in English, though, so it depends."

She gasped, then clasped her hands together with glee. "You're kidding me! Tell me! Tell me everything!"

"The thing is, it's a past life that I'm still living. I'm not sure...it's like I have something more left to do in it."

She leaned closer. "Yea? Like what?"

Embarrassed, he hid his face behind his glass and sipped. "Like marry my one, true flame. Someone I left there, you know. That's what's been haunting me. Why she came back."

"Who? Who?"

Carl hesitated again. "It's late. So next time we talk, let's pretend this conversation never happened. Late night talk. Dreams. You know."

"Okay...okay...who?"

"This chick who keeps coming around. Says we knew each other in a past life. Keeps coming and going, but wow! I can see her in my dreams now. Everything fits together. I dunno. It all seems so real."

"If it is, go with it. Look, you're working. Keeping your head on straight. Don't call yourself crazy. You're allowed a little recreation," Isabelle said, fascinated by Carl's outlandish story.

They both laughed.

Isabelle touched him on the arm with affection. "Guess what? Remember when last time I said you needed to come back? To meet someone?"

"Yea."

"He's coming right now. I told him to wait until I prepped you. Just called him."

Intrigued, Carl turned his head toward the door. "Really? Coming right now? Now that I've confessed I'm a lunatic?"

"Neat. Creative. He already knows that about you. I told him."

Carl looked back at her. "Who is it?"

Isabelle's voice became excited. "Name's Brian Huntsman. Really great guy. Runs a new software outfit, and well...I heard about him through the grapevine. Then met him at a party.

Told him I knew this crazy, really creative guy at the bar. But a guy who's a fully competent programmer. You know what the first thing he said was?"

"No."

"He says what, creative? And a programmer? If I could find a guy with a little imagination for a change…someone with a little vision…and a little passion…and can write code on top of that? That's what I want."

Carl sipped his drink again. "Cool."

She draped herself languidly over the table, scolding him with emerald-blue eyes. "Maybe he'll think you're Einstein. Hire you on the spot."

"Guy was a shipping clerk. Lacked credentials," Carl quipped.

"Yea…they'd outsource him today."

They exchanged rueful smiles.

Suddenly, Richard walked into the room.

Carl looked up from his drink, taken back by the sudden entrance, but felt mollified by his Central Park friend's soft demeanor.

"Look here. If it isn't my main man…working late and counting his cash!" Richard announced, slapping palms with Carl in camaraderie. "You know all I know about this guy?" he joked, looking at Isabelle.

"Do you know all I know?" she asked, turning to Carl. "I invited your old friend, too."

Flabbergasted by this unexpected convergence, Carl gulped and said, "My fellow hustler. What's got you down here in the Bowery so late at night?"

"I wanted to see your reaction, although a man's hanging outside on his cell phone, looking like he's casing the joint… wait, here he is."

In walked the entrepreneur. Only slightly older than Carl, and confident and smooth without appearing too slick, Brian came inside, looked once at Carl, took a mental note, then pulled up a chair. "Hi, guys. Good night for a drink. I'd like to join you but I've got more funding issues. Have to talk to Tokyo…you know…I'll be up all night. So I'm all business today. Sorry." He turned to Carl. "You're the programmer? Looking for work?"

Carl felt on the spot. "Yes and no. Yes, I'm always open to the right situation, but I'm gainfully employed right here. Not in any hurry to get back on the bandwagon, so to speak."

"Good. Glad to hear that. Let me tell you about myself. We're a start-up. Got our phase one funding in January. Hiring people like crazy now. Selectively, though. You understand. You miss business?"

"Yes and no, again. I wouldn't go back to what I was doing."

"As in—"

"As in, doing nothing but write code all day long to someone's arbitrary spec. Not getting plugged into the customers enough."

Huntsman allowed himself a thin smile. "Oh? That's why when I ran into your friend Isabelle here and she told me about you, I wanted to meet you. I like guys like you. A little business, a little technical, a little creative…you think outside the box. So do I. Listen, I never do the whole executive recruiter thing. Built the team with common sense. Go down to tech shows, find gamers, check out blogs…basically, I'm wherever the dreamers and poets hang out. I slip into their conversations, then," Brian said, looking around the room, "evaluate their choices. And I make a judgment. So this gig wasn't beneath you?"

Carl shrugged. "Nah."

The man shrugged. "Looks good on your resume. To me. Here's my card. Call me next Monday. Okay?" Carl nodded, then said he would, for certain. Satisfied and in a hurry, Huntsman stood up, thanked Isabelle for the personal tip, and disappeared into the night.

Watching him go, Carl shook his head. "Wow. That was unexpected."

"I think he liked you," said Isabelle.

"Yep, looking good my man," Richard said. "Real glad I caught you, too, because I'm shipping out first thing Monday. Found out you were still here when I lobbed in a call. Spoke to Isabelle here. Cousin's got a job for me down in Georgia. Says he'll set me all up, find me a Georgia peach. Know what I mean? Think I've had enough of hustling these streets. Had enough of New York. Seems all I can ever do is break even here. Now it's time for old Richard to cut himself some slack."

"Yea? Good for you. I'm glad. You sure helped me out here," Carl said. "I was just talking to Isabelle here...we can't do much about other people, but we can do all kinds of things about our own situations. But we need to have our own vision, then make it real."

"I'm feeling you, my man. I'm feeling you."

The trio laughed and drank until daylight.

CHAPTER TWENTY SEVEN

Carl lay around the apartment most of following day and into the evening. At least, he thought, he could afford food now, and hope stood on the horizon. Although he'd eaten poorly lately, as evidenced by the blemishes on his skin and the slight tire around his waist that would have, in better days, dissipated after one or two workouts, he felt he'd recover.

A young body can bounce back, he thought.

He flicked on the radio and soft, soothing music wafted over him. He failed to recognize the artist and didn't care. The important thing, he knew, was to focus on his breath, which he did with no further agenda.

I was a pleasant respite.

Life will get better, he thought. *But I still have this situation with Dasha to resolve.* As his mind flickered back and forth between sunlight and dark, waking and sleeping, modern madness and dreams, he began to see visions: a horse, bridled and saddled, standing on a wide open plain, guns flashing in the distance, dark rain clouds moving over the land, casting shadows across placid lakes, and hostels where he might need to stay when it poured. In his inner heart, he felt beauty, loss, and flickering images of love. He imagined Dasha standing on gold-tipped grasses that swayed around a flowing, white dress. She smiled at him, opened her arms and beckoned him by blowing a kiss. But he stood his ground, not wanting the risk.

"How long have we known each other, anyway?"

"More than a lifetime," she replied, her voice crystalline and tender.

Then slowly, softly, he faded out, and as he faded, the images disappeared

Suddenly something startled him, and he felt a pair of hands tugging on his shins. "Come on, sleepy head. Wake up… wake up I've come to see you," a beseeching voice whispered. "Marik, my lost Marik…I'm here! I've come back at once! As I said I would."

His spirits lifted, then soared. *It's her, it's her,* he thought, almost disbelieving. He threw open his eyes.

"Yes, it's me! You've had your dream. My potion worked! Now I've come back for you. This time with full permission! Oh, how my prayers were answered! The hoops I had to leap through to get this permission, though. Oh! That's another story. And how I wailed when you disappeared that day. I felt then, oh…it seems like yesterday, I would never see you again. But here you are! And here I am! I'm really here! Can we not do this at once. Once and for all? Your guilt will pass forever now, my dear," she said, her voice racing excitedly. "I've come back for our wedding."

Chills running through his body, he reached out a hand, gingerly touching her face. "My dear, I see everything now. As you promised, I saw it in a vision."

"Then at last let's go," she cried. "I'm a modern lady now. I'm dragging you off, my dear Marik. But won't you ask me, as well, so I know our hearts agree?" Her eyes shining, she looked him over, then leaned down, kissing him on the lips. "And you'll see so much more in time. But quickly, quickly…I must tell you. Time's running out now!" she warned, anxious and excited. "We must run to the park at once! That's where they're waiting! Here…take my hand. Get up! Get dressed! No time to shower, either!"

Puzzled, he inquired into her eyes.

"Quickly! There's no time to explain! Oh, this will be a glorious day! It's still light out, and I must leave by sundown. It's all been arranged and planned in advance, but we must go…go! There's no time to waste!"

"Why? What no time to waste? We get married and you have to leave? So you truly are a spirit and not…as I imagined… someone who shared a past life?" he stammered, jumping to search for his shoes.

"Sssh! Hush! There's no time for that now! Here," she said, searching around the room, "take this glass of water. Drink, drink! Wake up…come on…come, my love!"

He stood up, heading for a closet. "What happened after my dream? After I rode off without you?"

She gasped. "You were killed in action two months later to the day. I received a letter. Oh! I don't want to talk about that now. Come, come. There's little time. We're wasting time!"

Dark shadows descended over his heart as he imagined abandoning her again, and the pressing matters of his life, the realities of circumstance, and the chance this was not real, all faded in his desire to be with her, if only for a moment.

Hurriedly, she rummaged through his dresser, pulled out a wrinkled shirt, a belt, and a pair of knickers. "Here, here. These will do. It's not important! Wear this shirt and belt. No, I don't like those pants. Try the others! And wait…here…here…comb your hair. It's messy."

With grudging compliance, he obliged her exhortations, hoping to make peace; in return, her eyes glowed with satisfaction and cheer. "Hurray! You did it," she announced, pulling him by the shoulders to the mirror. "See, look in there, what do you see?" she beamed.

"A happy couple."

"Yes!" she cheered, kissing him again, this time on the cheek. "I see we understand each other. No more need to play the monk! Frocks are not my style. Oops! I shouldn't have said that!"

He responded with a surprised expression. "It was you—"

"Yes, yes, but I shouldn't have said that," she continued. "Anyway, hurry! Let's go, no time to waste! You're so slow today," she scolded, whacking him playfully on the rear. "Go, go! To the door!"

They hurried down the stairs, joyous and confused, bumping into the banister and walls as they went, until they reached the front door, which they burst through into the waning sunlight. "Run," she said. "Run! I'll race you!" Responding, he picked up his pace, grabbed her hand and ran, their bare feet pressing into the cement. "And where are we going?" he asked, pulling her hand into his.

"Our wedding, my dear Marik!" she said, as if dancing on air. "Hurry! Hurry! We're late, we're late!" she cried.

They ran through the northwest entrance of Central Park, racing toward their destination, squeezing each other's hands as they flew, laughing aimlessly. Benches, rollerbladers, and bicycles sped by as their hearts pounded and their legs, pumping as hard as they could go, carried them forward through summertime air. They sped down the street, crossed onto a sidewalk, entered the grass, a central nook, then turned south again, running as fast as they could. Carl began to pant and sweat, but she urged him on. "We're almost there!" she exclaimed. "Hold out for me only a moment longer, then we'll be there," she said, her voice loud and assuring.

They sprinted the final distance, anticipating their event, the skies continuing to redden. Then they came to a clearing: all around there were trees and benches and stainless steel fences, but oddly, he realized, the place was otherwise deserted.

She pulled him to a halt. "Close your eyes," she said.

He closed his eyes.

"Now open them."

And suddenly, it was all clear.

Standing on both sides of them were rows of men and women: officers and ladies, gentlemen and priests, all dressed to the nines in the best, 19th century fashion and all amassed there on the lawn. Many men wore beards and mustaches, and the ladies wore silken gloves and diamonds. Many of the gentlemen were uniformed in red sashes, dress swords and ribbons. All applauded the couple, who raced down their line, a band playing the background. "You see? You see?" she shouted. "This is our day!"

Without questioning the scene, as it was too much to absorb, he tugged her arm. "And our night?" he intimated.

"Night divides into day, my dear," she responded, dismissing the thought. "I must return. I'm duty-bound to God, on my sacred oath, to give you my purest of intentions. However agonizing that may be...and I was not prepared for the agony. I'd forgotten it all!" she exclaimed. "My mission is singular and nearly complete: to bless you on this day with all my heart and love and make you more strong."

Perplexed, his heart sank. "I still wonder whether you're a mirage."

"As you wish," she sighed.

He thought about kissing her again, to make sure, but the sincerity in her eyes and the strength in her voice made him feel as if every crevice of his body filled with warmth, and this, for the moment, was enough.

They ran to the end of the corridor, where a Russian Orthodox priest, dressed in a long, ebony robe, a bushy, hard-scrapple beard, and a silver cross, awaited them. He smiled at them warmly, encouraging them forward. "Where's the fight?" she sounded, whirling around to face the audience. "It's not a Russian wedding without a fight!" she teased, scanning the crowd, which responded with raucous laughter. She gazed wistfully into her groom's eyes.

"I almost forgot," he said, dropping to his knee. "Will you marry me?"

"Yes, yes! Now get up, fool! It's all been arranged!" she cried, tugging him in earnest.

The priest married them at once and to thunderous applause.

Looking askance, Carl recognized all of them, although he couldn't place them, exactly. And in his lifting, soft heart, he felt warmed by their presence.

Immediately, the band struck up again, playing a waltz. From there, they danced and laughed, swinging themselves in circles around the grass, the sun peeking down and gradually lowering on the horizon. Beyond, Venus began to shine faintly, a white crescent rising in the distance, coming to join them.

They danced for two songs, then, with star-studded eyes, she halted, kissed him, and rose on her tiptoes, as he knew she loved to do. Then clearing her voice, she embraced him.

They kissed to cheers and applause, then proceeded to dance again.

As they spun and whirled, however, the sun trickled down in the sky, and along it went sunbeams; gradually, the orb sank beneath and beyond the earth. They gazed into each other's eyes, the love of infinite truth shining brightly between them.

Then, with a nervous glance, she pulled him closely, searching his face. "My love, it's time for me to go now." She dropped on her feet slightly, energy draining. His face turned soft in response. "It's true," she continued, searching his eyes. "This was all I could negotiate. I thought they were quite generous in their permission. I've done my best for us. When I saw you there, hurting so, I decided I must. Mostly for you. I give you all of my blessings and all my love, right this moment...I give you my piece of heaven...a gift I can replenish many times over, however. Now I must go."

With her words, Carl felt warmth and comfort inside, yet the same time, he felt befuddled by this female rollercoaster ride.

His eyes misted.

"Perhaps I've settled the score," she said. "But it's unintentional. I'm not The One for you here," she said, tenderly.

Noting her wan expression, he pressed his hands into hers. "We've had what we could."

"Yes, and we must take it with us," she said, smiling through tears. "If we do, it's been quite the union!" With this, she let her hands slip from his. Then she spun on her heels, tossed a glance over her shoulder, and shuffled toward an officer nearby.

Carl scanned him closely, then dropped his jaw. "Wait... that's me. From the dream...it's Marik."

Looking back at Carl, she took Marik by the hands, raised herself up, and proceeded to dance with him across the lawn.

"Goodbye, my dear Carl! May you find love and happiness in this life! Listen! It's a fugue! Nikolai Rimsky-Korsakov! Don't you love him? And this man right here? Don't you love him as I do? I'm not modern enough for you now," she announced, turning with love toward Marik.

The band continued playing their joyous song.

Carl watched them in silence. They appeared to know each other intimately, Carl felt, and the man's physiognomy was certain. It was him.

Onward they danced, the moon hanging low in the clouds, until at last the sunlight disappeared altogether, and a breeze picked up, and a feeling of magic filled the park, and moonbeams shined on the whispering, fading ghosts, their figures turning dark, featureless, and distant.

Marik whirled her around, but Carl could see her face leaning back, savoring a last glance, and then, with a twirl and a leap, Marik spun her around, they faded, and all disappeared.

The field became dark.

Now by himself, Carl smiled grimly, both joyful and sullen at the same time, and digging his hands into his pockets and leaning back on his heels, he heaved a quick sigh. "I have her, though," he said, sullen and soft.

A man approached him.

With white, scraggly hair and ragged clothes, the stranger looked homeless. "*Katory sichas chas?*" he asked, pointing to Carl's watch.[xviii]

Considering the man more odd than dangerous, Carl sighed and pulled up his sleeve. "Sorry," he apologized. "Battery's dead." The man thanked him in Russian. Carl excused himself, then began traipsing his way toward the park exit.

Once he arrived there, he stopped.

He caught his breath, swallowed hard, and with a wondrous feeling intermixed with joy, hope and suffering, he stepped onto the sidewalk, turned left, and disappeared into a crowd.

EPILOGUE

Over the ensuing months, Carl's encounter with Dasha and their sudden ending weighed on his soul. The love she gave him seemed more a gift than something mutual, in hindsight; it had not been meant to be. Yet she stayed with him in a spiritual sense, as if she were truly his guardian angel.

But unlike an ordinary angel, he felt he could summon her smiling face, her support, and her love, at any moment. There seemed reserves of her to last until the end of time. This he felt inside himself, and he suspected she had carried this lifeline straight from heaven.

Sure, they were born more than one hundred years apart. *A mere age difference*, he joked. Her presence seemed immediate, but his images of her faded as the days and weeks and months passed.

Dasha. How could he ever thank her enough? Sometimes, he would gaze into the heavens, searching for her pirouette.

Yet none came.

Carl bided his time.

The following year, when asters and knapweeds and trumpet vines bloomed, he began to feel whole again. He thought about his career again, although he took the job with Huntman's startup and loved it. They loved him, too, calling him a star. He also felt grateful for the solid ground bartending had placed under his feet. At least he could work and stay engaged in the world around him while searching for something more suitable. He also thanked Isabelle with a card and kept in touch through email.

He thought about joining a leftist newspaper and railing against the corporate mess and everything else he had abandoned—at this point he realized it was a mutual decision, in truth—but he eventually dismissed this idea as off-base. No, he thought, it's better to use his hard-won talents and go run a company the right way and as he saw fit. The crooks running his old company would pay through karma soon enough, and he was determined to makes his own set of rules for his own circumstances. He would remain true to his métier and continue on his career path, but in the future probe the character of the place where he would work.

Maybe he would breed horses someday.

He didn't know.

But the truth was, the job didn't matter so much anymore.

He decided to contact Valerie, the feisty-and-nice woman he'd met at the penthouse party. Somehow, if he could find her, he reasoned, he'd be fully present and available for her now: things might work out for the better. He considered it worth a try.

So he tracked down her last name, De Luca, through Tabitha Murphy, who relished the subterfuge required for such a latent quest, and soon had her phone number. They went out on a date but keep things light for starters.

Frontier Re went under.

According to the newspaper, Kerry White had taken kickbacks in exchange for helping Jack Baker and other executives backdate their stock options. When the feds came down hard on the company, subpoenaing documents and so forth, a major client considered this the last straw and switched firms. From there, it was a matter of months before the stock had reached zero and the firm closed its doors.

EPILOGUE

With a wry sense of irony, Carl noted the destruction behind him and considered himself, if anything, all the better for it.

Valerie received him graciously, offering to buy dinner on the first date, to which Carl eventually agreed. Soon they habitually bickered over the check and many, sundry issues of scant importance in the big scheme of things. In his mind of mind and heart of hearts, Carl could imagine himself growing old with her, lying their bones side-by-side as deathless gods buried them in moon dust.

Huntsman's company was a Stamford-based firm, but Carl did the reverse commute, feeling it was more fun and rewarding to stay in the city for now. Despite their ardent passion, Carl and Valerie decided to keep separate apartments for now, coveting the space, flexibility and independence, even though they soon discussed marriage. All along, they struggled with the meaning of the word forever, however, and neither appeared in a hurry.

Naturally, sensing a match, their parents begged them to tie the knot.

Carl and Valerie, even the modern couple, imposed little pressure on themselves, however, having determined over the past year that such decisions of life resided with them and them alone. But they filled this uncertainty with an old-fashioned sense of wonder, awe and respect. Dasha might rap him on the noggin for his deliberations, Carl thought. In this life, she might say, one must take such steps on the strength of faith, and to a large extend he agreed.

A part of him refused to let Dasha go, too, and Valerie sensed something else was at hand, holding her beau back. Resenting his ambiguous heart, she often asked Carl, "Who is she in your secretive thoughts?"

"There's no *she* there," he responded.

"Yes, but is there a she *here*," she would say, pointing to his brain.

A smart woman, he thought.

Carl's parents were proud again, although he resented having won them over through performance. As he learned on a weekend trip home, they made him a celebrity in his home town, where everyone talked about Carl Moretti and his big move to the city, where he was the most successful man in the universe.

And so forth.

As for Dasha, she never returned. Although Carl often woke in the middle of the night, having imagined her sudden appearance in a dream, she was never there while he awoke. His eyes would dart around the room expectantly, but realizing she was gone, and noticing his beloved Valerie beside him, he would snuggle closer to his mate, sigh, and drift back to sleep.

The couple's practical life gave way to moments of carefree bliss, and even to thoughts of ditching it all for a windswept beach—for miles of coolness and sand—and always a pair, they ambled, hand-in-hand, along the same paths of Central Park where Carl and Dasha had roamed.

Day upon day, they pressed over Carl's memories with their feet, making new ones that shined with an everglow and grace that one expects, after all, from moments like this in a park.

AUTHOR BIO

D. F. Whipple has a varied history spanning an eclectic life, including writing, theater, film and business. He holds a BA degree from Washington Lee University and an MBA from the University of Pennsylvania. After an 11-year career on Wall Street, he left the world of finance to pursue acting at the New York Conservatory for Dramatic Arts. He is the author of two previous books, *Shadow Fields* (2005) and *Snooker Glen* (2006).

ENDNOTES

[i] Russian for "pleased to meet you." This is also a transliteration from the Cyrillic alphabet.

[ii] This French idiom translates literally as "tastes and colors aren't disputed." To those who communicate in French, this phrase roughly means "live and let live" or "to each her/his own." Members of the Russian upper class commonly used French instead of vernacular Russian in conversation, considering their own language comparatively vulgar.

[iii] A kopeck is the Russian equivalent of a penny. One ruble, or rouble, the main unit of currency, is divided into 100 kopecks.

[iv] Dasha Konstantinov is conveying subtleties of Russian names. As a matter of manners, she has conveyed her respect for Mark Kuzmin Andropov by addressing him with his formal name. However, she has displayed awareness of a class distinction by using his patronymic Kuzmin, since the suffix – min was exclusive to lower classes.

[v] With this reference to pinning notes on trees, she alludes to Shakespeare's *As You Like It*, wherein a young gentleman named Orlando posts love notes for Rosalind in the Forest of Arden.

[vi] Russian names include the patronymic, which is a middle name taken from the father's first name. By giving her full name, Dar'ya is establishing their polite, formal relationship as a matter of propriety, but she's also conveying her upper class status because the –na suffix to her patronymic is reserved for gentry. Despite this distinction, she goes on to suggest a more casual, and perhaps scandalous, relationship with him

by dropping formalities altogether and insisting on Dasha and Marik, the more informal and familiar versions of Dar'ya and Mark, respectively.

vii A Latin phrase meaning "Every man is the artisan of his own fortune." Dasha demonstrates her erudition and background, once again, with this classic aphorism.

viii The rank of cornet was grade (level) fourteen of the cavalry rank in the Russian military during Russia's imperial era.

ix Spanish for "a delicate sense of death and decay."

x The Spanish phrase "en...poder" translates to English as "in the form of a sardine can."

xi This French barb means "an imbecile with a knack for rummaging through dumpsters."

xii The scathing remark from a French critic suggests Alois "found inspiration in his own bile."

xiii Often abbreviated as *sapienti sat*, this Latin phrase means "a word to the wise is sufficient." The idea is that the illuminati "get it" with little explanation.

xiv An arshin is a unit of measurement once used in the Russian Empire. Equal to 71.12 centimeters and 2 1/3 feet, the unit was abandoned in 1924 when the Soviet Union adopted the metric system.

xv A unit of measurement equal to 1.0668 kilometers and 3,500 feet.

xvi Divided into grades (levels) and categories, then into service designations of army infantry, cavalry and artillery, the Tsarist military's system of ranking ground forces was complex during this era. A poruchik, or lieutenant, was an über-officer in either the army or cavalry; über-officer was one full category above under-officer, in which the highest cavalry rank was wachtmeister.

ENDNOTES

[xvii] The feldwebel is the artillery service's equivalent to the cavalry's rank of wachtmeister, so Marik and the officer, although in different services, share an equivalent rank.

[xviii] Translates from Russian into "What time is it?"

CPSIA information can be obtained
at www.ICGtesting.com
Printed in the USA
BVHW040847200820
586898BV00013B/298